"Have *you* ever fal

He winked at her. "All the time."

She'd have the last word, something she realized was important to her. "I think it's wrong, all these women you lead on. Don't you? I mean, they may get attached, fall for you. But you seem to use them, to see what you can get out of them for your own purposes. I think that's wrong. They're human beings, after all. With feelings."

He turned around, his eyes drained of any light. "They use me, too. It's not like they're not getting anything out of it."

"What am I getting out of this?" she asked him, if not rhetorically.

He stood on one hip, a move that made him appear more rakish than usual. "I really don't know, Miss Todd. I wondered that myself. I thought perhaps you were bored or intrigued. Or maybe you're a control freak." He took a step toward her so he was within half an inch of her face. "Or maybe you're just like the rest and can't resist me."

Hadley stood her ground. "How do you know when it's over? The moment when love, or lust, turns into something else. Something not as passionate?"

"I don't think about it," he said, returning her gaze. "It's something that happens. Maybe it's not one moment. It just *is*."

He turned around and walked out of the room.

Babe in the Woods

by

Jude Hopkins

Babe in the Woods

Cover Art by *Tina Lynn Stout*

The Wild Rose Press, Inc.
PO Box 708
Adams Basin, NY 14410-0708
Visit us at www.thewildrosepress.com

Publishing History
First Edition, 2023
Trade Paperback ISBN 978-1-5092-4843-8
Digital ISBN 978-1-5092-4844-5

Published in the United States of America

Dedication

To my mother, Gloria, and my sister, Carol

"And she tried to fancy what the flame of a candle is like after the candle is blown out, for she could not remember ever having seen such a thing." — *Alice's Adventures in Wonderland*

Chapter 1

September 1995

By the time Hadley reached the old Universalist Church, she was cold enough to have wished she had worn a winter coat instead of a raincoat. The fall evenings, as they wore on, were already turning chilly, electric-blanket chilly. That's what single women with few illusions use to keep warm at night, she mused. That or a large dog who sleeps at the foot of the bed. Hadley had chosen the former for the sake of convenience. Blankets, after all, had a control setting and didn't require letting out in the middle of the night.

Hadley Todd, thirty-five and tall-ish on the outside, and more than a little heartbroken on the inside, clomped down the church's old wooden stairs.

A familiar voice rang out.

" 'My God, Felicia,' he said. 'My God. I can't get enough of you. You're… you're… absolutely *ravishing.*' He mounted her in one fell swoop then expiated his masculinity in a—" The voice stopped.

It was the latest torrid scene from the pen of Delores Malvern, local accountant and aspiring romance writer.

"Hadley?" Dr. Marsha Culpepper interrupted. "You're just in time." She pulled out a wooden Sunday school chair at a table low enough for a pre-teen. "Delores is reading a new chapter from her novel."

Culpepper was the ringleader of the writing group because as the writing teacher at the nearest community college, she was the closest the group had to a pro. The rest of them, whose core members were rapidly dwindling with the onset of fall and its dark evenings, numbered only two, beside her and Culpepper.

"I'm sorry I interrupted." Hadley scraped the chair across the hardwood floor. The basement smelled of must and crayons, a cask for generations of children who had sat at this table coloring pictures of Moses, Daniel, and Adam and Eve in splashy Pucci colors, oblivious to the spiritual weightiness of their subjects. Instead of the great Biblical cast, the now-abandoned church walls were filled with the one-dimensional feral characters sprung from the accountant's fervid imagination.

"Go on, Dee," Culpepper instructed.

"Hiya," she said to Hadley, still keeping her index finger on the passage she'd just read.

"Delores?" Culpepper peered over her horn-rimmed glasses at the accountant. "Go ahead. Read more."

"Let me see, where was—oh yes, '… gush of passion…' "

"Excuse me? But what exactly is a 'gush of passion'?" The inquirer was Sal DeBrozzi, the town's only plumber, a self-described "student of the arts," and the other member of the group. He wrote frequent letters to the town's newspaper, *The Tillsdale Town Crier,* about the need to establish some sort of civic society in the area. "The town's cultural I.Q. should be 'kicked up a few notches,' " he'd say, quoting his idol, Emeril. Tillsdale folks knew Sal did his part by whispering snippets of bad poetry in the ears of all the women he seduced, poetry he himself had penned, created through

2

this self-same writing group.

Delores stared at him. She seemed rapt with attention whenever he spoke. "I think one's imagination can figure it out without going into graphic detail."

Sal shrugged. "Show, don't tell. Isn't that what you're always saying, Marsha?"

Hadley stared at the group's leader. Had there ever been anything between her and Sal? It was impossible to tell. Dr. Culpepper seemed so above any earthly desires, seemingly content to exist between the pages of a book. Her sensible clothing reflected her desire to remain above the coarser concerns of the world, her uniform of preference being an A-line tweed jumper hanging over a white turtleneck, dark brown tights, and loafers. Once she had worn patterned white tights with Mary Jane shoes to a meeting, and Hadley had deduced Sal was on the make. The return to her regular togs may well have indicated the affair had fizzled, never having led to the gush of passion Delores wrote about.

"I must agree with Dee. I think we can all let our several imaginations make the necessary leap." Culpepper cleared her throat loudly before checking her watch and turning to Hadley. "Unfortunately, you've come so late, we've all but finished for the night." Her tone couldn't hide her displeasure. "We've started meeting an hour earlier now that fall is upon us." She gazed heavenward at the flickering fluorescent lights.

Hadley was the errant child, transformed into one of her own high school students. Now she realized how they felt when reprimanded: shamed.

"Better late than never," Sal said. He flashed Hadley a wide grin, exposing an uneven row of front teeth framed by long incisors giving him a vampire-like

3

quality.

"But as long as you're here," Culpepper continued, in a higher voice, "are you working on your—what was it? Short story?"

"Play." Hadley corrected her.

"Play, yes, of course. How's it coming?"

Hadley ran her index finger over the word "piss" that had been etched into the old wooden tabletop. Maybe joining the group hadn't been such a good idea. It wasn't the muse-prodder she had hoped it would be when she signed up. They were good people, nevertheless, and she liked being around new faces.

"It's not. I thought it was, but…" She glanced around at the group. Sal sat with his arms folded across his chest, and Delores gave her a half-smile capped by a crinkly brow.

Culpepper now took a different tack, one delivered in her teacher's voice. "You have to share your work to stay in the group. Those are the rules. Didn't you get the letter about the time change and the rules?"

Sal leaned forward, his hairy forearms still intertwined. "To get, you gotta give, capisce? Same's in life." The chair creaked as he leaned back.

"I'm sorry. And, no, I didn't get the letter. I came here tonight," Hadley said, "because I was hoping you could help me. I've had a bout of writer's block that, with a bit of a push, may be on the verge of breaking up."

Delores squinted as if reading Hadley's lips, then struggled to get up from the chair, her husky torso and short legs making her less limber than the long, lithe ladies she created. Once on her feet, she came over to Hadley, and hugged her. "Don't you worry, honey. If you want, call me and we'll talk." She was too close; her breath was sour. "Funny, I never have writer's block. Maybe together, we can get you working again. Maybe you'll have a few pages for us by next week?" Delores nodded, first to her, then individually to the members of the group, as if to signal a group nod, like a wave in a football stadium.

Hadley smiled at Dee Dee's heartfelt attempt to cheer her on.

After all, what could Hadley expect of them? This was no Learning Annex in Los Angeles, workshops where you could learn from industry professionals, a place for aspiring, ambitious writers to network and spur each other on—and hopefully make some connections. This was simply a well-meaning knot of small-town folks who wanted to push back the blandness of their lives, to enlist others to cheer them on so they might feel better about themselves than if they had been home watching inane reality shows all evening. That, in itself, was admirable. But if she wanted inspiration and support, Hadley realized, then and there, she'd have to provide it herself. She hoped her personal rejuvenation would go well even though her nuclear family had imploded with atomic proportions while she had been in L.A. for the past decade. Oh, sure, she intended to go back there one day. But this time, she'd go back a lot more triumphant than when she'd left it.

"Delores is right. We'll do all we can to help you, won't we?" Culpepper said, dropping any hint of recriminations.

Sal muttered a "Why, sure," as he unfolded his arms and uncrossed his legs. Hadley imagined how he'd spent the day cramped up in crawl spaces staring at pipes and the underside of weary housewives. It was time to leave.

"So, it's agreed. Hadley will have the floor for next week's meeting. Bring what you have, and the whole meeting will be devoted to you." Culpepper appeared to force a smile. Her mouth had square parameters, like a robot's. "By the way, what's your play about?"

Hadley's gaze went from one set of eyes to another. They regarded her with interest. "It's about loss of innocence. When exactly we lose—women, that is—when we inevitably fall into disillusionment and despair. I want to know the exact moment before we lose our illusions about romantic love."

An awkward silence ensued. Nature filled the vacuum with the sound of wind swirling through every gap in the old brick building, as well as the ancient pipe organ a floor above. It seemed to Hadley this moment of non-speaking was fitting, given that all Sunday School lessons delivered in this room deserved reflection.

Had *she* made them think?

****

Walking back to her car, Hadley mulled over her all-consuming desire to write this play. She wanted, first of all, to figure out why she—and many other girls and women—were attracted to the same type of guy over and over, the ones who always seemed to break her heart. Sure, she understood the initial attraction, but why stay when they proved to be veritable will-o'-the-wisps in terms of faithfulness? Why did women cede their romantic innocence to these heartbreakers? Weren't there clues they should watch for? Once figured out, she could educate the female sex in her play, including that decisive moment when girls unwittingly stepped into the muck with their kitten heels only to find them irretrievably stuck. She would break the code. And it would be there in black and white, to be read, re-read, and acted out on stage. That would be Hadley's mission.

And, most of all, by writing the play, Hadley herself would avoid these blackguards once and for all. Like Derek, her ex-boyfriend from L.A, a walking heart smasher. She once overheard him talking on the phone to God knows who: "She's old. She can't put up with this much longer." Old? Maybe thirty, thirty-one at the time? What a bastard! OK, he was a good five years younger, but that didn't make her old! She'd show him. She'd write her play and have it staged while he still flirted with younger women who might be interested in him until they found out he had everything but money.

But it had stung, the insult and his subsequent leaving. It had been etched into her soul, the opposite of lovers' monograms carved into trees. Both, however, seemed permanent. She had believed Derek to be the real thing, laughing with her, putting his muscular arms around her, saying he loved her and always would. She fell hard for him when he seemed to adore her sense of humor, the books she had in her bookcase, the way she could imitate any female celebrity. She missed that. And she wanted to be in love—and loved back.

As she'd flown back home last year, she thought of how tucked away it was in spite of the "N.Y." in the address. If the Midwest was called the fly-over states, what was western New York state? It was more the buckle-up-and-secure-trays-onto-back-of-seats part of the country. It seemed like the perfect place to think and write, what with the slow pace and all the damn trees. In returning home, she hoped she could become the writer she believed herself to be instead of the high school English teacher she was. This much different environment, she had surmised, would be more conducive to writing given that Tillsdale did not have memories of Derek on every corner as did the City of Angels. So, in truth, home was an escape, too.

Yet, the writing wasn't forthcoming. Writing the play was proving difficult. Writer's block, she had come to find out, can be a stowaway, no matter where you go.

And then, there was the self-imposed deadline. She'd given herself five years before the millennium. She'd have to get something accomplished before her 40th birthday or the world blows up. It'd be all over then. Either way.

The chill she'd felt upon arriving had now turned into cold. The bursts of late summer weather in the daytime would only last a few more weeks in Tillsdale. Like all upstate cities, its winters were rough— impassable roads, bitter wind—and its summers so hot and humid that blow-drying one's hair was as futile as finding a decent bagel. It was, above all, not a town of pretense: The elements always exposed a person first. Perhaps that's why L.A. remained so inscrutable. Weather, she concluded, made people real.

And she was real all right.

Chapter 2

Hadley's self-diagnosis? She needed a jolt.

She scanned the library. This was supposed to be a class full of students with promise. Unfortunately, they still fell into the old ranks: the attractive ones at one table, the geeks at another, and the outcasts on benches or in line for the restroom pass to sneak a smoke.

"I wish these kids weren't so territorial," she said to her colleague Brenna sitting beside her at one of the library's tables. "They're as bad as we are. But they're young, for Pete's sake. They're supposed to be more open to life."

Brenna shrugged. She had been reading coeds as long as she'd been reading their essays, which was about fifteen years longer than Hadley. "Just human nature, I guess."

"Excuse me, Miss Todd," a student said, standing before the table where Hadley and Brenna sat. "I don't understand this assignment."

It was Jennifer, one of the students in two of her classes. She was on the cheerleading squad coached by yet another colleague in the English Department, Anise Blaine, still in her 20s and often mistaken for one of her charges.

"Did you take notes when I gave out the assignment?"

The student, tall, gangly, and awkward in spite of

being a cheerleader, shook her head slowly.

She studied the young girl before her, who was sickly pale yet had piled her magnificent black hair atop her head in such a way that became her. She had outlined her bright blue eyes in black eyeliner, raccoon eyes, emphasizing at once their forlornness and wildness.

Hadley bit her lower lip. "What author were you assigned?"

"Samuel somebody."

"Johnson?"

She answered with a shrug. Hadley was struck by the girl's appearance. Her clothes didn't match. Her striped top clashed with her magenta shorts. The cuffs were stretched out on her pullover, too. Her shoes, flats, were from a dollar store, a knock-off of the more expensive leather ones.

But lower-class kids, of which there were plenty in this school, still tried because they were young. They tried to be trendy, to be fashionable, to be cool. That innate desire—to be cute and attractive and stylish—wasn't quashed by meager budgets. It was part of that fleeting stage of life.

"OK," Hadley said in a voice low and soft. "First let's find a book about your author. You might want to check the computer to see what the library has. Or if you run into a dead end, I'll help you."

Jennifer stared out the window. The calendar said September, but she was still dressed in summer clothes, mismatched though they be. Around here, in western New York state, the weather, always unpredictable at best, seemed to get hot during the day when the kids went back to school. The relatively short summers affected them as it always had her, deepening the homegrown yearning.

The girl glanced from the forest outside to the row of computers in the library. "They're all being used."

Hadley smiled in spite of catching a whiff composed of equal parts cigarette and marijuana. "I guess you'll have to search for a book in the shelves until one opens up."

Jennifer hesitated.

"I'll help you," Hadley said. She was familiar with almost every book the library offered and its location because so many were the same ones she had read when she attended this school. She used an index finger to loosen the anthology that featured many of the authors and their poems and essays Hadley loved.

"Try to picture old Samuel sitting around in his wrinkled, and no doubt dirty, underwear," she suggested to Jennifer. "It'll make him seem more human."

Jennifer, her face expressionless, took the book and returned to a table far away from where Hadley and Brenna were stationed.

"Another thing I wish I could change," Hadley said, after she had returned to her seat next to Brenna, "I wish these kids loved lit like I did at their age. It might help them through the doldrums instead of a spliff."

"A what?"

"Nothing. Never mind."

"C'mon. You can't really blame them." Brenna clasped her hands in front of her, as if preparing for a game of "Here's the Church and the Steeple." "We're talking about an old fart who lived and wrote a million years ago. Do *you* give a damn about Samuel Johnson? Or even his *johnson* for that matter? They're kids. You can still remember how you felt at that age."

"You're right, at least about Samuel Johnson." Hadley closed her eyes. Her concerns with the students had nothing to do with their lack of interest in dead white authors. She could identify with their frustration. "I'm thinking of starting a writing club for some of the ones with promise."

"Be careful. These kids might be poor, but they're proud. They'll know if you're trying to patronize them."

Hadley shifted uneasily in the uncomfortable chair. "I'm a teacher. I'm trying to make them love reading and writing. That's not patronizing."

Brenna pressed her lips together, which Hadley interpreted as disapproval.

"I know what both their problem and my problem is," Hadley said, changing the subject. "We all need a jolt."

Brenna nodded. "You used to be a much more contented teacher before you left for L.A. How long have you been back now?"

"This is year one of the rest of my life," Hadley said. "And still nothing fast here but the food."

Brenna shook her head. "Hey. Have you forgotten I'm from here, too?"

"Yes, I mean, no." Hadley managed a smile for her friend. "And you *are* special."

Some things had changed. When Hadley had left this town for Los Angeles, she'd not only left her parents here in Tillsdale, but her teaching job as well.

While Hadley was on the West Coast, employed not as the writer she'd hoped to be but as an assistant in the music business, her parents divorced, her mother moved away and remarried, and her father became more reclusive by the day, fading more and more into the hills surrounding the small town of ten-thousand people.

Her father having had a mini-stroke became one of several reasons she'd come back to her hometown. After all, she was his only child. And he had never been good at caring for himself.

Brenna broke the silence. "How's your book coming?"

Hadley groaned. "It's a play. And it's not. I think I've got writer's block or something."

"What about the writers' group? No help?"

Hadley shook her head. "Not yet, but it's early. It consists of only the leader and three of us. One lady is writing a steamy romance I can't compete with, what with all those flailing appendages and guttural noises. But at least she's writing something."

"What's your play about?"

Hadley put one of her feet on the seat of the library chair opposite her, a verboten act she hoped no student would observe. "It's about that last moment before the inevitable realization that Happily Ever After is a lie." Hadley leaned forward, her arms tucked under her chest. "You know, the tipping point when a girl learns love isn't all it's chalked up to be."

Brenna tapped on the table with her pink pearlescent nails, either out of boredom or impatience, Hadley couldn't tell.

"Remind me," Brenna said, chuckling in spite of herself. "I've been married forever. What should love be?"

Hadley sat upright in the chair. "Monogamous, eternal love. You meet, fall in love, stay in love, and the guy cooks and does all the dishes, too. My play is exploring that last moment before women wise up about these fickle Romeos and move on. I want to know what comes before that point of no return. Then maybe it can be avoided."

Brenna creased her brow and pulled at the pearls encircling her neck. "That guy in L.A. obviously made you jaded. Why don't you come over for dinner tonight? It's only me and Wes. Nothing fancy. We'd love the company."

For a moment, Hadley mulled over the invitation, which she envisioned as something wonderful like meatloaf parked on a cloud of mashed potatoes. Besides, she hated to cook.

"I'm not jaded, just wised up. As for dinner, may I get a raincheck? I'm supposed to meet Neil at The Cork."

Neil was a childhood friend who had long had a crush on Hadley, one unreturned because she'd always viewed him as an older brother. He'd never left Tillsdale except to go to newspaper conferences in Albany or Rochester. Nevertheless, he was a big deal here: He was the editor at *The Tillsdale Town Crier* and a dedicated one, too.

Neil was also an anchor in her life. Unlike herself, with her restless desire to be more than what she was, he seemed content with his life, writing columns that unflaggingly nagged the residents to wash off the pigeon scat on the World War I statue in the public square or pony up for the poor at Christmas. The reason for the dinner meeting tonight, he'd told her, was to enlist her help in some new do-good project. Because that's the way he was.

"I wish you could find someone who appreciates your…"

Hadley gazed into Brenna's eyes, waiting to hear

what adjective she would pick out of her glossary for the eccentric. But Brenna simply trailed off, apparently at a loss for words.

Hadley laughed. "So do I, but I don't think such a creature exists."

She gave Brenna a conciliatory smile. Amazingly, she could pass for a young Joan Fontaine, one of the most regal of Old Hollywood's actresses, minus the perfect French twist. Brenna had been her mentoring teacher when she had first left college, armed with an English education degree, ready to rid the world of dangling participles and run-on sentences. She had used her seniority to get Hadley a teaching job in this school before she left for L.A.

Now she was back, with nothing to show for it except a bad case of wishing and hoping.

"You missed your calling." Hadley wagged her finger. "You should have been a matchmaker."

Hadley never forgot that Brenna had provided a shoulder to cry on when she had first returned to Tillsdale from L.A. She still was a close friend, although lately she'd seemed somewhat preoccupied. Brenna had been good to her. It wasn't her fault Hadley felt fidgety since she'd been home.

"Even if it's not Neil, you need to meet a nice man like him, one who appreciates you," Brenna told her, casting her eyes over the sea of familiar faces. "I wish there were more of them around here." She checked her watch, its face encircled by rhinestones. "Hey, first period is almost over." She pushed her chair back, preparing to leave. "Don't forget—talent show fourth period."

Hadley twirled a limp right index finger and said,

"Whoopee," but her attention was diverted to a tall, young stranger entering the library. He was so electrifyingly handsome, he made her feel woozy, as if she had skipped six meals. She grabbed Brenna's forearm.

"Oh my God, who is *that*?"

Brenna peered over the top of her half-rim glasses, also sprinkled with rhinestones. A man, probably in his mid-20s, his back turned toward them, was tapping out a drum solo on Anise's lower spine while she laughed and wriggled out of his grasp.

"That, my dear, is Trey Harding." She wrinkled her nose. "Sounds phony, doesn't it?"

The young man in question stood next to Anise, now parked in front of the librarian's desk. Hadley waited to see if Trey would turn around. When he did, she caught sight of a young man with huge eyes peeking through a shock of light brown hair with a few golden streaks running through it. A real heartbreaker. Just her type.

"My God, I feel like Keats when he stumbled across the Elgin Marbles."

Brenna hesitated, like someone who hated being outsmarted in her field. "Is that bad or good?"

"A little of both." Hadley was struck by the young man's resemblance to Derek. "What does Trey Harding do?"

Brenna shot Hadley one of her maternal glares usually reserved for students who misbehaved. "Forget it. He's too young for you. How old are you now? Thirty? Thirty-two?"

"Thirty-five. And ready to lie about it." How old she appeared in her New York state driver's license photo, the dark circles under her eyes the result of late hours grading essays on the imagery in Coleridge's "Kubla Khan." She had been mistaken for Carly Simon once at a Hollywood magazine stand and felt flattered, but now she simply felt deflated. "OK, what's his story?" She was interested for all the wrong reasons.

Brenna glanced again at her watch. The students sensed the bell would soon ring. They were as instinctual about the end of class as animals before an earthquake.

"Kind of a mystery. I know he's a stringer for the radio station. Reports on sports here at the school."

Hadley scrutinized her friend's smiling face. "What else does he do on the side?"

Brenna was ready. "Rumor has it he does it from all angles." She snorted rather unladylike, which endeared her even more to Hadley.

The young man in question had moved his arm to encircle Anise's waist and was whispering in her ear. She responded with a loud throaty laugh and removed the hand that seemed uncertain as to whether or not it would go a-wandering.

Hadley nodded in the direction of the library desk. "That answered my next question."

Brenna stared at the giggling twosome and shrugged.

"He's sleeping with her, isn't he?" Hadley was sorry to have asked the question. The answer was obvious.

"Rumor has it Sara, the school secretary, is also seeing him."

"Our Sara Yarborough?" The coupling was incongruous given Trey's magnetism and the secretary's more or less retiring nature. "He's seeing both women, then?"

She was surprised at the sting of jealousy and

chalked it up to his remarkable resemblance to her ex-flame in L.A. The height, the broad shoulders tapering down to a slim waist, the cherubic face with high cheekbones—not to mention that smile, nicely offset with a dimple. He reminded her of a host waiting for a game show.

And, boy, did she love game shows.

Chapter 3

What would be Trey's first impression of her? She was at least five years older than he, no, more than that. Who was she kidding? She tugged at a barrette and let her hair fall to her shoulders. Why hadn't she let her hairdresser put some wild blonde streaks in it? Because she didn't want to become Debbie Harry trying to recapture her halcyon days with Blondie, that's why.

As long as he was turned away from her, she could feast upon him. What a figure he cut. Even dressed as he was in a pair of khakis, Hadley could make out his perfectly rounded buttocks. He shifted his weight to one leg, jutting out his hip.

She frowned as she analyzed his posture. "Are you sure he's not more of an Oscar Wilde than a Lord Byron?"

Brenna answered her with a blank expression.

"You know, gay."

"Not a chance. According to Anise, he's a jackhammer in bed." Brenna's smile morphed into a smirk. "He knows women right down to their…"

"Thongs." Trey would undoubtedly be a thong man. She pictured him nodding approvingly along the sidelines of a Victoria Secret runway show.

Brenna frowned. "C'mon now. The way we talk, we could write our own steamy romance."

Hadley nodded. "You're right. I'm sorry. I forgot

where I am and with whom. I'll clean it up."

Hadley could *think* dirty, though. No harm in that. She tried to imagine what Trey's prowess in the sack might be and felt a pang quickly followed by a stab in the same nether region. Those types of guys understood how to hook a woman, get them to do their bidding, then drop them without even a backward glance. But, oh, the first leg of the journey! Absolute ambrosia. The first part stayed with her, no matter the dead end it led to. That's why she never forgot those guys. Screw the shrinks and the self-help books and Oprah and the rest of them. They'll show up in your dreams, in your dates, in your doggerel. She'd never experienced anything like those guys, and she'd never forgotten them, no matter how badly it ended. And it always ended. Badly.

"I hate him already," Hadley said a bit too loudly. A few students turned to observe her.

"Somehow I thought you would," Brenna said. She sneered as much as a lady known for her niceness could muster, as if to reinforce Hadley's belief he wouldn't be worth pursuing on any level. "He's OK for a fling, but anyone with half a brain can see right through him."

She eyed his hand, remaining parked above Anise's backside. "Then, why do those women allow him…" Hadley couldn't finish her sentence. How naïve she had been with Derek. She felt the heat rise to her cheeks. She was with her ex for almost half the time she'd been in L.A. And for what? To train him for the next one?

Brenna answered her anyway. "Anise is fresh off a divorce, and Sara's probably never dated anyone so delectable."

"Not many have," she said out of compassion for the ones eternally passed over. Yes, she had had dashing

Derek herself and others of his ilk before him. But they had ultimately not been a good thing. "Maybe he sees something in her the rest of us haven't taken the time to discover." She repeated it as if to convince herself.

Once again, her imagination took a different tack. The pairing of opposites wasn't so haphazard. Trey could have Anise in a cheerleader outfit and Sara in an apron. Hadley squeezed her eyes to blot out memories. How she had tried to be all things to Derek.

"Still, that's all rumor isn't it? I mean, just because he's beautiful doesn't make him a cad. Maybe he's ambitious." Hadley found herself too afraid to hope he could be different, as she had hoped with Derek. But her ex-beau had wanted so many things: a lover, a mother, a manager, a femme fatale. Hadley was, at best, two of those things, and she wasn't always sure which two.

"He fulfills a few fantasies, gets what he can, and moves on," Brenna said, waving her right hand upward. "That's all. *You*, especially, need to stay away from that sort, as downcast as you are."

"I'm not downcast. OK, maybe a little. But you're right about one thing. He's probably just another asshole." Hadley said this in the lower registers of her voice, what she called her radio voice. She gathered up her books from the end of the table and stood up, glancing out the same window her inquiring student had been eyeing a few minutes before. Brenna cleared her throat loudly.

"That profanity will cost you two hours' detention, young lady." The voice was distinctive, a little like Mr. Vegas, Wayne Newton, but with testosterone.

She spun around, only to find herself face to face with Trey. She stared, transfixed, into his eyes, emerald

21

encircled by topaz, like some exotic hybrid gemstone sold on a home-shopping network. The smile was blinding. She shivered.

"Hope I'm not intruding on some private girl talk," he said.

His presence was striking—a glass of champagne, smarting her throat with bubbles. Why did she always fall for this type? She could have had a steady, loving boyfriend or husband with a guy like her friend Neil, but no, she was still fourteen when it came to what attracted her. But then she remembered she wasn't alone. Wynona Ryder had gone for the hot slacker played by Ethan Hawke over good guy Ben Stiller in "Reality Bites."

"C-course not," she stammered, feeling like an idiot.

Smiling, he turned to Brenna. "How are you?" He extended his hand. "I spotted you over here and thought I'd stop by to say hi." He glanced at Hadley. "And meet the new girl, I mean, lady."

So Brenna has already been introduced, probably by Anise.

"I'm doing fine," Brenna said. She took his hand. Even the usually cool Joan Fontaine now seemed flustered—like in those scenes in *Suspicion* when Joan couldn't tell if Cary Grant was really planning on murdering her.

"I'd like you to meet Hadley Todd, one of our wonderful English teachers. Hadley, this is Trey Harding."

He saved his best smile, an orthodontist's dream, just for her. He was perfection.

Hadley wished she had more of what she called a "bar face," a face that draws men to a woman as soon as they enter a joint. She wanted to wow him as he did her.

She wasn't sure why, other than beauty translated into power. She'd been told she was attractive, but her whole presence wasn't show stopping in the same manner as his was. Or maybe she was down on herself because of past relationships. "You're an acquired taste," Derek used to say to her. He could go screw himself! In her 20s, she had a "bar body"—tall and curvy, with a nice round ass and shapely legs, and a waist so narrow she could touch her fingers when her hands encircled it. But, now, she wished for a bar face.

"Our names form a chiasmus." Trey waved his hands in a horizontal Möbius strip.

Chiasmus. She had studied classical rhetoric. But she had to pause. A chiasmus? She prayed to Aristotle that she'd not be outsmarted.

"Almost," she said before clearing her throat. "But not quite. I believe you need to invert words, not just letters, for a true chiasmus." Had she guessed right?

He smiled. "I stand corrected. A chiasmus is more like, 'Never let a kiss fool you or a fool kiss you.' "

Good Lord, sex appeal and brains! Precisely the combination that sent her libido blasting into the stratosphere. She stood opposite him, trying to push away the same electric reaction she'd had the time she'd first met Derek. It was something physical traveling from her brain to her stomach, then straight to her toes. The vasovagal nerve, if she remembered her college biology correctly. Why hadn't she outgrown such a reflex?

"Yes, not bad," she said in her schoolmarm voice. Don't ever let the star pupil think he's more special than he is. Brenna had once told her that, but no longer seemed to practice it, at least with Trey.

"Thank you, Miss Todd. Do I get an 'A'?"

She was thrown back. "An 'A'? No-o. No. That's what you call a hasty generalization, when you decide too soon." She tried not to appear too interested. "You have to prove yourself. At least in my class."

He unleashed another great half-smile on her and made a clicking sound with his tongue. "Shouldn't be too hard."

Before she could reply, he said, "I must run. Great to have met you!" Guys like him were always going someplace else.

He nodded to Brenna and walked away. In his Oxford shirt, khakis, and deck shoes, he came across as more suited for a party at Martha's Vineyard than for roaming the halls of a high school in the middle of God's country.

"So you know him." Hadley tried to act as if his presence hadn't caused her to lose her composure in the same way ghosts of boyfriends past had always done, no matter how much time passed. If Brenna knew him, was she telling her all the inside scoop?

Brenna shifted uncomfortably in the old wooden chair. "He stops in the faculty room to see Anise once in a while." She quickly recovered, the old pro. "Maybe you should come down there more often."

"Where's he from?" Hadley asked, smoothing down the few frizzies always popping up on her hair. "Can't be from around here."

"What makes you say that?"

"He actually pronounced 'chiasmus' correctly." At the expression on Brenna's face, she added, "And, yes, I know I'm a snob!"

Brenna shook her head as if it was best not to say all she was thinking. "He got to you. Just like all the others."

Hadley blinked, almost keeping her lids shut, as she'd seen cats do. "Seriously, where's he from?"

"Someplace in the Midwest. I guess he has aspirations of being a rock star or an actor. He's *inching* his way downstate." In spite of the innuendo, Brenna was all business now. It was as if she had spent too much class time on misplaced modifiers and was ready to move on to comma splices. Hadley again got the impression she was clearly not telling all she knew about this guy.

"Listen, I'm going to head down to my classroom before the stampede starts." Brenna took a few steps, then turned back toward her friend. "Oh, and don't forget to give Sara your absentee list."

Hadley had already entered a new zone, but at the mention of Sara, she began to picture Trey mounting the school secretary. She was surprised at the envy she felt, as if he had been her boyfriend instead of someone she'd just met.

"Go on ahead. I'll see you later."

"One more thing," Brenna said, her furrowed forehead conveying equal parts concerned and weary. "Today's the talent show, remember? You'll need some carbs. I understand last year's dairy princess will be singing a Celine Dion medley."

She waved Brenna on. The last thing she could think of was food what with the brackish taste now in her throat. Meeting Trey was like running into a young Derek, the Derek she thought she knew, who was an entire species apart from the Derek he actually was, or at least had ripened into. He, too, had wanted to be a star, the next big thing. But that was the past. She shook her head as if clearing her brain were as simple as shaking an Etch-A-Sketch.

Notwithstanding the bad memories, Trey could be useful to her for the play she was writing. "Our names form a chiasmus," he had said. Merely repartee or a come-on? Could the word "chiasmus" even be part of a come-on? She smiled. It reminded her of the playful overtures with which she and Derek had started out. Of course, those sparks had eventually turned into a case of arson after he grew tired of her and moved on.

If anything, she'd overcorrected after her last relationship. She was the one in control now. She would analyze love and the last luscious moment before a girl wised up, but she wouldn't fall for any b.s. again. And she'd write about it.

She restacked the books in her arms. She felt alive, all senses on the alert. If Trey reminded her of Derek, then they must be part of a type, members of the same genus and species. What was the proper name for a conclave of these guys? An assembly of assholes? A gaggle of gigolos? A bundle of bounders? Oh, but they had something, these guys. They could make her life a dream whether she was sipping Dom Perignon with him at The Plaza or swilling moonshine with him on a back porch. Those guys could change the lens all right.

Trey would be easy to observe, too. He was an alpha male in a jungle of willing women out in the middle of nowhere. He had enough girlfriends around here that she could easily watch and record his interactions with them. As long as these women were OK with being snookered by such a playboy, she might as well learn as much as possible and make the proverbial lemonade out of a bowl of sour fruit.

"Have you forgotten? You were one of them," an

inner voice reminded her.

She corrected her posture and straightened up to her full 5'8" height. All of a sudden she was twenty again. It wasn't only the play that interested her. *He* interested her. Besides, their names were linked. They formed a chiasmus—almost.

Chapter 4

Hadley bounced to her car after school. This was
usually the time of day she dragged her feet. But now
there was purpose to her life again, a tangible paper cone
around which the cotton candy of her days could now
swirl.

Brenna spotted her in the parking lot. "Hey, you!"
She loped over to Hadley's car, her French twist now
collapsed into a short flip stabbed with Bobbi pins.
"Lord, but you walk fast." She pressed her free hand
against her necklace. "Did you see who was sitting with
Anise at the talent show? My dear, your mascara's
running. Here." She licked her finger.

Hadley took a step back. "No, no, that's fine. I've
got a tissue." Hadley bent down to peer into her car's
outside mirror. Her face was flushed, the dark circles
turning her into one of her Goth students. "I didn't
notice. I cut out early. I had some work to do."

Brenna fiddled with the flip at the nape of her neck.
"You sure you're OK?"

"Of course! What makes you think I wasn't?" Was
she that transparent?

"I dunno," Brenna said, crinkling her nose. "You
seemed a bit down, saying you needed a jolt and all.
Then you were positively unmoored after meeting Trey."

With her mother now living far away, Hadley
usually appreciated Brenna's maternal gestures toward

her but wanted to be free to think of Trey. "Yeah, I'm fine. Only preoccupied with a bunch of things," she said. "As I told you earlier, I'm supposed to meet Neil." She climbed into her car. "You're a sweetheart, though, for worrying about me. I'll see you tomorrow!"

As she pulled out of the school parking lot, she caught a glimpse in the rear-view mirror of the petite figure of her friend, one hand waving, the other attempting in vain to re-wrap her tumbled coiffure. She had plenty of time before she had to meet Neil, but she was afraid Brenna would pick her brain like any mother hen would do. All afire, she wasn't up to being analyzed like a Wordsworth poem in one of her student's textbooks. Besides, she couldn't shake the feeling Brenna seemed to be hiding things concerning Trey, painting him as bad news. He seemed quite the opposite to Hadley.

The stoplight turned red. She glanced at the town's dilapidated buildings, some of which were now a century or more old. Hadley viewed her old hometown in upstate New York with new eyes since returning a year ago. How tucked away it was in spite of the "N.Y." in the address. If the Midwest was called the fly-over states, what was western New York state? It was more the buckle-up-and-secure-trays-onto-back-of-seats part of the country. It seemed like the perfect place to think and write, what with the slow pace and all the damn trees.

White's Drug Store still had the mortar and pestle logo on the window. The soda fountain was no longer part of the store, but she could still remember the chocolate shakes as thick as quicksand and gooey toasted cheese sandwiches served there. There was Offenbach's shoe store where her mother had bought her special shoes to accommodate the arches she had to slip in for her crooked toes. Across the street was Hoffmeir's furniture store, whose rickety old elevator intensified the joy surrounding the advent of riding to the upper floor to choose a new twin bed.

If the Tillsdale Bank had kept its temperature globe, it would have been cornflower blue. The globe, a big Humpty Dumpty-shaped thing once hanging on the bank's façade, would turn colors depending on the temperature—orange for warm and cornflower blue for cold. Rumor had it the bank took it down because it was too often blue, so the townsfolk were getting even more depressed and spending their money instead of saving it. Efforts at rejuvenating the town's dying businesses— like adding the temperature globe to the bank's front— had ultimately been futile.

The light turned green. She considered driving by to check on her father. He had taken to gambling a bit too much ever since her mother had moved away and remarried. The old man had been devastated when his bride had tied the knot with an old high-school flame, a man he'd always been jealous of, one who fancied knit shirts in pastel colors and plaid pants—a real estate agent of all things. At least he'd taken her to some place warm, North Carolina, the paradise for all Mid-Atlantic dwellers. Yes, she should check on her father. He was all she had near her as far as flesh and blood was concerned, and she loved him dearly. Maybe it was time he moved to some assisted living where he would eat better, talk to more people besides his jolt-deficient daughter.

As she slowly drove down Main Street, she caught a glimpse of a couple standing under a streetlight, probably crazy in love. Something about the way the guy jutted out one leg seemed familiar. He then scooped up his lady love and planted a passionate kiss on her, if passionate was defined as heads twirling around like dolls with magnets in their heads. The moment she passed them, he came up for air. It was Trey. She was sure of it! But the girl?

The driver behind her honked his horn. As she pulled away, she adjusted her rear-view mirror to try to catch the identity of the girl in Trey's embrace, but it was too late.

She clutched the steering wheel. "Trey," she said softly. A name with both the soft vowel sound of "e" and "y," and consonants, the "t" and the "r," signaling unpleasantness or discomfort. An English teacher could find meaning in anything.

Instead of driving to her father's, she swerved her car to the right and drove a few blocks to the humble home of her old high school guidance counselor, Winifred Maxwell. Aunt Winnie, as all the school kids called her, had long since retired, and some, including Hadley herself, said she was waiting to collect her reward after a long career listening to the most troubled demographic in the human spectrum. She was nobody's aunt—or wife or mother, for that matter—but all the kids had called her Aunt just the same.

It was Aunt Winnie who had first known of Hadley's anxiety over starting her period when she was 12, her first date, her first kiss, her first everything because she was much less preoccupied than her own mother. Aunt Winnie never told any of the kids' secrets. She retired when school statutes made it so she couldn't keep those secrets anymore, but those still left in the town confided in her, knowing she'd take all their confidences to her grave.

And she'd heard it all: sex, pregnancies, abortions, alcohol, dope, the works. That was the best gift she could give to young people, she'd always told those who still came to visit. Keep their secrets and let them think they're coming up with their own answers. She was the open ears to their self-disclosure.

When Hadley had first returned to Tillsdale a year ago, she had gone to Aunt Winnie's house and sobbed until she couldn't even breathe. She'd fallen asleep using the old ottoman as a pillow while the old lady sat on her sofa, patting her head with her fingers gnarled from arthritis. When she awoke, Aunt Winnie brought her a warm cup of cocoa and told her so long as there was living to do, she'd damn well better do it.

How could Hadley tell her there was living, and there was *living*, the heightened moments of being with someone you're crazy about? Otherwise, it was merely existing.

She knocked on the wood framing the side door, which was the only one Aunt Winnie ever used.

"You home?" she yelled through the screen.

"Come on in."

"Don't get up," Hadley said. She motioned to the old woman to stay put in her easy chair.

Aunt Winnie was a fright on first sight, mainly due to her wild salt-and-pepper hair, clipped back from her creased face with a sole tortoise-shell barrette. She was 70-something, tall and gangly, with extraordinarily long limbs that might have been pulled out from her torso like saltwater taffy. She fancied wearing the same old maroon sweater in her retirement, topping a variety of tweed skirts and the most god-awful putty-colored hose, which she once secured by garters right above her knee. Come to think of it, this ensemble, with a few dreary variations, was basically the same uniform she had worn most days in school.

"Make yourself some tea if you want some," she told her guest, flashing her protruding teeth.

"No tea—unless I can make you some? Or a sandwich, maybe? You need some calories."

Aunt Winnie shook her head. "C'mon in and sit down, Kathy."

Even though Hadley had changed her name to Hadley when she went to L.A. because it sounded more literary, being Hemingway's first wife's name, Winnie still called her by her old name. It only reminded Hadley that she hadn't yet earned the name change.

Hadley did as she was told and sat down, probably from force of habit from her school days. "What's new?"

Winnie shrugged. "What could be new? I wait for you kids to tell me what's new. How's your father?"

Hadley shook her head and played with the buttons on her raincoat. "Whenever I bring up assisted living, he changes the subject. But it would be good for him. His place is a mess. He doesn't eat right. What with school and all, I don't get to see him as often as I'd like." She held her head up with her arm propped on the old couch.

Winnie scowled. "You got your father all wrong. The mess is a symptom. No assisted living for him. He doesn't feel useful as a man, anymore."

As his daughter, Hadley loved him but perceived him differently. He drank. He gambled. The nearby casino was a constant worry. As his only relative left in town, she was responsible for him and weary because of it. It seemed like ever since she was a kid, she'd been taking care of him. It was always a tug of war between what he needed and her life apart from him.

"How about yourself?" Winnie's voice, still a beacon from a lighthouse, broke her reverie.

"I met a guy today. A young, handsome one." Hadley checked to see if her hostess had reacted, but only a poker face greeted her. Winnie never wanted to control the conversation, she told her charges. Let them open up, that was still her motto. Be as tough as hell, sarcastic even, but let the students talk. They'd spill that way. She believed talk was catharsis.

"Where'd you meet him? At school?" She pulled her buttonless sweater around her thin frame.

"Yeah. And guess what?"

The elderly lady shrugged again.

"He made me think of Derek."

Hadley came out to Winnie's humble home at least two or three times a week to check in on her, bring her a meal or groceries. She and Neil shared caretaking duties. So many needed so much: her students, her father, Aunt Winnie. Might there ever be a time when the days were cleared for herself?

She loved Winnie, though. Hadley remembered how, in high school, Winnie hadn't laughed when she told her how awkward she'd felt the first time she had gone to a movie with her first real serious boyfriend, getting a bit too dressed up. Winnie had said, "It's OK, dear. You were merely expressing yourself."

Winnie hesitated before speaking. "Is that good or bad, meeting this new guy?" She squinted her eyes, as if sizing up Trey in the flesh. Ever since Winnie had adopted Hadley as one of her regulars, she'd become suspicious of anyone who might treat her charge less than nobly.

"Probably bad. Except, as I said, he made me think about Derek, which, for some reason, made me feel good."

This time, Winnie reacted with her this-is-trouble expression, a drawing together of her untweezed still-black eyebrows.

"I want to write a play based on Derek. This guy I met not only reminded me of him, but sparked some ideas I've been struggling with for some time."

Winnie did a double take. "What, specifically, would you write about?"

"The loss of innocence. Not the physical deflowering. The mental one, where your heart gets busted so bad, you can never put it back together again." Hadley smiled faintly. "Call it your heart's hymen."

Winnie flinched, perhaps because she had taught English Lit before she became a counselor and believed that John Donne's conceits still ought to be the touchstone. "You can't think of another topic?" She knew about Hadley's play, and no doubt remembered the details of Derek's effect on Hadley's innocence like she remembered the number of absences every kid had in high school. "Can you even remember your last moment of innocence?"

"Can you?"

Winnie stared back. She never talked about herself. That was her success as a guidance counselor. Don't let them see your hand. There was a rumor she had once been a nun, or a nun-in-training, then left after she fell in love with some guy. Sort of like the plot to *The Sound of Music* but the guy she loved wasn't rich or handsome and probably couldn't sing "Edelweiss" either. And he stood her up. But no one had ever confirmed it. The only proof was the occasional reference to a Catholic education, the trivium, especially rhetoric and logic. Perhaps the nun thing was an urban myth of sorts. Anyway, myth or not, her destiny as either nun or bride was never realized.

"I don't know if I can remember," Hadley responded after several seconds. "I can remember moments, days, certain times."

"Such as?" Winnie's small black eyes bored into Hadley's soul.

Instead of answering, she noticed how much Winnie's lace curtains had yellowed over time. Her old arts and crafts home was a long way from the French restaurant in California that sparked a remembrance, a scene there, so long ago, when she was in love. And it all seemed so innocent.

****

SCENE: *Upscale French restaurant with solicitous waiters. Two people, a woman in her early 30s and a handsome man in his late 20s, are seated at a two-top next to a window dressed in lacy curtains.*

HADLEY: Did you see how the waiter stared at us when we came in? I thought maybe we weren't up to the dress code.

DEREK: He was the host, not the waiter. And why wouldn't he let us in? We're young, tan, and gorgeous.

HADLEY: You make us sound like "The Couple From Ipanema." Anyway, you're young, tan, and gorgeous. Me? Well, two out of three ain't bad.

DEREK: [*sounding slightly annoyed*] Oh, God, not again. OK, I'll take the bait: Which two out of the three are you?

HADLEY: Take a guess. I've got a beautiful tan,

I'm at my fighting weight, and I'm sure you noticed the Strawberry Festival Queen trophy near my bed, which leaves…

DEREK: [*sighing*] I have never known anyone so obsessed with age. What exactly happens when you turn 30? You turn into a pumpkin or something?

HADLEY: Have you seen those big creases in the average jack-o-lantern's face lately?

DEREK: [*Re-rolling the cuff of his sleeve.*] I wish you'd relax.

HADLEY: Easy for you to say. The bloom's still on your rose. Just wait, in a few years you'll know how it feels.

DEREK: I don't know about that. [*In an exaggerated motion, he throws back his shoulders.*] Time imparts a certain ruggedness to a man.

HADLEY: If you ask me, I wish you had a little more of Mount Rushmore about you right about now. I thought the host wasn't going to let you in without some proof that you'd passed puberty.

DEREK. Yes, but then when he saw I was accompanied by my mother. [*Laughing*]

HADLEY: You are vile, despicable, and insulting. I won't dignify any more of your insults tonight. [*She rises in mock outrage.*]

DEREK: [*He grabs her wrist.*] Unbutton your top button. [*He gestures at her blouse.*]

HADLEY: [*Her hand at chest.*] I will not! [*She puts the back of her hand on her forehead, mimicking a Victorian prude.*]

DEREK: C'mon, honey. Only the top two buttons. I like that little suggestion of cleavage.

HADLEY: [*leaning forward*] What do you mean

"suggestion"? I suppose if I were nineteen and had boobs that sprung out like a Slinky, it would be more than a suggestion. It would be a damn proclamation then, right?

DEREK: Honey?

HADLEY: Yes?

DEREK: What's a Slinky?

HADLEY: You're joking. Of course you remember those little toys made up of coils that moved when you put them on the stairs.

DEREK: Oh, sure. My grandma used to tell me about them.

HADLEY: I will finish this drink and leave. I do not need this torture. [*She sits back again and sips her drink.*]

DEREK: Oh, lighten up. Quit acting like an old crone.

HADLEY: What? I display a little restraint and that's menopausal. You drink a little alcohol and your testosterone level falls to zero, but that, somehow, is not hormonal.

DEREK: Now hold on! That "little bit of alcohol" you're referring to was four Bacardi and Cokes. So I got a little drunk. So I passed out.

HADLEY: So I noticed.

[*A waiter brings them their drinks, does the amenities, then leaves.*]

HADLEY: Did you hear that?

DEREK: What?

HADLEY: The waiter calls me "Ma'am," but didn't call you "Sir."

DEREK: So?

HADLEY: So, he could have called me "Miss," but he didn't. Where is that fine line of demarcation between "Miss" and "Ma'am"?

DEREK: Ever hear of the Mason-Dixon line?

HADLEY: Yes, so tell me: Where's Virginia compared to Pennsylvania?

DEREK: I'd say it's as much mental as physical. C'mon. Drink up your bubbly and let's go.

HADLEY: Oh sure. Aid and abet me in destroying a few more precious collagen cells.

DEREK: You know, I never dwell on the differences in our ages until you start yammering on and on about how five of the longest years in the history of the cosmos separate you from me. That when you were starting college, I was starting eighth grade. And when you were making out for the first time at a drive-in with some football player, I was making like a Star Wars Jedi in my backyard. When you...

HADLEY: All right, already. [*She buries her face in her hands.*] I'm obsessed and I hate it.

DEREK: Why not consider it as a definite advantage instead? I mean, you got to see a lot of the classic TV shows first time around, and I got stuck with re-runs.

HADLEY: Did you know I was one of the people who went to CBGB's in New York?

DEREK: You see? A definite advantage in perspective.

HADLEY: No, I'm serious! And I remember Watergate and disco and punk rock and...

DEREK: Yeah, and look what I got—Boy George and A Flock of Seagulls.

HADLEY: Yeah, I see what you mean.

DEREK: Besides, I don't know any nineteen-year-old who has a credit line as high as yours. You should think of your autumn years as a culmination of all that time letting your investments grow.

HADLEY: [*brightening*] Oh yeah? Wait'll you see what we can do with my Social Security checks!

DEREK: I understand there's a great resort in Acapulco with wheelchair ramps.

HADLEY: Terrific. I'll wheel you up.

DEREK: Hon?

HADLEY: Yes?

DEREK: Let's go.

HADLEY: To Acapulco? Don't you think I have a few years left before I draw my first Social Security check?

DEREK: No, I mean home. Let's go home. My place. I would love to raise your blood pressure.

HADLEY: Don't you think that's dangerous for someone my age?

DEREK: If I misbehave, you can tie me up with your support stockings.

HADLEY: And chase you out of the room with my cane?

DEREK: You can even take my teddy bear away from me.

HADLEY: Or unbutton the back panel of your jammies and spank you?

DEREK: You're quite the sport, old girl.

HADLEY: We'd better go. It's past your bedtime.

DEREK: Promise to tuck me in?

HADLEY: With these arthritic fingers? [*She wiggles her perfectly straight fingers.*]

DEREK: C'mon! You love a challenge.

HADLEY: Obviously. I'm with you, aren't I? Hey, help an old woman to her feet.

Chapter 5

"I said, help an old woman to her feet, will you?"

Hadley stirred and glanced at Aunt Winnie, struggling to get out of her antique horsehair chair.

"Of course." She grabbed underneath the old woman's bony left elbow, an overworked joint that had coupled together two parts of an arm, each half the size of a thigh bone.

"Thinking of your lost youth?" Winnie walked, bent over, to the kitchen where she filled the tea kettle with water and grabbed two mugs from the cupboard.

"Yes, I was, actually. Wondering what happened to that girl."

Winnie turned on the gas underneath the kettle. "Oh, for Pete's sake. Everybody was innocent at some point." A smile played on her thin lips.

"I was thinking of how wonderful the world was when I was in love."

Winnie glowered at her under furry eyebrows. "About this guy you've met," she said. She steadied herself with the edge of the counter in spite of the ballast her sturdy orthopedic shoes provided her. "Listen, why not pick on someone your own age? You need a solid guy, not some flibbertigibbet with hair. A man either is or he isn't."

"I guess I do always choose the ones who are *becoming* something."

There it was. The logic. The principle of the excluded middle. Catholic education again, courtesy of Winnie.

Hadley made a motion to help with the tea things, but Winnie pushed her away.

"Let me put a point to it," Winnie said. " 'It was always the becoming he dreamed of, never the being.' That's Fitzgerald, in case you forgot. F. Scott, not Edward."

Winnie was undoubtedly thinking she should give Neil a chance. But he was like a brother. And one doesn't romantically love one's brother. At least not most of the time.

"I was thinking of this guy, Trey, as inspiration, I guess."

Winnie, as usual, shot Hadley darts from her dark eyes. "Is this scheme you've cooked up strictly about the play?"

Hadley ignored her last remark. She needed to think about that.

Winnie adjusted the flame under the kettle. "So, it's a do-good project, is it?"

"Yes, in a way. I know there are other women like me. Maybe some right in the place where I work." Hadley stood in the entranceway between the living room and the kitchen. She was losing Winnie, and maybe herself. "Listen, while driving through town today, I had this idea, and believe me, it's been so long since I've been inspired. I checked out the movie theater and remembered one of the first movies I'd seen there—a revival of *Gone With the Wind*."

The old woman folded her arms, an indication of interest, Hadley knew, from countless trips to her office as a troubled teen.

"And I thought of how my affection for and affinity with Scarlett has actually intensified the older I get. In fact, popular wisdom holds that…"

"Seldom is *popular* wisdom very wise," Winnie interjected. The bony fingers of her hand crooked over the handle of the whistling tea kettle. She was careful to pour its contents in the mugs without plunging the dangling part of the teabag into the steaming hot water.

"…that she was ruthless and willful, especially with those men who found the Civil War a cinch compared to tussling with her."

Winnie's wrinkled face creased into a smile. "She *was* a tough character, wasn't she?"

Hadley returned her smile but continued almost breathlessly, as if Winnie would lose interest before she finished. "But I've always seen her in a different way, more as a sad, dependent heroine trying to get someone to love her in the way she loved the unavailable guy. I think it's her unrequited passion more than anything else that makes me, and millions of women, identify with her."

"You identify with her?" Winnie offered Hadley the mug of tea, perched on a saucer. "Most people only like her for her ambition. Her survival instinct. That's why *I* liked her."

Hadley pressed on. "Yes, like me, I always went for ones I couldn't have rather than the ones who loved me. Let's face it, all the crevices in my heart are the result of the elusive dreamers. Whereas I've flung all the solid heroes I've known by the wayside."

"Like Neil?" Winnie's once piercing eyes were now red-rimmed and rheumy from taking a sip of the steamy brew.

Winnie was aware of Neil's affection for her, starting way back since Hadley herself had told her. Neil must have confided in Winnie, too, in one of his frequent visits. But Winnie never squealed—merely hinted. Why were Winnie and Brenna always trying to push Neil on her? Hadley told Winnie countless times that she had a great affection for him, but she couldn't change her feelings into something more romantic.

She returned to her earlier subject. "That faded print of *Gone With the Wind* I saw right here in Tillsdale so many years ago," Hadley said, cupping her hands around the warmth of the cup, "has been replaced by a restored and rechanneled-for-stereo sparkler."

Winnie nodded and walked back into the living room. There were no VCRs in this room. Only a small color TV and books stacked like stalagmites on the floor.

Hadley continued, renewed and inspired. "In this new version, the definitive Southern belle has the blush added back into her cheeks and in her cinched-up party dress, all deep green and white chiffon, greets her adoring beaux."

"What are you trying to tell me?"

Hadley plunked down on the old ottoman and faced Winnie. "Unlike her, I've become a bit faded and weary, can't you understand?" The tears clouded her eyes. "No one can restore me. I'm no longer the belle of anyone's ball. And I hate that... I hate it. I'm so tired of taking care of others and worrying about others."

Winnie remained stolid. "As I said, everyone gets older. And if they're lucky, they'll pick up a little wisdom along the way."

Wisdom. The kind that comes right out of Proverbs,

Hadley thought.

Why did Winnie always refer to the collective? As if anyone else had any bearing on what she, Hadley, experienced. She missed being in love. Didn't she deserve that? She was tired of taking care of others.

"I'm sorry. I realize I'm talking too much." Hadley made a sweeping gesture with her arm near one of the book piles in the room. "Which of these many editions are you reading these days?"

Winnie left the question unanswered before continuing in a softer voice. "So, what's all this have to do with your play?"

Hadley took a few deep breaths before answering. "Like I said before, I'm going to use this young guy, Trey, the one I met today, sort of like field research."

She studied her old guidance counselor's face. In spite of its impassiveness, Winnie disapproved of any type of scheme, be it bullying or using other people for one's research or revenge. Hadley didn't add that she was attracted to Trey.

"Can't you see? It'll put the blush back in my cheeks to have the score evened, on paper this time. Even if I'm several degrees removed."

Winnie remained passionless, listening intently.

Hadley picked up where she'd left off. "After all, guys make girls fall in love with them, and not all of them are clever or strong enough to fight back when the guys lose interest. Maybe my play, once it's finished, will make all of them wiser."

Winnie took several more sips from her teacup, saying nothing for the longest time, but locked her gaze on Hadley. "I don't want you to get hurt again, or him either. That's the bottom line."

Hadley closed her eyes and sighed. "But at least I'll feel *something*. And, by the way, those types of guys never get hurt."

How could she ever relay to her mentor the passion and intensity she'd experienced with these men who everyone said were so bad for her and yet made her feel so alive? Yet she had to break her reliance on them for boyfriends. That much she knew.

The older woman set her cup down, folded her hands, her fingers so long they almost tapped her wrists. She looked right at Hadley.

"I should think you'd be sick of being hurt." The New York was back in her voice. "You've got a lot of holes to fill. For starters, your dad left a deep one that's never healed. Love is supposed to be mutual, not one-sided. People ought to rise above their past, that's my belief. Don't return to it by plugging all those holes for the rest of your life with the same spackle. Open yourself up to someone completely different than what you think you want."

Hadley sighed. Winnie's eyes narrowed further.

"And I have to say, my dear—it's never right to use someone, no matter their want of character. And that's not even anything you're sure of. That's what I would say if you were asking for my advice."

"Please don't worry about me," Hadley said before setting down her teacup and pulling her coat too forcefully around her as she matched buttons with buttonholes. "Please rest. I'll bring you something delicious next time I come. Good night."

She planted a kiss above Winnie's still scowling brows before carefully shutting the door behind her, calling back to the old woman to make sure she'd lock it, which she never did. As she worked her way down the old steps, she noticed the sky was the color of slate. In this town, it could be summer one day, winter the next.

All the more reason to get her plan rolling.

Chapter 6

She chose to walk, not drive, to The Cork to meet Neil. It had been a warm day, but, as was now the pattern, a chilly night. She dreaded the advent of a long, bleak winter.

At five sharp, Hadley walked into The Cork and Kettle, one of the town's many beer joints. The management actually referred to it as a "beer garden," although nothing verdant could ever survive its smoke- and grease-choked atmosphere.

Dutiful Neil was already there, sitting at a booth, sipping a draft beer. Facing the door, he waved her over as soon as she arrived. His eagerness upon seeing her was something she'd come to expect, and rely on, frankly. His freckled face like cinnamon on an uncooked sweet roll only added to her belief that Neil was an indelible part of home.

"Wow, get a load of you," he said, watching her slide unceremoniously into the booth to face him. "What's the occasion?"

She smiled. His eyes, as soft and uncritical as always, comforted her. Since their early days together, playing kickball and walking to school together, he had always taken care of her, stuck up for her. She was ashamed to think of the times she had snickered with her girlfriends about him or ignored him at school dances because of his predilection for nerdy clothes and dorky

Hush Puppies. She wanted to make up for it somehow. Maybe she could really contribute something to his new project, whatever it was.

"Oh, you! These are my school clothes." She fiddled with the tie on her blouse. "What's up?"

He smiled. "Always in a hurry." He signaled to the waitress. "Relax. Have a beer."

"Just coffee. I think the dam finally broke on my writer's block. I went to my writers' group earlier. I might be inspired to work on it later."

"Writer's block? You in some group?"

"Yes. It's nothing, really. Only a few locals. But I hope to write a play."

"But that's good." He held up his hand for a high-five that she returned. "I'm glad to hear it."

Asking the waitress for "a cup of joe," Neil then took a sip from his beer, leaving a foamy residue on his upper lip like one of the "Got Milk?" advertisements. "We can skip dinner then. Even though we haven't had much of a chance to talk lately. And I do need to update you." He smiled again, exposing the gap in his front teeth.

"I miss our times together," Hadley said. "Like the surprise birthday party you threw me last year. Only you would do something like that."

"Gee," Neil said, reverting to his habit of employing words his grandfather would have used. "That's what friends do."

"You're right. You absolutely make the rest of us seem cold-hearted by comparison. Now what's this idea you want to run by me?"

Another project. Neil was the most selfless person she knew. His pale blue eyes were framed by almost

49

invisible lashes. His freckles never faded with age, making him appear more adolescent than young for his age except for the sprinkling on his pumped-up arms straining the sleeves of his shirt. He must be working out. She nodded for him to continue.

"I'm starting a five-part series on drugs for the paper."

She took a few sips of her coffee. It was strong and bitter. She hated to think of her quaint hometown, as run down as it certainly was, being riddled with big-city problems, but she was aware that several of her students, if not more, were on a dark path.

"Drug use among the kids, illegal stuff, substance abuse. They do it all." He shook his head. "But by publishing the facts in the paper, maybe we can attract the attention of the state and get some money for programs."

She tried to guess which of her students might be using drugs, among them pale and distracted Jennifer who had asked for help that morning in the library.

"I know what you're thinking," he said. "More work when you've got all those papers to grade. But, it's important." He took another foamy sip from his glass.

"Yes, it's important," she said. "I have an idea to start an after-school writing group, but that seems so inadequate compared to what you're doing." Hadley shifted in her seat. Her heart beat too rapidly. The temperature in the old joint seemed to rise. "What about it? How do I come in?"

"I've gotten permission from the school to take surveys from the kids...the drugs, you know, whether they use or not, stuff like that. We need the facts to make it local, if you know what I mean. It'll all be confidential, no names."

A lot of kids in this town were bored and depressed—and taking desperate measures to deal with it. When she was young, she escaped into books or biked for hours on the country lanes surrounding the town. It was a different world now. She admired her old friend for wanting to help the youth in concrete ways that didn't involve writing a poem. But, who knows? Expressing themselves in other ways was important, too.

"What would you like me to do?" This time, she delivered her words with a smile.

Neil drained his glass and plunked it down with a thud. "I wanted to see if I could come in some morning and talk to your students. During one of your classes. I've already got the principal's OK. I think he's making up a schedule."

All of a sudden, returning home to work on her play didn't seem like such a good idea. Instead, a terrible force hit her, like getting the wind knocked out of her, one as strong as her writer's block had been. She remembered their childhood friend, Joshua, who had died of an overdose years ago. She fought the tears that were at the ready. Goodness came naturally with Neil. She loved that about him. Why couldn't she love *him*?

She swallowed hard. "Of course. When are you scheduled to come in?"

"Soon. This week, probably. The principal will send around a memo, he told me."

She nodded, wishing she could slide out of the old banquette and run home. She didn't, though. Neil would rush right after her.

"Hey, kiddo. You could use some red meat. C'mon. Are you sure you don't want to order a steak or something? My treat, of course. We'll pretend it's your birthday." He studied her face first, then the menu, even though every Tillsdalian had memorized the bill of fare as soon as they could read, which was essentially the same from restaurant to restaurant in this neck of the woods. No chopped salad, no bistro food. Just plain old comfort food.

For a moment, she wanted to stay and let Neil take care of her, order food for her and pay for it. But she reminded herself she was on a mission to write something, anything. She put her hands on the banquette. She could feel the slashed skin of the booth, held together by duct tape. Life seemed fragile all of a sudden. "I think I want to go and start working. I'm not hungry."

Neil nodded. "I'm sorry. I didn't mean to—"

Hadley beheld him, a force in spite of himself, what with the thinking and planning this project must have engendered. "I know. Like you said, it's important." She wanted to think of life, quickened with possibility. And her play, yes, that gave her hope. Her students needed something to hope for, as well. "You made me realize I need to do so much more with these kids. There never seems to be enough hours in the day. But, as for your request, of course, yes, come in anytime."

Neil's forehead was furrowed. He always had an accompanying physical reaction to his emotions.

"I'm so sorry to have dampened the mood," he said, taking her hand. "I only hope to avoid, you know, these kids sliding more…" He squeezed her hand instead of finishing what was obvious. "We need another celebration soon, or something like it, right?"

"Yes," Hadley said. She found the warmth of his big hand comforting. "Good idea."

"May I drive you home?" he asked, deepening the rows in his brow even more.

"No, I left my car at Winnie's. Thought a nice brisk walk would do me good."

Neil slid out from the booth as she did and planted a kiss on her cheek.

"See you soon," he said. "I hope."

She nodded as she walked to the door, wishing, once again, she had more than her thin raincoat around her.

****

When she got home, Hadley called her dad. The chill of fall always brought with it the reminder that she wouldn't have her parents forever. Besides, she worried about him. Her mother had someone now to look out for her after decades of thanklessly taking care of her first husband. He was from a generation that considered cooking and cleaning to be women's duties, so she tried not to think of his messy house and how it was somehow up to her now to clean it up without her mother around.

"Papa?"

"That you, Kathy?"

"Listen, are you OK? Did you eat anything good today?" That was a question both Winnie and Brenna often asked her. Maybe there was something magical in nutrient-dense foods to make people happier as well as healthier. She might never know. She was a poor eater like her father.

"Now, now. Don't go worrying about me. What are you up to? Go to bed."

Hadley checked the clock on the wall: 9:05. "I've got some stuff to do yet. But I wanted to hear your voice. And tell you I love you."

Her father cleared his throat. "I know you do. I don't

know much, but I do know that. Now you go and get some sleep."

She nodded, as if he could see her. "Good night, Papa. I'll see you soon."

The unopened mail lay before her. Her eyes gravitated toward an envelope with a return address from a literary magazine to which she had submitted some poems. Slowly, she opened it, afraid it would be another rejection. But the letter's first line read, "We loved your poem 'Metamorphosis.' We have accepted it for our next edition."

She pressed the letter against her chest. "How wonderful," she said to the books in her small apartment's living room. "How very wonderful." The poem was set during a time when her parents took her on vacation and stopped at a Tucson motel in the month of March. Hadley had asked the manager if she could swim, but was told it was off-season. Instead, she imagined what it would have been like, an Eastern girl ready to advance spring by diving into the pool and slowly rising to the surface, "splitting open winter's caul."

A win under her belt, she was more than ever ready to start writing, wriggling her fingers in anticipation of typing. Writing would help her—and help her father and her students by extension. How? She didn't know. But writing energized her.

She sat in front of her computer screen. Her intention was to sketch out the bones of The Plan and maybe type out the scene between her and Derek that she had dreamt about when she was at Winnie's.

She brewed herself a cup of coffee, then started typing. Furiously.

The Plan

Goal: To show the waystations a player takes while wooing a woman for his purposes (which may vary) right up until the woman wises up and realizes she's been duped. Use as inspiration for the as-yet-untitled play ("The Moment Right Before?"), an early draft of the beginning, which I need to have finished by next Wednesday for the writers' group.

First Stage: Done! The attraction blossoms like a fresh hickey on someone's unsuspecting neck. Everything's funny, faults are brushed aside, lust is in the air. They find each other irresistible (even the guy does). Pure heaven!

Second Stage: Still a closeness, but usually the girl notices the guy is less available, tries less to enchant and/or engage her, seems distracted. Observe Trey's visits to the school to see Anise or Sara. Try to catch him in the act. Eavesdrop if you must! Enlist Brenna for help (even though she seems to be hiding something about Trey).

Third Stage: The girl (usually) becomes needier (watch Anise's and/or Sara's behavior). Either the girl will beg for more "talks" about where their relationship is headed (or not), or she'll drop him like a hot cast iron pan.

Fourth Stage: Watch for signs of forlornness (izzat a word?) if the girl is hanging on—probably Sara. Or insouciance if she dumped him—more likely Anise. The latter possibility means the girl has saved herself from going over into the deep end. She has control, even though she loses him. But does she still have innocence at this point???? Or only wisdom????? What distinguishes girls hanging on indefinitely at this stage or deciding to take charge and leave before he dumps *her*?

What is the quality these girls-in-control have?

Fifth Stage: It's over. Too late to find that last moment of innocence 'cause the girl has waited around too long. Girl realizes it. Guy may be unavailable at this point or has ditched her for someone else. What's the aftermath like????

Hadley rubbed her eyes. She was in the Fifth Stage. Such a realization, right before her in black and white, made her sad.

The clock said midnight. She had to go to bed, even with the weight of her new insight bearing down on her. Maybe, just maybe, with her plan, she could help others like her before they reached the point of no return.

In spite of all the coffee, she felt sluggish, full of wet sand. "Am I at the point of no return?" she asked the spirits in her apartment who often showed their presence by causing the seemingly incessant static electricity in her hair.

Chapter 7

On the way to school the next morning, Hadley had the misfortune of getting stuck behind a school bus that stopped every few seconds to pick up its human cargo. The fog had now condensed into droplets on her windshield. She turned on the wipers and scanned the sky for a glimpse of the sun. But the sunrise, along with all other events in Tillsdale, whether divine or secular in nature, was more insidious than dramatic.

"Once you're in, you can't get out," Hadley said out loud. She watched as the bus door opened for children whose families often went way back in the region.

Seeing Trey yesterday had brought back Derek in living color. Trey had momentarily taken away the ache only to leave her with a new one. The damn worm of yearning was always choosing her to be its host.

Maybe she was never meant to be with Derek for the long run. He eventually drifted away, then after a while, quit calling. She remembered the old wives' tale that when cats know it's their time, they go away to die. But there she was, still yelling "Here, kitty, kitty, kitty" long after he'd gone.

But she would have the last word. In her play, her heroine would triumph.

The windshield wipers tapped out the rhythm to The Rolling Stones' "Let it Bleed." She preferred the classic rock station these days with real guitars and drums instead of today's processed music, no matter how "sick" the beat of rap and New Jack Swing.

She then mused about the stages of love she had worked out last night. How sweet it was in the beginning! Trey had brought that feeling, that volcano-in-the-gut feeling, back. When people were getting to know each other, everything was new and wonderful and fascinating.

Like when she had met Derek in L.A. at You Can Be A Star!, a place offering people a chance to sing against a pre-recorded track like real singers and go home with a cassette. She and her friend Bryce were there, bickering over whether to choose a Whitney Houston song or go with "Over the Rainbow," the standard default song for all histrionic amateurs.

"Why not go with both?" Derek, who worked there as the engineer, had suggested.

He was charming, pretty, even. Dark, with expressive eyebrows arching over eyes of deep blue.

"Yes," she had said to him. "Why not?"

When Bryce and she had finished butchering both songs, they emerged to find Derek carefully labeling the tape of their performance before handing it over.

"Stevie and Tom?" She read his writing. "As in Nicks and Petty?"

"Exactly," he said, flashing a disarming grin.

"I'm taking that as an insult. They're so...well, '80s." Bryce reached inside his leather jacket to pull out the tips of his shirt collar. "He could have said Peabo Bryson and Regina Belle, at least," he whispered to Hadley.

"Not meant as an insult," Derek answered, winking at Hadley. "You sounded a bit like Stevie, scolding, even though it's a love song, right? You sounded like you were singing personally to that rainbow to get you over it. And for the record, no pun intended, I like Stevie and Tom."

The plastic cassette case also included his business card. On the back of the card was written a telephone number with the message, "Call me. We can listen to 'Stop Draggin' My Heart Around.' " And she did. The next night, in fact.

Soon after, they went to see a showing of the French version of *Les Liaisons Dangereuses*, when he found out she was a fan of *Jules et Jim*, and later they kissed under streetlights on Santa Monica Boulevard. She went home with him, too. There, she learned he was a waiter in addition to his gig at You Can Be A Star!, but what he really wanted to do was act or sing, preferably both, he told her. Acting, he had said so prophetically that night, was what he was really good at.

Before she knew it, they were an item, at least in her mind. Until, one day, they weren't. And somewhere in between was the moment she wished to recapture on paper, in her play, so she could savor it and analyze it and return to it and wonder until she had salt-and-pepper hair like Aunt Winnie and recount how in the hell she had lost it and crossed over from Toyland into a land from which she could ne'er return again.

But another side of her, perhaps the deeper, more authentic side, understood that Aunt Winnie was right. Involving Trey wasn't right.

It wasn't long before she found herself a parking place in the outer edges of the school lot, as convenient a spot as any in which to think.

She longed to talk to Roxie Sanchez from L.A., her

wild friend who always sided with her against the dogs of the world but found herself too often in the dog pound herself, especially with the love-'em-and-leave-'em record executives she worked with and fell for.

By the time Hadley had touched up her makeup, she spotted Trey in her rear-view mirror, bounding down the sidewalk from one of the back entrances of the school. The sight of him, all youth and optimism, charged her spirit instantly. He was hopefulness in a perfect package.

He was headed in her direction, too. Should she crouch down in the seat or confront him head-on? She held the mirror closer: Her nose was unbecomingly red. The decision was quickly made for her when he chose to wend his way right by her car.

"Hadley?" He squatted, bouncing on his heels, and tapped on the window. She was forced to open it, letting in all his exuberance along with the morning mist. A wafting of spearmint accompanied him.

"It is Hadley, isn't it? Or shall I call you Miss Todd since we *are* on school property?" He offered her an up-close beaming smile, his all-access pass to anywhere.

"*Hadley's* fine." She flattened her hair with her hand. Damn the mist. She'd be a frizz fest in no time. And the blotching. *Please, God, don't let him notice.*

"I'm curious about something. How'd you get the name Hadley?"

She scrutinized his face, a combination of planes and angles; he was handsome and pretty at the same time. Along with a strong jawline, he had those luscious eyes, big expressive eyes like Dondi, that round-eyed orphan of the comic pages from years past. And his smile, framed by pouty lips and one dimple, not two. Two would have been perfection and everyone had to have a little dusting of humanity.

She defaulted to what she considered to be her most unattractive expression: pursed lips. She caught herself in the act and stopped. Damn his questions anyway! "I legally changed it when I lived in L.A."

Although she hadn't dreamed it was possible, his smile got even brighter. "Really? What was it before?"

"Kathryn. There were a million Kathys, so I changed it."

"But why 'Hadley'? I've never heard that name before."

Her stomach growled. Had she eaten breakfast? Or just drunk coffee? "It was Hemingway's first wife's name. His favorite wife, by all accounts. And if I ever became a writer…"

"Wow, I like that. I mean the fact you had the…I don't know, whatever it took, balls, maybe…to change it. Such a show biz move."

She kept her eyes on the mirror. "And your name? Trey, isn't it?" As if she hadn't said the name over and over to herself since meeting him yesterday.

"That's right." His lovely mouth opened like an archer's bow. He ran his hands through his thick hair and stared at her, causing her to shift in the car seat. "And that's what it says on my birth certificate, by the way."

When had that certificate been issued? She wanted to stop him from thinking whatever the narrative was accompanying his gaze. "The only 'Trey' I've ever heard of was Old Dog Tray in the Civil War song. And it's a homonym."

"A what?"

"A word pronounced the same but spelled differently. 'Old Dog Tray' is spelled with an 'a.' I assumed you're spelled with an 'e.' " *How could he know "chiasmus," but not the basic "homonym"?*

"Hum a few bars," he said, grinning.

She wouldn't take the bait, afraid he'd make a sarcastic remark about her remembering it from the pop charts back then. "Sorry. The melody escapes me." It was a lie. She could sing it in her sleep after learning to play it on the piano years ago, one of the songs in her Big-Note beginner's piano book. "But, I do remember your namesake was described as being ever gentle, ever kind, and ever faithful."

A sexy chuckle erupted from the back of his throat. "Well, two out of three ain't bad."

She glanced at her watch, reluctantly tearing herself from the feast of his face. "I must be going. A legion of young Shakespeare fans awaits me."

He leaned in closer, smelling of fabric softener, spearmint, and fresh air. Sara must be quite the laundress.

"So you like music, in addition to homonyms?" he asked, ignoring her remark about school.

"Yeah. Even stuff that came *after* the Civil War."

He tapped his fingers on the car door. "Listen, I was wondering if you'd like to come down to The Cork and Kettle tomorrow night around six." He waited a beat or two before continuing, fidgeting.

Hadley liked that he seemed nervous inviting her. She must intimidate him to some extent.

"I'm giving a little acoustic set." He paused again, as if awaiting her reaction.

Who would she go with? Who would be there? She'd like to see him in action before a crowd, though, but scolded herself for not having memorized her plan of action.

He studied her face. "Oh, c'mon. Torture yourself. Say you'll be there."

"I'll try. No promises, though." She paused. Her eyes searched the school entrances to see if Sara was coming out. "By the way, did you know I used to work in the music business?"

His smile momentarily faded. "Yeah, sorta."

"Who told you?" As if she couldn't guess.

"I don't know. Brenna maybe?" His face lit up again. "That's how I knew you liked music."

It was her turn to tap out her annoyance on the steering wheel. How much had Brenna disclosed to him about her? "Actually, working on the business end is often a sure way to make you hate music. So, if you're on the prowl for pointers, I must warn you, I'm a tough audience."

"I'm not worried. I've worked more difficult rooms."

At one time his confidence would have charmed her. Yet, she didn't feel she could trust him, given that he appeared to be involved with two women. She wanted to change the subject. She was not prepared yet on how she planned to enlist him to help with her play.

"By the way, what brings *you* here so early in the morning?"

He stood up to stretch, replacing his face with his blue Oxford shirt in her realm of vision.

"I had to talk to the coach about covering a game." He stretched before crouching down again, leaning into her. "Actually, I spotted you from a distance and wanted to see for myself if you were wearing my two favorite colors today, pink and gray."

Only a v-section of her dress, whose alternating stripes were indeed pink and gray, was visible underneath her raincoat.

He laughed. "See you tomorrow night," he said and tapped her car door with his knuckles before springing off.

"Mental note to self," she said aloud. "Always leave before they do."

Chapter 8

She didn't like what Trey's desirability and self-assurance elicited in her, which was pure mealy-mouthed mushiness and hot animal lust. If attraction to the opposite sex was supposed to be such a pleasant experience, why did she feel weakest at such moments, least like what she imagined as her tough teacher persona? What would Winnie say to that?

On her way to her classroom, she passed the office and noticed Sara, on the phone, staring into space. She must have seen Hadley passing by before turning to face her computer.

"You're so bad," she said, laughing from deep within her chest. "I know, I know. I'll be there, OK? I love you."

Hadley shifted her books to balance the weight better. Sara must have been talking to Trey, newly outlaid with a cellphone at her expense, who might have said "I love you, too" back to her. He was the type who would be expected to date someone with a more outgoing personality like his. Sara was always quiet. But he got the flash with Anise. It was rumored Sara's uncle in Albany, who had recently died, had left her some money. There were bets going around on how long it would be before she'd quit, now that she was "sitting pretty," as the locals termed it. Brenna said the buzz was she was ready to start her life anew, preferably with Trey, but was letting him have his freedom so he'd come to her of his own will.

Or maybe he was truly into her? Maybe Hadley didn't know men at all.

Sara, whatever her intentions, would have to wait. Hadley needed Trey to be her muse. He'd come over to speak to her, hadn't he? Oh sure, he was the one in control this time, but it pleased her that she had been able to catch his eye. But she reminded herself he was only interested in her connections, just as he was only interested in Anise for sex and Sara for dough, right? Suppositions were dangerous things. Playboy though he might be, he was impossible not to like, that was for sure. She liked him, all right, the few times she'd interacted with him. She even liked the way he smelled—fresh.

Even the advent of teaching "Othello" to a reluctant group of students couldn't stanch the rush of excitement Hadley felt. The challenge was on. It was fated to be. This showdown was destiny. Shakespeare's Emilia had said, "Why we have galls, and though we have some grace, yet have we some revenge." If Hadley followed through with her desire to avenge her own heartbreak by means of the play, she'd be putting those words to the test. She wondered if she were more like the spiteful blackguard of the play or the world-weary, but wise, woman.

She decided she was a little bit of both, a conclusion affording her no consolation whatsoever.

****

By the time Hadley met Brenna to walk to the faculty room for lunch, Brenna had learned that Trey's musical debut was scheduled for Friday night at The Cork and Kettle.

Hadley didn't tell her he had already invited her.

"Do you think you'll go?" Brenna asked her on the way. "Anise has asked me to be her beard for the evening, but even beards need beards."

Hadley stopped walking. "I'm curious. What will he do about Sara?"

"Oh, she'll come alone and sit by herself, her preference, hoping against hope he'll grab her and go home with her at the end of the night instead of with Anise. Please say you'll be there." She touched Hadley's forearm with both hands. "I need to get out and have some fun."

"Does Anise know I know about her and Trey?"

A slight scowl crossed Brenna's brow. "Oh, sure. She's nothing if not upfront about what she's doing. I think it gives her a thrill to be the other woman." She paused. "Or *one* of his women."

"Speaking of being frank, I ran into a certain someone who seemed to know I once worked at a record company, compliments of you." She feigned mock indignation by pursing her lips.

Brenna paused for a good five seconds. "Golly, I didn't think you'd mind. He was in the faculty room one day and happened to mention his music. I thought it was a good lead-in."

"To what?"

"To conversation. I have so little in common with him. Although I feel as if I know too much about his abilities in a certain department." She smiled and winked, hoping to regain the balance she had clearly upset.

"How did he react?" Hadley's heart thudded.

"Oh, he wanted to know all the details. What record

label, and of course I forgot, and what you did there, all that stuff. I told him he ought to talk to you." She tittered. "I knew you wouldn't mind spending an hour drowning in those sea-blue eyes, and elsewhere, if you dare. Do you think he stuffs a catnip toy in his pants?"

Hadley ignored her comment. "But if I come with you Friday, what about Anise? Wouldn't she mind if I went?"

"Of course she'll mind. She changed the subject when I mentioned it, as I recall. But, the boy's certainly shown he's public domain anyway, hasn't he? Say you'll come with me. Please? Without you, I won't have anyone to gossip with."

The challenge could begin with her accepting the date this time around, only to engage him in her plan. If she snuck in on Friday and caught his act, she'd have a better chance of observing his women already knee-deep in love with him. Not to mention his behavior. The vasovagal nerve once again pinged. She remembered reading that a surge of adrenaline causes a twitch in this nerve, located somewhere in the seat of emotions, tangled as it was around an organ or two.

"OK. I'll meet you there."

"Wonderful. We'll have a ball." Brenna wrinkled her nose. "Think of all the intrigue."

****

After school, Hadley wanted to see Aunt Winnie to update her, or maybe soothe her own conscience, but instead she called her father during study hall to tell him she'd stop by and bring him a burger and fries, his favorite meal, after school.

Her parents' former homestead, a modest Craftsman set back from the road, had been remodeled with white siding and forest green shutters over 10 years ago. The remodel was her mother's last stab at trying to save the marriage by dressing up the exteriors. How ironic that for years her mother had begged her to return, and, once she did, her mother had already moved away.

The house seemed so small and unassuming whenever she'd visit from California. The house was on a treeless street, with only low-lying shrubs around it. The fact it still seemed like home grated Hadley's nerves. There, within its unyielding wainscoted walls, her life had been shaped and cast. If this had been the chrysalis to her pupa, no wonder her dreams still seemed so hard to realize. No gusset could be found in the house's fabric to accommodate sickness, change, or growth.

"Papa?" she called, rapping on the screen door attached to her father's humble kitchen door. "You in here?"

No one answered her call. The air was heavy with the odor of unwashed clothes. A pile of dirty laundry had been stacked next to the basement door. The sink was full of dirty dishes. It seemed like he'd go a few days cleaning up after himself, then abandon doing so. Why couldn't he be consistent? It was the same reason he hadn't been consistent as a father.

She walked across the small patch of green sod, approaching the garage that doubled as her father's workroom. He was sitting there, yet unaware of her presence, smoking a cigarette. His hair was uncombed and his shirt crinkled. Men were so damn helpless without women! A row of beer bottles lined one of his work shelves, little amber soldiers fighting the war of depression. Mercenaries, not soldiers. They could turn on you.

"Papa." This time, it was a statement, not a question.

"Here and accounted for," he said. He swiveled around on his stool. "Hi, honey. What's in the bag?"

"You know. The usual," she said. She found it difficult to muster much enthusiasm after a long day at school. Her feet hurt, so she sat down at one of the two chairs at either end of the small table. "You shouldn't smoke with all the wood chips." She nodded toward the shavings lying underneath his feet. "Not to mention your health." He had such a deep bronchial cough.

He still did occasional work. Carpentry, mostly. He loved to work with his hands, to be the master of a piece of wood. As a little girl, she had watched him work on his lathe, in this same garage. He'd show her a piece of wood newly smoothed out and point out the whorl in the wood grain and ask her what she saw there. A horse's head? A cat's face? She still thought of whittled wood as a stilled fantasy, figures swirling therein caught in motion.

Since he had retired and had the mini-stroke, her father's workplace was more a crypt than a center of creativity. She wished he'd get himself a widow or a nice divorced woman. Men were supposed to be so strong, but the only way they could go out and fight the big wars was if they had women at home fighting the little battles—the congealed egg on plates, the grease on clothes, the dust on the TV screen. That was certainly true in his case.

He dived into the bag and laid out the cheeseburger and fries on a napkin.

"No coffee?"

"Damn. I left it in the car. I'll go get it."

"Sit down, little girl. I'll make some later. Sit down

and talk to your old Pa."

As much as she loved him, there were times Hadley wished he were more independent. Her mother had infantilized and spoiled him. Then she took off for a new life and left him helpless. He grabbed the burger, so tiny in his huge hands. He could lift anything in his prime.

She remembered when, as a child, she had broken her leg. Her father had been so worried, arriving in the emergency room soon after. When she awoke after surgery, he was there, in the corner of her hospital room, his big workingman's hands covering his face. It was one of two times she had ever seen him cry, the other being when his childhood sweetheart left him for another man.

"Talk to me," he said through bites of fast food.

"Not much to say, Papa," she said. How could she talk to him about her problems with men or writer's block? Silence fell between them like the shaft of late afternoon sunlight on his work table. She remembered a verse in the Bible that said if you're ever at a loss for words during prayer, you should ask the Holy Spirit to intercede. She needed such an intercession now, but she considered herself to be off the list unless she made some changes.

"So, what's new at school?"

She picked up the piece of wood he had been whittling. "Nothing much. It's a job."

"You don't sound much enthused. Ain't that what you went to school for? Why else did you come home for?"

The circles under his eyes emphasized his weariness. There were times she wondered if he could ever muster the passion of his earlier days. Perhaps her mother had had a fling decades ago, and she was the product of the real estate man in the plaid pants, her new stepfather.

"Yeah. I like it all right. I'm tired, I guess."

Her father began to cough, the result of stuffing his dinner into his mouth with nothing to wash it down.

"I'll get you something to drink." She welcomed the chance to escape from the garage for some fresh air.

His face grew beet red. He gestured toward the corner of the garage. "Get me a pop over there," he said.

She retrieved a cola from the ice chest, popping it open before setting it in front of him. "I'll get a glass."

"Nah. I'll drink it as is," he said. He took a swig from the can. "You're awful gloomy tonight. You missing that guy in L.A.?"

She steadied herself. She hadn't told him anything about Derek. "What guy?"

"There's always a guy, right?"

She nodded. He could still be as sharp as his whittling knife. It was a relief, in a way. She didn't have to pretend.

"What else can I get you?" She wished she had cooked him a healthy meal. But between him and Winnie, she was weary, too.

"Nothing, you go on. You've got things to do." He waved her away.

She scanned the room. Old oil cans shared the shelves with the spent beer bottles. He had been a dreamer, her father. She had remembered his dreams when they had all been younger. He was going to win big money, he'd periodically tell her and her mother. For years, she'd heard him speak over the phone about exactas and trifectas, repeating wonderfully florid names like Rose Dust or Rapid Fire. But the big money never materialized. She couldn't really blame her mother. People can't live on the ether of dreams forever.

"Don't be so gloomy, girl," he said, proffering a smile.

"Didn't know I was." She smiled back, so he wouldn't think she was sad.

He finished off the soda. "Do you know that as a child, you always said, 'I'm gonna be like Elijah and go to Heaven without dying.' Yessir, you'd tell me you was so scared of dying you'd ask God to take you up in a chariot and bypass the whole thing." He chuckled before belching. "I think you said that after your grandfather died. We should never have let you see him at the funeral home. Made you morbid."

Dust motes danced in the mottled sunlight. She got up to shake off the thought of *him* at a funeral home, a thought that was more than she could bear. "I'm going to take off now. Goodbye, Pa. I'll call you tomorrow."

"No need. I'll be fine."

"What do you mean? Of course I'll call you. You worry me."

He waved her off again. "I keep busy here. You go. You've got your life. We'll talk soon."

She started to leave, but instead wended her way through the junk in her father's workshop and gave him a kiss on the forehead. He was only one of two people whom she could call her flesh and blood. Her father put his arm around her.

"Go on, now," he said, quietly. "Your papa will be all right."

She walked through the house on her way out. Perhaps, after all, her father's plans were to clean up the house, do the dishes. No one should have to clean up someone else's mess, Tennessee Williams had once written. And she understood now what he meant. Nevertheless, she rolled up her blouse sleeves and tackled the mess. A little housekeeping might make him feel better, too.

He learned about wishing to escape early in his life. His father was an inveterate gambler, and his mother was not the working kind, herself preferring a life lost in books and dreaming. Something had to give in such a household.

When her father was about eight, he was sent to live with his paternal grandparents on a farm in rural upstate New York, north of Tillsdale, a god-forsaken place. Such a solution, it was believed, would allow his father to get the gambling bug out of his system and his mother to save some money. They were ill-equipped for such a gauzy solution. His father who worked in the oil fields one day, injured his leg, carving out a wound that would never heal, eventually causing his death several decades later when it became cancerous. His wife was always who she was: a flighty belle never meant for marriage, struggling pathetically in a world she could never negotiate, even when she, too, was forced to live on government surplus food after her husband died.

Hadley's father as a child struggled to adjust to farm life, one whose atmosphere was colored by his stern grandmother. He said he often went to bed hungry, listening to the rats in the old farmhouse walls. He loved his grandfather, though, who taught him how to milk cows and be kind to the farm animals. But his life was hard. Many years later, Hadley found a letter he had written home to his mother during this time that implored her to come get him and return him to the household he had once known. It is pathetic in its entreaties: He was cold, he was hungry, he was lonely. "Please, Mother," he wrote in his schoolboy script, "take me back home. I miss you so much." What could be worse for a child than to have a mother, but not be with her?

So he married, in effect, a woman not averse to being his mother on some level. She was only eighteen when she became his bride. She was willing to cook for him, coddle him, make excuses for him. But he continued to drink and gamble because she was not his mother, after all. It was too late. Sometimes we can't get the timing right, which can upend all that follows. He had not been returned to his own mother until he was well past the important years, a teenager to attend high school in his hometown. The kids weren't like those he knew from his time with his grandparents. He went back to his rural high school to graduate, a year ahead of his classmates, his restlessness—and brokenness—evident in his desire to wrest control in spite of being a "motherless" boy.

So Hadley had come into this life, her father actively playing out the childhood damage—damage so deep and broad he didn't think of its effect upon the lives he had created. So, their relationship was lacking; without that extra something he craved, she would never be enough. None of those in his world would. Without that extra something to lift him out of the world he secretly despised, he was angry, spotlighting his daughter, in particular, for not being personable enough toward him, for not eating the food he worked for with the gusto he felt it deserved, for not condoning his spates of alcoholism.

For expecting too much of her.

Maybe, she mused, she had trouble with men because of her family. Her mother babying her father, waiting on him, then getting antsy and leaving, perhaps to live a little before calling it a day. And maybe her father simply didn't have enough time for his daughter growing up, preferring the immediacy of the bottle and the thrill of the track to the winsomeness of a little girl. Maybe that's why she attracted the unavailable types. To make history right.

Still, her father loved her. And it was mutual. Blood mutual.

But it was time to let it go. Hadley would love him, but would have as one of her goals not to allow him to hurt her anymore.

****

She drove through the dusk-smudged town on her way home.

She put her foot on the brake pedal as she approached the stoplight in front of the newspaper office where Neil was undoubtedly slumped in his chair, reading copy or editing a story. She should have called him to follow up about the school survey. She ought to call him more often. He was good for her.

These red lights were ridiculous on nights when no one was around. What was the point?

The town had dwindled to a hamlet. How wrong her father had been about her! Gloomy? Far from it. She had no desire to bypass death and go straight to Heaven. She wanted to live. That was the whole problem! She wanted to live! She choked back a sob and wiped her nose, unladylike, with the cuff of her raincoat. No one was around to see her anyway.

The streetlight rinsed Tillsdale in an unrelenting

melancholy. Nighttime was closing in again, along with the tree-dense mountains, doubly insulating her. The rain mixed with the evening's mist. For half a second, as she waited at the interminable red light, she closed her eyes against the darkness.

When she got home, she called Roxie, simply to hear her voice. They spoke about men, mostly. What they didn't say, but what was understood between them, was their desire for the self-same men they trashed. Roxie was having an affair with Benny, the married A&R guy at the record company where she worked.

"Benny's driving me up the wall," Roxie said, taking a long drag of her cigarette. "Would you mind being my therapist for a quick second? Pretty please? That's what friends do, right?"

Roxie had always been there for her when Derek had given her heart a thrashing. Roxie could never speak to Derek after that. How is it people could be so certain about knowing what was the right thing to do with their friends' lovers but less so when it came to their own?

"I'm here for you," Hadley said. She cradled the phone between her ear and shoulder, spending the next twenty minutes trying to convince Roxie that she was a way better person than Benny would have her believe.

Chapter 9

By the time Friday night arrived, Hadley wanted nothing more than to soak in a hot tub and listen to a Beethoven's pastoral or maybe something baroque to make her feel civilized and noble again. She'd read that people's heartbeats synchronized to the tempo of baroque music, inducing relaxation. There was no time for that. She would have to take a quick shower and reconstruct herself for Trey's musical debut.

Her plan was to see what his effect would be on Sara and Anise to determine what stage of the love train they were on.

She checked her answering machine. A message from Neil. "Are you OK?" His disembodied voice said he was still concerned with the way she'd fled their last meeting and he hoped he hadn't upset her. Good old Neil. She'd call him later, or sometime.

What time was it? She intended to be late for Trey's show by at least a half hour. She took a shower then went to her closet to choose something appropriate to wear. Did she want to come across like a respectable English teacher out for a safe and early night? Or did she want to transform herself into a sex goddess to catch a certain someone's already overtaxed eye? She tried on several outfits, only to be content with a slightly looser version of the schoolmarm she fancied she had become.

By the time she pulled into the parking lot, the

swamp noises in her gut were vying with the reverb issuing forth from the bar's interior. Hadn't her stomach failed her all the other times she had gone to smoky venues to hear Derek play?

It was wrong, her going, she could hear Aunt Winnie saying. Anything duplicitous was, although Winnie would never bring it up without Hadley first doing so. Instead, it would lie there between them until she couldn't bear it any longer. As a result, she hadn't lingered when she dropped off a bag of groceries recently.

The Cork was located at the end of a street in a no-longer-so-good part of town. The parking lot was full, so Hadley was relegated to a spot on a neighboring side street, one lit by an old-fashioned streetlight, a relic of a time when Tillsdale might actually have been quaint and bustling. Now it needed markers to proclaim its historical value.

A round of applause was in progress as Hadley stepped through the doorway and handed over a wadded-up five-dollar bill to a man standing at the entrance. How much of that five-spot would go to Trey and what, if any, would filter down to Anise or Sara—and in what form?

As she stepped into the room, Hadley scanned the crowd for Brenna. Instead, she caught sight of Sara, sitting by herself at a table in the back. She was wearing a leather jacket with, of all things, fringe trailing from the shoulders and along the sleeves. Her attempt at dressing for a dive bar touched Hadley's heart. Sara managed a quivering smile that, in truth, was probably a reflexive response more than a deliberate greeting, but Hadley smiled back.

Finally, she spotted Anise's platinum hair, lit up

from the recessed lighting. Brenna sat beside her at the table, sipping from a creek-colored drink. Trey was between songs, so Hadley walked to the bar and ordered a drink, although anything too potent would surely put her to sleep. While she waited at the bar, Trey introduced his next song.

"Now here's a song I can relate to." The sing-songy inflection of his wildly intoxicating voice came through the speakers. His beauty blazed under the sole spotlight as he adjusted the pick-up on his guitar's frets and flashed the audience his winning grin. "But maybe, just maybe there's someone sitting out there now who can change all that."

The room had become quiet with anticipation. Most of the audience was female, of all ages. Hadley was not alone in her attraction. Hadley fancied she had been the one to discover him, but realized she had had nothing to do with his ability to charm. Brenna was right to point out that she was like all the others, at least in some ways.

There was but one solitary chord before Trey ended the suspense by singing the first word of an Eagles ballad, which like some magical incantation, evoked a low, knowing communal moan from the spectators. With one chord and one word, he had found any number of girls who would have taken him up on the song's challenge to find love.

Anise was saying something to Brenna but stopped when Hadley slipped into a chair at their table. Like the other females in the room, her co-workers stared rapturously at the stage. A triangular wedge of pizza bisected a white ceramic plate in front of Anise.

Trey sang the last line, attempting valorously to add a little melisma on some of the words. But he was ultimately too pitchy.

Hadley tapped Brenna on the shoulder and got a welcoming wave in return. Brenna pointed at Trey and made a fanning motion. There he was, in the spotlight, with only a microphone and an acoustic guitar as accoutrements, unless his perfect face could be considered an accessory. *You don't get over these guys.*

The response to this number was an even more rousing round of applause. A few girls even whistled, prompting a chorus of wolf whistles, which elicited an endearing smile from the target. He waved his hand to the crowd and said, "Thank you very much" in a parody of Elvis, which brought forth an even more animated response in the form of a pelvic thrust or two. This part of the state would always be Elvis territory—Elvis and classic rock. Someone threw a set of keys onto the stage. Trey started to put them in his jeans pocket, but said, "No room—too tight," then tossed them back into the crowd with a laugh.

"Without those keys, she's out of the tractor pull," Hadley said to Brenna, who responded by wagging her finger at her.

"I've got to take a little break now," he announced still channeling Elvis. A disapproving murmur arose from the crowd. His "I won't be long" was followed by another chorus of wolf whistles and, this time, foot stomping.

Trey laid his guitar in its red velvet-lined case as gently as she imagined he'd lower a lover onto his bed. His fingers slowly encircled the neck of the guitar. It was a sensuous gesture. A few of the girls approached him as he stepped off the stage, but he pointed to the clock over the bar and frowned in mock dismay, a gesture that deepened his dimple, and undoubtedly their desire. One girl jammed a piece of paper in his back pocket, cupping his ass as she did so. His face registered the faintest of smiles.

He glimpsed Hadley on his way to the bar and backtracked. "Well, what did you think?" He stood close to her in an upright missionary position.

"You were unbelievable, baby." Anise answered for her, outstretching her thin bare arms in his direction.

"I was asking *her*," he said without taking his beautiful seafoam eyes from Hadley's face. "What did you think? Have I got what it takes?"

What would it be like to have him peer into her eyes like that without an ulterior motive? Nevertheless, she had to stay on track. She was on a mission.

She studied him, making mental notes. He certainly seemed guileless, even vulnerable, in some respects. She savored the moment. He was so lusciously attractive, every feature complementing the others. Could he be attracted to her? Was that what she wanted? She didn't know. But as the Magic 8 Ball says, "Signs point to yes."

"Well?" His eyes took on a strange tint, a somewhat unpleasant luminescent green. His cheeks were flushed. He had what the Victorians referred to as high color.

"I agree with Anise. You were good."

His face relaxed. "Really? You're not just saying that?"

"I mean it," she said, pretending what he had asked her was instead, *Do you really and truly want to go to bed with me?*

He laughed outright and grabbed her drink, gulping it in one swallow. Hot guys had presumption. Hadley didn't like it.

"Come over here and let me give you a big hug, honey," Anise said.

"Gotta drain my two-incher first," he said, beaming. He kept his eyes locked onto Hadley's.

Brenna said, "Me, too," then laughed after realizing what she had agreed to.

"Don't move," he turned and said to Hadley, pointing at her.

Hadley chafed under his command. Apparently he hadn't gotten the memo that she no longer took orders. Besides, it would be a good time to strike.

The three of them walked toward the back, leaving Anise to squeal about being left alone. On the way, Trey stopped, turned around, and grabbed Hadley's arm while Brenna went on ahead. She hadn't realized he was aware of her whereabouts.

His lips seemed colorless. The smile was gone. "Were you serious about me being any good up there?"

She hesitated before speaking. "You need some work, some pointers." Reluctantly, she shook off his arm. "Gotta go, Brenna is waiting."

"You gonna help her take a piss?" He took a step closer. "What pointers?"

She was strangely invigorated by his needing her. The crowd was jostling both of them, trying to get to the bar and the bathroom. Hadley half-wished they'd jostle her right out of the place. She recognized the yearning in his voice, layered though it was, over his fake machismo. He was still a believer at this point. She smirked, in spite of herself. "I don't yell out professional secrets in a juke joint. Let's talk some other time."

"Only if I pick you up this time. I don't trust you."

She narrowed her eyes. "Then why would you want

my advice?"

"I don't." He hesitated. "I want to…weigh it."

She smiled broader, feeling victorious. "Give me a call. I'm in the book."

"Screw the book. What are you doing tomorrow night?"

Maybe that was the best way in order to observe him firsthand. She'd get the results a lot sooner. Was he just another Derek, a master at the con game, or was he instead as innocent in his desire for recognition as she had been for love with Derek? It couldn't matter, for her purposes.

She answered clearly and firmly. At last she understood the power Derek had felt with her. "Tomorrow's fine."

He turned his back to her when a girl approached him and whispered in his ear. They both laughed. In his deepest FM voice, he said, "Your mother wouldn't approve of such language." The young lady, with a pretty face, albeit too much blue eye shadow, turned to watch him as she walked away. She could have been one of her students with a fake I.D.

"You did say tomorrow?" His voice sounded pinched. How quickly he shifted from his radio tones!

"Never mind."

"OK, then. Tomorrow it is." He started to turn, then stopped. "Wait. Let's make it the day after. Sunday. Eight o'clock. Where do you live?"

Foiled again! She was the one who was supposed to manipulate him. He was obviously busy Saturday night, Date Night, U.S.A. She had been relegated to Sunday night, the night for safe dates, a real dud of a night, socially speaking. Sunday was recovery night after hangovers and lost weekends. But wait— He wasn't asking her for a date, after all. It was business, on her part as well—or was it?

She wished he'd take her in his arms, aglow from the excitement of being the cynosure of every woman's fantasy, yet struggling to create one of his own.

"You know who you remind me of?" She would regain control of the conversation the best way she knew how: her intelligence.

"Who?" He scanned the crowd as if Hadley had spotted someone.

"Eric Weiss. Know who that is?" She was certain he wouldn't know. After all, he hadn't known what homonyms were, and that was easy. The chiasmus reference must have been a one-off. She could always get a man back under control with her brains. Especially a younger one.

Trey paused only momentarily. "Yes, I do as a matter of fact. That's Houdini's real name."

She tried not to let the surprise register on her face. "Yes. He could have been you, the way you're here one minute and gone the next." She didn't wait for a response. She spotted Brenna in the crowd and walked with her back to the table.

"Wow. What happened back there?" Brenna asked. "You OK?"

Hadley hesitated. "Yeah, I think so."

Brenna stopped and blocked Hadley's way. "Listen. Don't get tangled up with him. You don't need any of that now, do you?" Her forehead was all crinkly like a pug's. "Take a gander at the crowd," she said. She swept the room with her arms. "Estrogen galore. He's not the jolt you need."

"It's something I must do," Hadley said, at the same time wondering why Brenna was always trying to keep her from interacting with Trey. "It's deeper than I imagined." She had even forgotten what "it" referred to. The room's atmosphere seemed blurry and dreamlike. Maybe she was having the beginnings of a migraine.

"You mean how you feel about him?"

Hadley shook her head. "How I feel about me."

But Brenna had been right. Hadley was indeed feeling something for him.

Brenna raised an eyebrow. The crowd began taking their seats once again, as Trey slowly made his way through the crowd to the stage. "What do you mean?"

"I realized something. I don't make memories anymore." She stared at Trey, who was pressing the guitar close to him once again, his shirt unbuttoned enough to expose a thatch of golden chest hair. "I just live on them."

"You'll feel better in time." Brenna grabbed her hand tightly to lead her back to their table.

"It's been a year. It's *time*."

Hadley was glad for her friend's concern. She scanned the crowd, catching sight of Sara, who was still sitting alone in the corner. She must have witnessed Hadley's exchange with Trey. There was a part of Hadley that wanted nothing more than to forget about the scheme and ask Sara to come join her. She was like her in more ways than one.

Instead, she squeezed Brenna's hand, grabbed her coat, and headed for the exit, just as Trey launched into his version of "I Love Rock 'N' Roll" in what could only be considered an elusive pitch.

"Must have been a case of unrequited love," Hadley

mumbled to the bouncer on her way out, giving Sara a wave.

When she returned home that evening to an apartment that seemed especially dark and cold, she had a message waiting for her. It was Bryce, her friend and literary agent in L.A.

"Hi, honey," he said in his nasally voice. "I was wondering how you are…how the play's coming. Guess what? Maybe I'll be in New York before year's end and we can hook up. Let's talk sooner than later. Love you. Bye-bye!"

She plopped into her chair and began to type.

When I have the upper hand, he's needy, desperate, and shows it by having an edge to his voice and refraining from outright anger. He's conflicted… wanting to explore what I have to offer him in advancing his career, yet troubled by having to change his freewheeling lifestyle (screwing any number of girls who all serve different purposes in his life) to find out. I've been firm, indifferent…but will he give up if I don't give in? Just a little?

And how do I write a play with this?

Chapter 10

There was a knock on the door as Hadley sat down with a bowl of chocolate-chip ice cream. She glanced at the clock: 8 p.m. Sunday night. She'd shot the whole weekend, mostly grading papers and sleeping the day before.

"My God," she said aloud, remembering Trey's promise to make good on a date. How could he possibly show up after she'd been so deliberately elusive? She had forgotten the resiliency of some guys.

"Who is it?" she trilled, bouncing a mound of the frozen dessert on her tongue. She cleared her throat and repeated the question, all the while picking up the detritus from the weekend—the pizza box, the ice cream container, the *National Enquirer*.

" 'Tis I, Old Dog Trey," he yelled through the door. "Ever faithful. We have a meeting, remember?"

She used her fingers to comb her hair and moaned when the mirror reflected a wan, puffy face staring back at her.

"I never confirmed any meeting," she said through the door. She hurried to straighten the cushions on the couch. "I'll take a rain check." Her heart was doing double time.

"C'mon. Please open the door. It's getting chilly out here." His voice was deeper than usual.

She brushed the lint off her sweatshirt and zipped up

her jeans before opening the door.

Trey was twirling the end of a white stick in his mouth. With a loud slurping sound, he pulled from his mouth a bright red lollipop before sticking out his tongue, which now matched the color of his shirt.

"Fire your secretary," he said, tapping his watch. He waited a few seconds. "May I come in?"

She let him in, the shame of her unkempt apartment equaled only by the shame of her own disheveled appearance.

He stood close to her. "I have to say, you are much more attractive without all that make-up." He talked with the lollipop stuck in his cheek. "Definitely younger."

It was an approach she remembered from her time with Derek. First you surprise them, then compliment them when they're at their most vulnerable. She made a mental note.

He walked toward the nearest chair, sat down, but quickly jumped up again, fishing in his pockets. "Where are my manners? Here." He extended a lollipop, grape flavor, her favorite.

"No thanks." It wasn't even on the level of the apple Neil had given her on the first day of school. Besides, what was with men and their semiotics anyway? Perhaps it beat communicating with words. And how in the world would he have known grape was her favorite flavor? Was she that transparent? Was there a grape type as opposed to an orange or cherry type? The grape type would be moody and dark. The orange type would be young, perky, sassy. The cherry type? Passionate, desirable. Like him.

Lollipops aside, he was lusciousness itself, the blood-red shirt adding to his angel-faced carnality. His skin glowed, no doubt from a day spent in the autumn sun with a frisky faun, the name of which she itched to know. What lovely young sylvan thing *had* he taken to the woods?

She also thought it weird that she should care. But she did.

Then she remembered the scheme, *her* scheme, and stepped over to him, her thumbs in her belt loops. "This wasn't planned. Neither my naturalness nor your coming over."

"As I recall, we had a business date."

"No, *you* had a date. It hadn't been confirmed on my end." It was easier to play hardball when she imagined herself to be plain and unequal to the challenge.

"As long as it's still early, would you mind going out for some coffee with me?" He articulated the words with what Minnesota Fats, the great pool player, would call a lot of English on the shot. He strolled around the small apartment before gravitating over to her bookcase. He ran his fingers across the books' spines, eventually plucking one out.

He opened the book and began reading, seemingly far more interested in its content than anything happening between them. Hadley was left standing by the door, wondering what to do next. How she hated vying for attention, especially with a dead author. She noticed his jeans, fashionably torn, exposing the golden hair covering his leg, right above the knee.

"I need to change."

Trey kept reading. "Don't put on any make-up. You're fine the way you are." He returned to the book.

How easily and freely he reacted to things and how different she was in that regard. Had she come down with a case of anomie from her last heartbreak, only to have it stay in her spleen like an incurable virus, ruining her humors? She would get at the source by writing her play. Play? Wasn't she supposed to read this week at the writers' group? Oh well, what was the good of a writers' group, anyway?

But the play was her ticket back to the world. And the people in the writing group were, at least, nice. OK, OK, think—what was the premise of the play? When *was* her last moment of innocence, the last time she had laughed so spontaneously and the *exact* moment she had lost it? She had to believe it was decades ago, when Jimmy Sinclair had tickled her as they played the game where you had to put a different appendage on various colored circles, causing her to pee all over the blue one. Or had such a moment been with Derek?

Trey never looked up from the book he was reading when she left the room. She gazed at her reflection in the bathroom mirror. What was this "natural" business? She filled in her eyebrows where she'd over-plucked them and applied blush and lipstick with the prowess gained from twenty years' experience. Derek would say the same thing about a woman's earthiness, then pay good money to see some tarted-up floozy throw her legs around a pole. Typical man. Black and white. Madonna / whore.

She darted into her closet to phone Roxie. Amazingly, she'd caught her friend at home, but it was, after all, Sunday night. No one, except losers, went out on Sunday nights.

"Thank God you're there. Listen, he wants to go out for coffee. What'll I do?"

"Where the hell you been? I've called a million

times. Dammit, I wish you paid a little more attention to call-back messages."

"I know, I know. I've got calls backed up and essays to grade. This guy, young guy. He's downstairs, wanting to go out. I know it's because he thinks I've got connections and he's an aspiring Bon Jovi, and…"

"Oh, for God's sake. Don't tell me. You gotta be kidding me. Another Derek? I hoped you would learn from your mistakes."

"Hey, no lectures, OK? And you're a great one to talk while we're on that subject. Should I go out with him? I'm using him, actually, as part of the field research for my play in progress."

"Then go. Do it. If you can use him back, do it."

One of Roxie's remarkable qualities was to be able to answer the phone and understand exactly what was going on without a lot of backstory.

"Yeah, I guess. But, he's never actually done anything to me."

"But he's just like Asshole, isn't he?"

"He sure reminds me of him. And he might be a narcissist."

"Oh please. Maybe he'll surprise you and be a nice guy. There are a few of them left. Gotta hope so. Otherwise, why inhale and exhale?"

Hadley detected Roxie weakening. "Are you in trouble with Benny again?"

"No. No, did I say that?" She could be heard clicking a lighter for another link in what had always been a continuous chain of cigarettes since, she said, the age of thirteen. "Go out with him, cut him down to size, then maybe he'll quit bugging you."

"He's not bugging me. I'm the one insinuating

myself into his life, and maybe…"

Her friend took a long, addictive pull on her cigarette. "Honestly, Had. Get over these guys, will ya? Like I said, go out with him, have a few laughs, and send the bastard back to Mommy."

"In this case it's back to a school secretary."

"A what? Whatever. But call me when you get home, OK? No matter how late. Promise?"

"Yeah, yeah."

When Hadley reappeared, hastily pulled together, Trey was standing by the door, obviously anxious to go. He pointed to the book he left lying on her couch.

"Do you spend your time writing marginalia in books instead of going out and enjoying life?"

"You make it sound mutually exclusive."

"Sometimes it is," he said. In straightening his shoulders, he made his leather jacket squeak. "Freud said work is desire held in check."

Freud? He knew Freud along with Houdini's real name? How many layers did this guy have?

"I find reading enjoyable. That's only one facet of my life."

He laughed endearingly, the kind of laugh that should be followed by a body tickle, although in this case it was not. He took a step closer to her. "You underlined and put a star next to Elizabeth Barrett Browning's lines about love being the fruit of experience, 'the wine that tasted of its own grapes.' "

"So? Did you go through all my books or what?"

He twirled the grape lollipop in front of her. "Obviously, to get that experience, you have to go out once in a while. You know, put down the books."

"You're impertinent."

"C'mon. You know what I mean. You're in the prime of your life." His eyes ran up and down her body as he said this. "You should be out making memories for your old age."

She studied his face. It was as if someone had told him about the conversation she'd had with Brenna on that very subject. "I have plenty of memories."

"I'll bet you do," he said with a chuckle. "But you ain't dead yet." He gave her an air nudge with his elbow.

She started to speak, but he stopped her. "I meant being in the music business and all. You have some good stories."

She could feel the muscles in her face tightening. "Aren't we supposed to be talking about your business? Your future in the music business?"

"I came to take you out as a new acquaintance, but it's no secret I'd like your opinion about my music, if that's what you mean. But I also want to hear about *you*." He must have noticed her expression. "Hey, you should be flattered. How many people in these woods have actually worked at a record company in Hollywood?" He smiled and moved closer to the door. "Come on. Let's leave this dungeon before your hot young shape sets my arteries on fire."

She stared at him, uncomprehending.

"Paraphrasing S.J. Perelman. Just read it in one of your books." He grinned.

She hid her smile. No sense letting him think he was charming her. Besides, she remembered how derivative narcissists were. That line probably cost poor old S.J. a whole week of his life, and here was this young bounder stealing it with nary a qualm. But then again, she'd seen pictures of S.J., and he looked nothing like the specimen in front of her.

She walked past him and opened the door. "What are we waiting for?"

Chapter 11

Trey drove Hadley into town, pulling up in front of The Cork. Few, if any, establishments were open. Not only was she relegated to a Sunday night, she was once again backdropped in the local dive. But she remembered her purpose: to study his approach.

Who was she kidding?

He opened the car door for her and took her hand. "Allow me," he said a bit too gallantly, and she struggled to her feet, trying not to make him pull her up and out like somebody's grandma.

The Cork, like any bar, assumed a whole different atmosphere on a Sunday. Sad, dingy, almost ghostly in the lurid hues of the jukebox. Only as Sunday night becomes Monday morning does it once again fit its skin. They sat in the same booth Hadley had shared with Neil the week before.

"What can I get you to drink?"

"Coffee's fine."

"Nothing stronger?"

"What's stronger than the coffee here?"

He smiled, showcasing his dimple. "Good point." He slid out of the booth and gave his order at the bar. As he waited, he walked around the room where he had performed two nights before. She wanted to know what he was thinking.

"So," he said. He placed a hot steaming cup of black

liquid in front of her, a great deal of it having already spilled in the saucer. "Tell me about yourself."

Hadley couldn't forget it was Sunday night. "Be honest. This is all about you, isn't it?"

He swallowed. "No. I want to hear about you, about the music business, about the world you left behind." He leaned into her. "Why *did* you leave?"

"A lot of reasons."

"Fair enough. Well then, how 'bout filling me in on your exciting life in L.A.? Meet any rock stars?"

"The music business is mostly that, a business. And business is often dull."

"C'mon. How could life in the fast lane be dull? Concerts, rock stars sitting on your lap, wild parties. Especially compared to this town."

"Here's an example," she said. "I had to go to a show at the Ambassador Hotel once…"

"The Ambassador?"

"Where Robert Kennedy was shot."

"You mean where Greg Brady took Carol Brady on their first date."

She ignored his remark, which she took to be another reference to their age differences. "It's closed down now. But at the time, it could still be rented out by companies for parties. So anyway, I went there with some friends to see David Cassidy try to make a comeback."

"Cassidy?"

"Teen idol. From the '70s."

"Yeah, yeah. Partridge Family. I know all the pop idols."

She tested him. "Oh yeah? You think you know pop idols? Who sang 'Easy Come, Easy Go'?"

He took a swallow of his draft beer. "Bobby Sherman."

She glowered at him.

"Sorry, but I'm a trivia expert. You'll have to dig deep to stump me." He grabbed his beer and clinked her coffee cup with it before draining it. "So, tell me about David Cassidy."

She giggled in spite of herself. He reminded her somewhat of her L.A. friends, who never minded talking pop culture. Except most of those men were gay. She relaxed her shoulders, which she realized she had been holding at an impossible angle. What harm would it do to indulge him?

"OK, so he was making his comeback at the Ambassador Hotel. But my point in mentioning him was that his comeback was ultimately all about the past—the glory days, the hotel, the singer." There! That should satisfy him, but he motioned for her to continue. "This event was held in the Coconut Grove, once *the* hot spot of Hollywood society."

He nodded, all the while gesturing to the barkeep.

"But when we got there, the place smelled, literally and figuratively. The walls were peeling, the whole venue was rotting in front of my eyes. On all levels."

"Yeah, but how was Cassidy? How'd he hold up?"

She studied Trey's face. He appeared to have sidestepped the point of her story. "Never got to see him. It was past midnight, and we were all tired, so we left."

"Bummer."

She could feel another ring added to her tree of life.

"But that, to me, is as good a metaphor as you can get about the whole business. Decadence. Soon after, I left town before I became Gloria Swanson in *Sunset*

Boulevard."

As analogies go, it was a bad one, given the age-gap between them that seemed to be growing wider the more she studied his baby face.

"Hey, you shouldn't paint it so gloomy. Just think, you still got to see the Ambassador. That's history, man. And hang out with people in the biz. Could have seen the hottest teen idol in the world. So what if it's a couple of decades late? If you really loved music, it would have been cool."

Hadley drank in his beauty. He was so young. In spite of his reputation, he was still enthusiastic, something she was not.

"What other rock stars did you meet?"

She shifted in her seat. "What do you honestly want to know?" She would decide the order of conversation, dammit. He didn't appear to be interested in anything beyond information. So, let him sweat over what he came for, which sure wasn't the pleasure of her company. She took a sip of the coffee, which had clearly been reheated, and sat up straight. "But first, I must tell you. You should always confirm a date before just showing up, especially when there *was* no date. Anyway, a phone call before is the classy thing to do."

He seemed to blush, but maybe it was the reflection off his shirt. "I'm sorry."

Ignoring his last comment, she tilted her head back and began to orate. "And, second, you could have thanked me in advance, sucked up, as they call it in the biz. A lollipop hardly ranks as payola."

She meant it to be a witty remark, but he turned away awkwardly and ran his fingers through his hair. There were large crescents of sweat under his arms. He was nervous. Nervous was good. He started to say something, but instead pressed his lips together tautly.

Hadley broke the awkward silence. "So you want to be a rock star?" she asked in an effort to cast herself more as a late-night companion than a jail matron.

"I'd settle for singer-songwriter," he said while gazing at the stage he had so recently commanded.

"I didn't know you wrote your own songs," she said, genuinely interested. Maybe the guy had talent and not only looks. Maybe the other night was an off-night. Maybe she'd find an excuse to get out of this imbroglio she'd cooked up.

Two or three restaurant employees had jumped onto the stage and appeared to be setting up equipment.

"Is there live music tonight?" she asked.

"There is now." He leapt onto the stage and spoke to one of the men. He grabbed an acoustic guitar pushed toward the rear and pulled up a stool. He hurriedly tuned the guitar and began to sing.

I used to start every day
With a heartfelt prayer
That I'd wake up and find
Baby, you still care
I was dying inside
Only you were the cure
Now you want to come back
But I'm not so sure

As he continued the song, Hadley was moved to think he could sing in such a heartfelt manner in spite of the insipid lyrics. Maybe this was a song he had written. Regardless of its shortcomings, he belonged on stage. That's where he seemed most at home. What right did she have to goose fate and stop him in his tracks if, in fact, he had even a monad of talent?

He placed the fingers of his left hand carefully and deliberately on the guitar frets. He even resembled David Cassidy, in fact, from his salad days. But even David had hit hard times after his peak. It was a tough business.

"I hope I passed the audition," he said in a British accent, mimicking John Lennon's famous words at the end of "Get Back"—the album version, of course. A few of the restaurant employees checked out Hadley as if she were a talent scout they ought to know, then glanced back at Trey.

He slid into the booth next to her. "Well, have I?"

"What's that?" she said, feigning insouciance.

"Passed the audition." He kept the British accent.

"Depends. Did you write the song?"

"Sure. And there's a lot more where that came from."

She leaned back into the booth's uncomfortable vinyl pleats. His nearness unnerved her. She could feel his body heat. She imagined herself to be the heroine in one of Delores Malvern's romance novels. "I assume it's autobiographical."

His smile reappeared. "Would that matter?"

"No, no. Of course not."

Too late. He'd gotten her on that one. She had, in fact, been wondering if it were instead a song a girl would sing to him since she couldn't imagine his ever having been dumped. She quickly shifted into manager mode. "I think you've got potential, certainly. Roughly hewn, but talent nonetheless. There, I've given you my professional opinion. What time is it?"

"Whoa, wait a minute." He clutched her wrist. "Unless you climb under the table, you're not getting out. I wanna know what you would do if you were me?"

"I'd certainly take me home."

"You know what I mean."

"I'd probably take voice lessons. I detect a bit of a pitch problem. Your song is OK, but the lyrics are… anyway, production is key. I mean where would half these so-called rock stars be without their producers? You'd need a good studio, a good producer, engineer. All expensive stuff." She paused to take another sip of the noxious brew. "And, of course, I'd have to monitor you exclusively all through this." She wanted to catch each moment of his thinking and operating processes because he'd be seeing his girlfriends through it all.

His eyes narrowed. "Monitor me? I was only asking for some advice. That's all."

For all his charm, he was hardly the essence of self-confidence. A small shaving cut marred his otherwise flawless upper lip, and a fast pulse beat in a vein in his neck.

"All those things you mentioned cost a lot of jack," he said with too much emphasis on the last word.

Hadley gave him a blank look. But why should he sweat it, if he had financial connections with Sara? "I could help, you know. In ways not involving expenses." She tried not to sound too mewling.

His eyes were a depthless pool, the kind Narcissus himself could have drowned in. "How? You've just shot me down, told me I can't sing."

It was time to pull out the maternal stop. "I never did. In fact, you're nothing if not potential itself. Some of it realized already." She tried to sound sweet. "It's tough out there. It's not like wooing small-town audiences."

"What are you proposing?"

She longed for a puff on one of Roxie's cigarettes, though smoking was one bad habit she had never succumbed to. "As long as you asked, I suppose I could help by giving you my two cents."

Surprisingly, he didn't jump at the chance. She suspected he worried about the curtailment of his freedom.

"You've given me that. It's connections I need."

It was a blatant statement, a bit too raw.

"I suppose I could help there, but you won't like the conditions."

He cocked a naturally arched eyebrow. "Which are?"

As the perfect specimen for her field research, she could watch him operate up close. "If you work with me and let me advise you on your career, start to finish, I'll see to it you get heard by people." Roxie would undoubtedly help her in any scheme. "But you've got to let me take creative control. And you have to hold up your end of the bargain. Let me run you through vocal exercises before a demo is cut, follow my lead, those things. That would have to be understood." She tried to read his face for a reaction, but found none. "Do we have a deal?"

It was a dilemma for him. Boy, did she know it. He was young and liked his freedom. Maybe, she could make him like her in such a way she could observe first hand when that last moment of innocence does occur.

There was one thing worrying her, however. If he didn't hold true to his promise and wanted no further contact, she'd have to let him go and write her play based on memories. Isn't that what she should do anyway? She certainly had a deep well to draw from. She had to admit she wanted a quick affair with a beautiful guy, to feel his closeness, to imagine, to pretend. Was that what was behind it? She didn't know. But she liked him. And, secretly, she wished he liked her.

"We have a deal," he said, his gaze locked on her eyes. "I have one stipulation, though."

"Which is?"

He drained the few dregs left in his glass. "We'll have to shake on it. At least the part about being heard by the right people." He extended his hand, even larger than she imagined once she finally had an excuse to stare at it.

Since she didn't know if he was as good as his word, she happily clinched the deal.

"Now that that's over, speaking of old teen idols, what's your favorite old teen idol song?"

"I don't have one." Somehow the spell had been broken. After all, she'd just sold her soul to the devil.

"C'mon. Everyone has one." He put an arm on the top of the banquette, right above her shoulders. "How 'bout 'I'm a Believer' by The Monkees?"

She shook her head. His closeness was truly beginning to unnerve her. She made a mental note of it. "Written by Neil Diamond. Did you know that?"

He ignored the opportunity to one-up her on trivia. "It would be helpful if you believed in me, you know."

In one smooth move, he slid closer to her, dropping one arm around her and sliding the other behind her back, drawing her face to his lips, whereupon he delivered a kiss worthy to be immortalized as cinch art on the cover of one of Delores' novels. She let him take control, tipping her head back. His lips were as soft as she'd imagined—soft-serve ice cream twisted with vanilla and strawberry, a kitten's toe beans, raspberry cream truffles. It had been so long, so awfully long, since she'd been kissed in such a way, meaningless though it might be. But she had to end it, at least in the moment, to stay in control.

"Hey, Cowboy, slow down." She laughed nervously.

"Suit yourself," he said before settling back into the banquette. "But you may not be as tough as you'd like to appear to be. There's a heart beating somewhere within."

She noticed his arm was now back in its pre-kiss position, a millimeter from her shoulders.

"Did you ever think maybe a kiss shouldn't be so casual?" she asked him, in the same tone of voice she asked students why they didn't hand in their homework. "That a kiss should mean something?"

Trey slid out of the booth, making Hadley's release now possible. He stood by the table, fishing bills out of his wallet. "It did mean something."

"No, no. Wait a minute. What exactly did you mean?"

"The kiss? It was a friendly little peck, that's all. I like women, especially women who seem to like me. I figure you're only young once."

"No, that business about not being so tough."

He tucked his wallet back into his pants, still a tight fit, she noticed. He was beautiful, even when he wasn't flashing his signature grin. "Sometimes a kiss is just a kiss. Not everything is a symbol waiting to be analyzed, Miss English Teacher. Ready to go?"

Her hams sliding against the fake leather caused an unbecoming squeak as she maneuvered out of the booth.

The squeak, an obtrusive bit of reality, reminded her it was Sunday night, and the realization that this stranger whom she had deemed an unfeeling playboy had understood something about her, that she was a romantic at heart and that, in itself, was not a cause for worry, a fact that no one—not even her friends—seldom mentioned. That this relative stranger knew this about her was almost more than she could bear.

"Sometimes a kiss is just a kiss." What did that mean? If it was so insignificant, then he or his kind couldn't be hurt. It would have to go a bit further. She was in it deep. She'd have to see this thing through. And she would this time, be the one in control. But only after she'd had a fling. To be the cynosure of someone's eyes, even for a brief period. She was tired of taking care of others. She needed the respite an affair with a non-committal, sunshiny young guy could bring.

"Shall we meet sometime this week to work on your voice? Say, Wednesday, 7 p.m. in the school's music room?"

"Sounds like a plan," he said, his dimple deepening.

Chapter 12

The cold metallic ring of the phone awakened Hadley who had fallen asleep with her head on the computer keyboard. A continuous series of consonants and vowels flatlined across the screen.

"Hello?"

"Girl, is that you?" It was Roxie's raspy voice.

"What the hell time is it?" She squinted her eyes. The clock on the computer screen read 4:17 a.m.

"Hey, how did it go? You were supposed to call me, remember? Son of a bitch, girl! You need to work on follow-through, you know?"

Hadley blinked at the computer screen in front of her, trying to remember what had prompted her to sit before it on a Sunday night. She remembered Trey, the business arrangement, the kiss. The desire. Then the determination in its aftermath. Then she realized she had been typing out the scene inspired by the one that had played itself out only a few hours before.

"I'm sorry. I got involved."

Roxie laughed, more of a wheeze. "I'll bet you did. That shouldn't excuse you when you promised a friend. I'm just saying."

Hadley listened to her words. "You're right. I'm sorry."

"OK, lecture over. Give it to me. Start at square one. Where'd you guys go?"

"To hell and back."

"What's up with this guy? Talk to me." She paused only long enough to take a long, inward pull on her cigarette.

Hadley straightened up, took a swig from the bottle of water she'd left by her computer and filled her friend in with the details of her play.

"Hey, speaking of assholes," Roxie replied, "I've got some dirt on Derek to pass along."

Hadley groaned. She did not want to appear too interested. She wanted Roxie to think she was completely over Derek, even though there was no fooling her. But she was ready to change the subject from Trey to Derek.

Roxie reacted to the groan. "Oh, come on. Trust me, it's worth it."

"OK, what'd you hear?" The crick in her neck made it difficult to stay upright. The familiar vasovagal nerve was acting up again. Actually, she was glad Roxie called. The early mornings were often the worst times for having a love-in with solitude. It was the time Sinatra sang about in "One More for the Road," that quarter-to-three isolation. But Derek? Hardly a comforting topic. She was curious about him, sure. She'd be curious for as long as she heard sappy songs on the radio. But wasn't it bad enough that she had the East Coast clone of Derek in her life now, albeit by her own finagling?

Roxie took another audible pull from her cigarette. A former hand model, she had parlayed her addiction to smoking as a way to showcase her beautiful hands—that's what Hadley believed anyway. Hadley pictured her now, holding her cigarette poised as if she were shilling for hand lotion or a cubic zirconia ring on one of those shopping networks.

"I talked to Dave, remember him?"

How could she forget? He was the guy who had helped set up Derek with people in the music business. She had been the one to introduce them.

"Dave said he met up with Asshole and Rachel in Branson."

Hadley was aware he had gone there with Rachel, having found out through mutual friends, but she didn't have the energy to explain to Roxie. Besides, she didn't know all the details.

"Branson. Branson frickin' Missouri. That's Branson, M.O. to you, girl. 'Cause you know he's always got one."

She sat up, trying to sound like it was 9 a.m., not five hours earlier. "Where in Branson?"

"Seems Derek tried to get a job as a stage manager for some Liberace-wannabee, but apparently the guy said no. He gets dumped by a guy with worse taste than he has. That's saying something."

Roxie paused briefly, but Hadley didn't fill in the vacuum. She tried to picture a Liberace manqué nixing Derek, possibly threatened by the whole pretty package. Why did she make excuses for these guys when she wasn't so forthcoming with others? Or maybe it was too many fairy tales as a kid. Or maybe an emotionally unavailable father who worried more about himself than his daughter—or wife. But Roxie was always trying to bring details into the moral they illuminated.

"Anyway, Branson guy ditched him, but apparently he got a job at some other joint down there," Roxie added. "But here's the deal. He *had* to take Rachel, if he wanted to eat, of course. Hey, what do you s'pose they eat at Branson? Hog jowls? Rocky Mountain oysters?"

Rachel. Derek's version of Sara. But this one had a BMW. What was with these girls with the Biblical names acting so terribly, well, unbiblical?

"Are they still on good terms, Dave and Derek?"

"I guess Derek left town owing him some dough. Now there's a surprise, huh? And girl, are you sitting down?"

Hadley nodded, even though Roxie couldn't see her.

"They're engaged. Not Dave and him, but Derek and Rachel. In order to get *to* Branson and set-up shop, he promised Rachel the moon. Which in this case is him, I guess, although me personally? I'd rather have the damn moon, craters and all." She laughed, which generated a frightening coughing fit. "That's something, isn't it? Your ex could always surprise us with the details, couldn't he? I mean, never the big picture, but the details. Branson. I mean, God."

Lines of unintelligible letters filled her computer screen as if the answer to her problems waited only to be decoded.

"Girl, you there?"

"Yes, yes. I'm trying to take it all in. It's so damn early." Hadley couldn't move without feeling the cramp in her neck all over again.

"And he's so damn predictable, isn't he? But listen, back to the future. When are you coming out here for a visit?"

Hadley squirmed in her chair to try to feel more comfortable. She felt inspired to resume her role as play maker.

"I don't know. But soon. I promise."

"Listen, just say the word. If there's anything I can

do to help you get out of those damn woods. Girl, you awake? Hello? You're so not with me."

"I'm here. I'm trying to rally." In truth, Hadley was reflecting on her days with Derek. How they'd walk down the sidewalk from Universal Amphitheater after a concert, laughing, holding hands, discussing the details of the show they'd just seen. She could remember how she felt in his arms, like a "lily-cradled bee," to quote the Victorian poet Alfred Lord Tennyson. She loved his broad shoulders and slim waist, as well as the sweetness of his lips in contrast to his day's-growth of beard. Men had contrasts she loved. What had gone wrong? People always say, "Move on. Find someone else." But sometimes certain moments, certain people, aren't replicable. Maybe it's the singular shake of pheromones, maybe it's the moment in time, but sometimes it's a once-in-a-lifetime feeling never to be recaptured, even if you spend your whole life searching for it.

"OK, listen, I'm gonna let you get back to sleep. But think about it. Aren't you glad you're rid of him?"

"Who?"

"Derek, of course. You could be stuck in Branson!"

But of course she wouldn't be in Branson. Derek had dumped her, after finding Rachel. Rachel was all Branson, and Hadley had been all L.A., or maybe upstate New York. And Derek was leaving all that was Hadley behind. She pictured him with Rachel, married and surrounded by children someday. Her time with him had obviously meant nothing after all was said and done.

How ephemeral are life's moments. How could you ever tell when a moment, a glance, a word might be enough to either rise like a seven-tiered wedding cake or be folded into the batter of someone's forgetfulness?

What did a girl have to do to make enough cherished moments for a guy that he'd want to keep them coming day after day, together?

She remembered an idyllic summer day when she and Derek went to a Dodgers game together. On the way to the stadium, the afternoon sky was streaked with pink with a touch of gold, making all things below appear surreal. As the sky darkened, the bright mercury vapor lights took over, illuminating the game as if it had been a movie set. The old Baldwin organ had provided the soundtrack. Only skating rinks, horror movies, and ballparks used an organ with such a distinctive sound.

During the seventh-inning stretch, Hadley and Derek sprang to their feet to sing baseball's national anthem, swaying in time with the old tune, arms intertwined. When the game was over, families streamed across the diamond, birthplace of a million fantasies. Derek had stood at home plate, surrounded by the stadium's lightning-bolt zigzag perimeter that harkened back to California's grand and glorious period of optimism: space-age architecture of the 1950s and early '60s.

"Someday I'll bring my son to a baseball game," Derek had said. Hadley should have known then. *His* son. Not *our* son.

"Yeah," she said, in response to Roxie's question, left hanging in the air. "Good riddance to bad rubbish."

"There's my girl."

She wasn't rid of him, though. That was the thing. People always said time heals and all, but it doesn't. It suppresses pain, but never heals completely. New men, new environments—they're the cocoa butter you put over stretch marks, but they never really eradicate the damn things. You don't recover from such hurts, F. Scott Fitzgerald had written. You turn into a different person instead.

As she hung up the phone, a thud hit the front door. The morning paper. Neil's lifeblood. She'd had the whole weekend and never reached him, this after he had been so sweet and worried about her.

She might as well start the day. No sense going back to bed only to be jarred awake by a heartless alarm an hour later.

Since as long as Hadley could remember, *The Tillsdale Town Crier* had been folded in a full lotus position, so when you read it, you had to constantly press out the creases. Palming the front page, she noticed the headline: SICKNESS UNTO DEATH: DRUG ADDICTION AT LOCAL HIGH SCHOOL. Neil had the byline. A nod to Kierkegaard? Someone else must have come up with that headline—Neil wasn't one much for philosophy. Or maybe he was. She questioned whether she knew him now.

She stumbled over to her bookshelf and turned on the lamp, mercilessly exposing the homely corner of her room like a light bulb on Blanche DuBois. She pulled out her condensed overview of Western Philosophy and ran a chipped nail over the index, searching for the Danish drone. Yes, it was Kierkegaard, all right. Instead of getting ready for work, she found herself buried in one of his works, condensed though it was like a can of cream of mushroom soup, and just as unpalatable. Where had her curiosity gone to? She used to love the pursuit of knowledge for its own sake. Now, these pages yellowed with age like her love life, representing nothing more than lost dreams. Trey, of all people, had noticed.

When she arose from the couch two hours later, a great load had been lifted from her, even though she had, at best, only a few hours' sleep in her.

Chapter 13

Later, after an uneventful day at school, Hadley drove over to Aunt Winnie's place with a take-out meal she herself would have devoured. A gaunter version of the old counselor came to the door, a rail wrapped in a chenille robe.

"My God, Aunt Winnie. You all right?" Hadley pushed open the screen and carefully shut the door.

"I assumed Neil told you," she said by way of answering. "He said he called you."

"I'm sorry, I got busy and—please tell me, are you OK?"

The old woman motioned her to follow her into the living room. A tray table filled with the remains of a simple repast sat on the TV table. Hadley quickly removed it to the kitchen and returned to Winnie in the living room.

"I had a cold," the old woman said. "Neil took me to the doctor. I'm fine now."

"It's this change in the seasons. Could you eat what I brought?" Hadley slumped, heavy with guilt.

"No, no, I ate. I'm as good as new," Winnie said. She finished off the remains of her tea. "Neil and some nice young girl from the paper have been bringing me food. I'm fine."

"I'm so sorry. I have no excuse. I'll put this meal in your refrigerator for tomorrow."

Winnie waved her off. "I'm no spring chicken. Stuff happens. Tell me how you've been. I've been worried, what with your young man and all."

Hadley propped up the pillows behind her old friend and helped her fit her lanky frame onto the old couch.

"Rest your eyes for a while," Hadley told her. "I'll stay here with you."

Hadley waited until Winnie fell asleep, then began thinking of those moments before love is lost. An understood love brings confidence to both partners, allowing them to take risks, feel free to be goofy, let more of themselves come out without fear of criticism or disapproval. Lovers smile and laugh, hang on to each other's arms, find their stride together when walking, say nothing when one of them pushes the hair out of the eyes of the other, share food from the other's plate, play footsie under the table.

But the moment before it's lost? There's a distance in one of them. Annoyance when any of the above is done to the other, a jerking back when hair is pushed out of the eyes of the other, withdrawing a foot underneath the table when shoe touches shoe, showing annoyance when food is eaten off the plate by another ("If you want this, then order your own"). Maybe eyes are rolled at a story told before, a dislike of the other's clothes or lipstick, a desire expressed to see more of others. Is there always a time stamp?

When is such affection worthy of a lifetime? Or do people settle instead?

She recalled Derek's personal ad in the *L.A. Weekly,* in which he claimed to be hotter than Evan Dando of the Lemonheads. She remembered the expensive car in his driveway, a car found to belong to his next-in-line,

Rachel. How he ghosted her while courting the new one, someone who worked at night at a TV station known for its soap operas, of all things.

It still hurt, all of it.

She remembered what an L.A. shrink had said to her: "Why must it be your fault?"

Why indeed.

She remembered Derek had once said life meted out only a limited number of purely happy moments. Said he was glad he got to spend some of them with her. She should have known when he said those words, it was code for his pulling away. All words in past tense.

Were happy moments really like coins in one's pocket to spend with others? Had he simply gone through all the happiness coins he could with her and was now spending the rest of them with his new woman? It didn't matter. She had her own pocket change, which she intended to spend.

Chapter 14

The next morning, Hadley was late for school. With good cause. A headache made her feel as if she'd already worked the night shift by the time she'd negotiated the first step of the old high school, crumbling now like concrete coffeecake under the weight of generations of students.

Who designed these horrible Edwardian structures, these fin de siècle monstrosities in which to supposedly enlighten young minds? It was the same way with old hotels. So grand on the outside with the magnificent pilasters, the columns, the ornate foyers, but once the key opens the room door, the grandeur stops, unless you've got the money for the presidential suite.

Hadley remembered the time she had stayed at the Beverly Hilton, that magnificent pink palace so much the Petri dish for Hollywood lore. Paid a pretty penny for a room, too, only to be given a rabbit warren, a veritable cleaning supply room. It was her first, but not her last, introduction to Hollywood hierarchy.

The first person Hadley noticed when she walked into the foyer of Tillsdale High School that morning was Neil himself. He was, as always, comforting to her heavy eyes, dressed as he was in the nerd's uniform: a short-sleeved plaid shirt, khaki pants, and Hush Puppies. She noticed, once again, how buffed his arms were, making the hems of his shirtsleeves tight.

"Hey, friend! You must be here for the survey." She smiled wider than she had of late.

He pointed to the rolled up newspaper under her arm. "Yep. I won't take up much class time. I promise." He walked toward her. Neil appeared to be happy these days. He seemed content in his job, which made her feel good. Was she happy in her job? She had been when she first began teaching, but she wanted to know if she was reaching any of her students? Maybe she still loved teaching underneath it all if she could dig through the layers of loam and humus.

Did any of her students find out she had attended Trey's debut? Had Neil been told? After all, he employed student interns at the paper. In fact, hadn't he just hired a part-time reporter, a teacher's aide at the high school who'd gone to a state college and come back with a degree in something that could be fitted into any number of professions? If he knew, he hadn't called her about it—or maybe he'd tried. She felt more than a little guilty for not returning his call.

"Say, wait a minute. I need to talk to you soon about some other things, important things. We'll have to get together for unofficial business soon, OK?"

Was Neil the only person in this century who prefaced his sentences with "Say"? Only people in old 1940s movies used "Say"—Spencer Tracy, Jimmy Cagney, Clark Gable—but not now, not in this transition-less era.

"Sure."

He chuckled, sounding like somebody's uncle. "Good. Terrific. I'll give you a call to set up a time."

Her mind was on the essays and homework still piled on her desk while she had indulged her little whimsy with Trey. She would never be as disciplined as Neil. He never lost control, never acted less than the gentleman, the concerned brother. She was the flibbertigibbet of the two—impulsive, passionate, a Turner painting to his paint-by-numbers. But he accepted her, weaknesses and all. That's what she needed. He scolded her at times, too, but he always followed any of that with, "C'mon, let's forget about it and have an orange pop," something his mother used to say to him.

"I heard you checked in on Winnie," he said as they lingered in the hall outside her classroom. "I tried calling you about her."

She nodded. But just then, a group of chattering teenagers had drowned out all but their adolescent noises.

Thank God she had no homeroom duties this year. She could sneak in late on mornings like this. The bad part was she'd have to sit through study halls and be on call for lunchroom monitor duty as well. Lunch duty was the worst. Standing on her feet while kids screamed to be heard in a cafeteria so old even the asbestos couldn't absorb all the noise. Did she truthfully love her job? Or was something else tugging at her?

"Go ahead and make yourself at home in the classroom," Hadley said to Neil. "I'll be in shortly. I'm going to check to see if I put my car keys in my purse."

"Well, it's about time, Mary Sunshine." Brenna spotted her digging in her purse. "Late night last night?"

"Yeah, sort of."

"Something wicked this way *comes*, perhaps?" She winked.

"You should have been teaching Shakespeare this

year, not me." Hadley felt too weary to try for more of a rejoinder. The crick in her neck was still there, like a nagging conscience. "No, I didn't do anything bad. At least not yet."

Brenna must have had an extra cup of coffee. "Thoughts are the same as deeds. Remember Jimmy Carter lusting away in his heart. Did you read Clymer's memo?"

Clymer was the school's unpopular principal. He was gangly, brusque, and enamored with suspenders and bow ties. For the most part, people considered him to be a dandified jerk who dwelled on crunching numbers and how well he photographed with his head tilted at a 45-degree angle in yearbook photos. Hadley, on the other hand, had always rather liked him.

Hadley peeked into her classroom. Neil was trying to find a place to put his briefcase on her desk. Student essays were stacked in untidy piles like Dagwood sandwiches filled with bologna of a much different sort. "No," she finally answered. "I can't seem to find the time. What's on his orderly little mind?"

"It seems like we're working with the newspaper," Brenna said. "Some sort of drug survey, as a way to show parents who don't care that their kids are, in fact, junkies. At least some of them." Brenna edged closer to Hadley. "Didn't you read the paper? Welcome to our nightmare, right? They're only a half a century behind the times."

Brenna was all overblown gestures today, when Hadley was least up to them.

"Yes, Neil from the newspaper is in my classroom now," Hadley said while rubbing her stiff neck. "My class is first."

The bell rang. Brenna grunted as she turned to go to

her classroom. She turned around to face Hadley.

"Hey, would you mind helping me with the computer later? I'm from the typewriter generation, you know."

"Absolutely," Hadley said. "Glad to do it. I spend my life staring at one when I'm home, so whatever you need."

Hadley's Shakespeare class was filing in. Oh, how she longed for a cup of strong coffee, the kind that had been percolated to blackness. The kind they used to serve at church functions or weddings. Or after Rainbow Girls meetings. She had once been a member. All those white dresses. Some girls had had their periods during those long meetings and had to stand around afterwards during social time with big red stains on their backsides like bullseyes. She wanted the coffee and the simpler times that went with it. That wonderful black liquid, steamed of any flavor, coming out of a jolly old coffee pot that actually spoke to you as it brewed.

Instead, she entered her classroom and stood with Neil at her desk.

He held a sheaf of papers in both hands. The freckles even covered his digits. All of Neil must be covered with freckles, Hadley deduced, then quickly shook her head.

"I don't have to take the whole period," Neil told her. "But I'd like your help someday when the results are in, your feedback."

"In what way?"

"What we talked about the other night. Your input on this project."

Yes, she'd promised him, but how could she reach them? How young her students were and how awful that drugs proved to be such a lure. The old line "sex is the poor man's opera" could be modified for the '90s kids. Life required boosts, something to get through, especially when money was an issue, as it was with so many of her students. Shakespeare and Samuel Johnson weren't cutting it. It had to be tactile, sensate, *immediate*. At some level, wasn't she the same way, using unavailable men as her drug? She needed some coffee to think, some precious few minutes to compose herself and drink her own drug of choice. Would a writing club make a difference in some of these kids' lives? Neil was her moral corrector, someone put in her life she could learn lessons from, especially lately. She would not abandon this issue.

"Take as long as you'd like," she told him. "I'll be grading papers in the teachers' lounge." Hadley wanted Neil to be in control of the class. She feared they might show off if she were there.

The hall was emptying as stragglers filed into class. Why was noise so integral a part of kids coming to class? Was noise the only way trapped students could get the world to acknowledge they'd prefer to be outside? She scanned the classroom and scolded herself. Most of these kids were disadvantaged. They needed to be heard in any way possible. She smiled at the late ones who took their seats.

Now that the room had filled, Neil was stuck. There was no cajoling Hadley into staying without making a spectacle. Before the clamor had died down, she turned to the class and announced in rather stentorian tones, "Mr. Martin is from the newspaper. And he's here to get your opinion on a survey."

"On what? How to dress for success?" Justin was always ready for fresh meat. A rumble of laughter ensued as the youth pointed to Neil's olive-green Hush Puppies.

"No, and that was rude. He's here to give you a survey sheet to fill out."

"On what?" Corynne echoed from the sidelines.

"On drugs. Whether it's a problem at this school, with you guys. You know what I'm talking about, at least some of you do." Teaching high school distilled life to the basics.

"The only problem is finding enough of 'em," Justin muttered, prompting those within hearing distance to laugh loudly.

"Again, Justin. You need to watch what you say. Drug use is nothing to joke about." She grabbed a few essays from one of the stacks. "Please be nice to Mr. Martin. Do what he says."

Neil lifted an index finger in protest, but quickly realized he was center stage, a mailman among a porchful of pit bulls, so he hastily began handing out the surveys.

"Ms. Todd?" It was Jennifer, the student who had approached her in the library the other day, stopping her at the door, as she was almost in the hall, the demarcation zone.

"Yes, Jen?"

"You never showed up after class," the girl said. "Or else you'd left. You told me to come up after school, remember? To help me re-write this essay that sucked? But your room was empty."

She had indeed left early. That was the night she had to hurry home to get ready to see Trey perform. Hadley had let her down. How often did kids like her make an effort to get extra help? Had it come to this? Was she pushing aside the few students who actually sought help in English, one of the most hated of all subjects in the curriculum, all because of her hideous plot with Trey? What was happening to her? Long ago, she had gone into teaching for the kids, seeing education as the only way out of these backwoods. Now where was her commitment? Where was *her* innocence?

"I'm sorry, Jen. I really am. Can you give me another chance, stop by another day after school in the next few days?"

Jennifer nodded and turned to go back into the classroom.

"Jen? Hey, hold on. You can slip back to class in a minute," Hadley said. "I wanted to say it's important you come back for help. I know, together, we can make your essay better. OK?"

The girl blinked her eyes slowly like a cat who signals it might trust you after all.

"OK," she said, barely opening her mouth to speak.

"Good," Hadley said. "That's great. I'll hang out after school's over for the next week. Stop by whenever you can."

Hadley made sure Jennifer went back into the classroom before she walked slowly down the hall, rubbing her temple where a migraine had settled. Once she procured some coffee from the cafeteria where it was fresh, Hadley headed for the faculty lounge. Neil would never leave without her being there to replace him. She was exhausted anyway. She was two weeks behind on these papers, too. Life was never balanced. Too many papers, too much undone business.

****

"I'm telling you, there's nothing like a divorce to make you love your ex-husband."

Before Hadley even opened the door, she could hear Anise. Once inside the faculty room, she caught sight of her sitting at the round table, regaling the shop teacher, George Herbert, and Tom McElroy, the psychology teacher, on her newfound singleness.

"So, is there a new guy in the picture yet?" McElroy was rumored to have little compunction in the commitment department, his wife a disenfranchised *hausfrau* taken to knitting her way to oblivion for bad choices made early in her youth, her marriage included.

Anise kicked off her shoes and put her feet up on the sofa, a horrible orange tweed number that would have been right at home in The Brady Bunch's living room. "Well, of course, there's *playthings*."

George Herbert laughed and shifted his position in his chair to get a better view of Anise. He put his arm on the top rung of the wooden chair and leaned his head against his hand, unconcerned that the sweat-stains on his shirt had now opened up like the cavernous mouth of Elmo the Muppet. George Herbert was the furthest thing from the 17th-century metaphysical poet whose name he shared. *That* George Herbert had likened God's love to a spiritual pulley, and had even written poems in the shape of a cross in an attempt to embody his manifold devotion. His modern day namesake, on the other hand, dealt only in what was coarse and palpable.

"*Playthings* in the plural?" he asked Anise, probably anxious to extend a conversation that was the closest thing to phone sex he'd had in quite a while.

But the talk soon came to a halt when Hadley came in and slumped into the corner of the couch, as far away from Guinevere and her knights as possible.

"Wow, you must be tired," Anise said. She wagged

a finger at the stack of papers on Hadley's lap. "Here's a word from the wise: Don't spend so much time grading those things. The students don't read what you write anyway."

What followed was a mumbled consensus on the state of today's students, a tiresome subject, but one all teachers defaulted to. Hadley could feel the heartburn. She had become the wistful percolator of yore, bouncing coffee up and down her esophagus.

"I should be getting back," George Herbert said. He sounded disgruntled now that the threesome had become a bridge party.

"I, as well," McElroy said, speaking like a country squire instead of the overbearing know-it-all his colleagues found him to be.

"And then there were two." Anise turned to Hadley. "So, I understand you've taken an interest in Trey's musical career?" She twirled a bleached strand of hair around her finger.

"What did he say?"

Anise rubbed her feet together. "Just that. And you were willing to give him a few pointers. You know, because of your background."

"Well, yeah." One of the things Hadley had learned was never to give the cross-examiner any more than she asked for.

"How nice of you," Anise said. "He's so talented." She waited a moment. "Don't you think?" She leaned in toward Hadley, her face closer than comfortable.

"Yes. Nothing *but* raw talent."

"You lit a fire under his perfect bum. He's been hounding me to contact my friend in New York who has a small studio. He said he'd give him a listen." She stretched, a gesture that turned her tank top into a crop top.

Without warning, Hadley dropped her coffee, the shadow of her wonderful church social-wedding-reception-Rainbow Girls percolated coffee, all over her lap, home to the essays. When did this plan happen?

"Shitski," Anise said. She quickly moved into action, attempting to salvage whatever she could of the musings. "Did I say something to upset you?"

Well, yes, as a matter of fact, Hadley thought, *I'm handling this boy. It's part of my plan! What the hell do you think you're doing?*

"No," Hadley said. "I'm clumsy."

By the time Hadley had cleaned up the coffee, with Anise's help, and herself, she was anxious to check on Neil, given, by now, he'd surely be eaten up by the likes of her worst students. She was grateful for an excuse to leave Anise, professing the need to get back to class.

So, Anise was going to take Trey out of town to have a friend listen to him? Clearly, she had a plan of her own. And it would be like Trey to have several plans, as well as women, in play at the same time.

She flew upstairs, prepared to walk into a room of fatherless children, wild waifs from *Lord of the Flies*, cannibalizing the remains of her friend. Instead, she stopped at the doorway and listened.

As she peeked her head around the doorjamb, she saw him, sitting on the edge of the desk. Students were listening intently to him, their hands under their chins or else folded neatly on their desks. Shakespeare had never commanded their attention in such a way. Perhaps therein lies the rub: Find them where they are.

Neil was speaking slowly. "When I found him,

behind the bowling alley, sprawled on the ground, he was already dead." He paused. His voice had seemed to crack momentarily, but he quickly regained his composure. "I called out his name. No answer. I remember it was 3:35 in the morning. I had recently left for the night at the newspaper. When I went over to him, he was lying on his stomach. I could tell something was wrong by the way his right arm was twisted unnaturally behind his back. When I rolled him over, his mouth and eyes were open." He paused, lowered his head, then spoke directly to the class. "He was gone. My best friend was dead."

Hadley's stomach dropped. A rush of blood to her head made the sound of the wind in her ears. She grasped the door casing for support. Even bad-boy Justin was quiet. All eyes were on Neil. "Now you see, you can understand, I hope, why this is important to me. So be as honest as you can be on this survey. Don't sign your name. It's confidential. But, please, be honest."

Another ten seconds of silence fell before Justin finally spoke out.

"Dude, that has to be the saddest frickin' thing I've ever heard."

Hadley tiptoed back into the hall and tried desperately to fight back the tears welling up in her eyes. She remembered Joshua, Neil's childhood friend—and hers—lost to drugs. But Neil spoke of him. She remembered Joshua's boyishness and his need to be liked. Her heart broke for the lost and disillusioned, including herself. Neil had a busy life at the paper, yet he was taking on this monumental program to help actual lives, addressing the problem directly, not through writing clubs or essays.

She remembered when she and Neil were kids. She had come home from school and spotted him through the back door. He was signing a card—it was her birthday after all, her 12th birthday—then he slipped it in her mailbox, along with a fancy chocolate-mint candy bar. By the time she got it, the candy had melted all over the card. She could only make out "Love, Neil."

She walked down the hall in an attempt to pull herself together. She did not want Brenna to see her. It was wonderful to have such a caring friend, but the last thing she needed was her fussing over her. So, she went where English teachers always go for solace: the library. Once safely hidden in the stacks, she spotted a volume of Matthew Arnold's poetry, yellowed with age. She checked the inside cover. The volume had been a gift from a teacher back in 1949. She then opened the book to Matthew Arnold's poem "A Buried Life."

"But often / in the din of strife / There rises an unspeakable desire / after the knowledge of our buried life / a thirst to spend our fire and restless force / in tracking out our true, original course..."

After Shakespeare class, she avoided Neil the rest of the day, using lunch duty and her landfill of ungraded papers as her "out." She could not think of Josh, of death and drugs and despair. She could not think of young souls gone too early, her parents far away from her, either literally or metaphorically, running away from grief. She wanted instead to think of life and youth and passion. She wanted to see Trey who represented all of these things to her.

And she would see him tomorrow night.

Later that night, she realized she had missed her writers' group. They had expected her to read what she had written.

That was a fact she resolved to change.

Chapter 15

Wednesday after school, Hadley had stayed long enough to give Jennifer time to show up for remedial work—she hadn't—before running home to fix up for her meeting with Trey. She would dress like a L.A. clubhopper, which wouldn't mean much to him given that he'd never been there, but he certainly had ideas about its inhabitants. She put on her tight black pants, a black tank top, and a leather jacket, and teased her usually flat hair, except for a few errant frizzies that refused to comply.

Inspecting herself in her bedroom's full-length mirror, she frowned. *You're more like Olivia Newton-John in the last scene of* Grease *than a hot young L.A. chick.*

She got to the school's music room early by a half hour, doodling around on the piano, wondering if he would stand her up. After all, he'd worked out some parallel plan with Anise.

What an operator!

She went over what she'd do tonight. Run him through a few warm-up scales, have him perform a song and critique his lyrics (words were her business, after all), take him through some phrasing. Commonsense stuff. Things she learned in church and school choirs.

She'd be in control all evening…and see how he reacted to being the clay, not the potter. And, yes, she'd

132

turn on the sex appeal. He said he loved women. Maybe she could take him to the point he'd feel vulnerable, in anticipation of being praised as he most assuredly was by Sara and Anise, to name but two. She reminded herself to dole out constructive criticism instead.

The clock, an old black-and-white model adorning most classroom walls, said 7:15. He was already late. She took it personally.

At 7:30 p.m., he waltzed in with his guitar case and a backpack, matching her jacket and pants with his own. If anything, he belonged in L.A. more than she ever had.

"You're late," she said in her teacher's voice.

"But I'm here," he responded with a smile. "I had to finish up some work at the radio station."

"Let's get started," she said. She swung around on the piano bench to face the keyboard. When she did so, she caught sight of a poetry book stuffed in his backpack. "Let's start out with some scales to warm up with."

"Do I need this?" he asked her, lifting his guitar out of his case.

She shook her head. "OK, let's go. I'll play the scale, and you sing along with it."

After several of these, during which she made him sing incrementally out of his key, she found her heart pounding. *Now what, Smarty Pants? You're an English teacher, not a vocal coach. You've misled him already. And that's wrong. Come clean! Get out while you can!*

"You should always warm up," she said, hoping to impart some golden nugget of wisdom he hadn't already heard a million times already in order to feel less guilty. "Saves your vocal cords."

He leaned against the piano. "What now?" he asked. "What do you want from me so we can call your musical connections in L.A. and set up an introduction?"

"Play a song then," she said. Her mind raced. "Play the song you sang at The Cork on Sunday."

He lifted his guitar from its case and did as he was told. This time, he emphasized the *Baby, you still care* line more.

"That was good. You sang the lines with more emotion this time, but the lyrics. Don't you think they're a little trite? I mean so many songs nowadays—"

He interrupted her. "Again? I know you're an English teacher, but love lyrics are love lyrics. People want them to be simple because the feeling of love is simple. If you're in love, that is."

They stared at each other. *As much as you want to criticize him, the parts are greater than the whole. You've seen worse get signed in the record business. It might be time to get out of this whole mess. It doesn't feel right. I hate deceiving people, and that's just what I'm doing.*

"You *have* been in love before, haven't you?" he asked her point blank.

"That's none of your business," she said, avoiding his stare.

"I disagree. It *is* my business when you're criticizing my lyrics, and I'm arguing that people in love hardly see simple declarations of love as trite. You don't always need John Donne's conceits to tell someone you love them."

John Donne! Conceits! He was a well of surprises. And Winnie had recently mentioned Donne. How would he pick his name out of the vast galaxy of stars in the Western Canon?

"Of course, I've been in love. But I wasn't satisfied

with clichés and platitudes," she told him clipping the endings to her words. "I had a higher bar than most."

He sat beside her on the piano bench, forcing her to move a little to make room for him. She could feel his body heat through the leather. "Maybe that's why you're alone now. Sometimes overthinking ruins things with guys."

She jumped up and walked over to get her purse and the satchel filled with ungraded essays now as attached to her as another appendage. He was humiliating her. Or maybe he'd figured out her weak side just as he had figured out other things about her. Maybe now was the time to make a final stab at control to see how he'd react.

She faced him from across the room. "OK, fair enough. But I'm going to be frank with you. I don't think you're ready for the big time. I don't think you're a good-enough singer. And your songs aren't cutting-edge. This is the '90s. People are doing different things, musically."

She hated how the acoustic tiles in the music room seemed to absorb her words, which she wanted instead to ring and echo with gravity.

He walked over to her, his shoulders back. "You could be right. You told me so the other night." He was within inches of her face. "But I know I've got the swagger and the smarts and the personality to make up for whatever I lack in vocal ability or lyrics literate enough to enthrall a lit major. Your age group is not my main demographic."

She gazed into his face, his high color, those light eyes comprising both shades of teal and blue at once. *If he kisses me again, I won't stop him this time.*

"Listen," he said while taking her right hand in his. "We shook these hands on a deal that said you'd introduce me to someone in the music biz, right?"

She nodded. His hand was smooth and dry. She ever-so-slightly tightened her fingers in his grip.

"Then let's skip these so-called lessons. I've already made arrangements through a friend to get a demo made this weekend. So all you have to do is honor that handshake and arrange for me to meet your connection in Hollywood, OK? Just a name, a phone call to introduce me."

Her play would fail with no inspiration. And stuck with carrying out the worst part of the deal! How did this happen?

"OK," she said, but not in a commanding voice.

"Good," he said. He released her hand, breaking what she worried might be the last physical connection she'd ever have with him.

He grabbed his guitar case and headed for the door.

"Wait!" she shouted at him, taking long strides to keep him from leaving. "One more thing. What about you?"

"What about me what?"

"You. Have *you* ever fallen in love?"

He winked at her. "All the time."

She'd have the last word, something she realized was important to her. "I think it's wrong, all these women you lead on. Don't you? I mean, they may get attached, fall for you. But you seem to use them, to see what you can get out of them for your own purposes. I think that's wrong. They're human beings, after all. With feelings."

He turned around, his eyes drained of any light. "They use me, too. It's not like they're not getting anything out of it."

"What am I getting out of this?" she asked him, if not rhetorically.

He stood on one hip, a move that made him appear more rakish than usual. "I really don't know, Miss Todd. I wondered that myself. I thought perhaps you were bored or intrigued. Or maybe you're a control freak." He took a step toward her so he was within half an inch of her face. "Or maybe you're just like the rest and can't resist me."

Hadley stood her ground. "How do you know when it's over? The moment when love, or lust, turns into something else. Something not as passionate?"

"I don't think about it," he said, returning her gaze. "It's something that happens. Maybe it's not one moment. It just *is*."

He turned around and walked out of the room.

In spite of herself, he'd had the last word. And he seemed to know her better than most. Was she a case in the book *Women Who Fall for Womanizers*?

He had guessed it: She was falling for him. She had gotten herself into the same old trap again. And that scared her more than anything. What did it say about her? Wasn't it time she learned? At least she recognized it. Now what to do about it.

Chapter 16

Hadley spent the next few days trying to avoid Anise and Brenna. She didn't want to discuss Trey or her plans or anything. She wanted to catch up on her grading and work on her play. She didn't want to hear about Anise's taking Trey to New York this weekend so he could return with a demo in hand. And she especially didn't want to see Trey. She came and went, as surreptitiously as one can in a public school.

Friday night, Hadley went over with groceries to cook dinner for Aunt Winnie and herself. She tapped lightly on the always-unlocked door and entered, fearful of what state she might find her former counselor.

"Aunt Winnie?"

She walked into the kitchen. "I gotta stretch. My legs are killing me."

"Sit down here. I'm going to fix us a little dinner."

Winnie did as she was told. "How are things?"

"I'm good. I think I figured out the answers to some of the problems weighing on me—thanks to Kierkegaard."

Winnie paused momentarily. "The philosopher?"

"Yes. None other. I've been on the wrong track here, blaming myself for not being better prepared for my loss of innocence like some damn rube. But, in truth, my lack of sophistication in matters of the heart had nothing to do with me at all. That's what I learned."

"Go on."

Hadley fried some fresh hamburger with onions and garlic, turning the meat methodically so all sides cooked. "I was intrigued by this whole 'sickness unto death,' what Kierkegaard said. He was talking about some existential crisis, but, to me, the phrase described the feeling I had, which meant I took to be more of a half-baked omelet, about loving someone who doesn't love you back any more, even though there had been a wonderful connection at some point. And then it's gone, just like that."

She mixed some macaroni and tomato sauce into the mix, grub fit for cowboys in the Old West, and stirred under a low heat. "Anyway, I read this other stuff he'd written, something about how when you want to wean someone off you, someone you don't want around anymore, you have to 'blacken the breast.' "

Winnie got up and walked to the sink to get a glass of water. "I have a good background in philosophy."

"Then you'll know what I'm saying. I read an overview of his *A Seducer's Diary*, and he puts that whole theory into practice, how he actually played with the idea of love, got the girl to love him, maybe even loved her at first to get that heady feeling of infatuation. Then after he's had his fill, he tries to make it seem like she breaks off the relationship by painting himself as a no-account bum, a worthless creep, far beneath her." She put the lid on the pan with more emphasis than was needed. "That's what I've been letting men do to me."

"So don't let them," Winnie said. She casually leaned against the sink.

"Sometimes you don't know they're doing it," Hadley said with a slight shriek at the end. "It's the worst type of deceit. It's cowardly." She crossed her arms as if doing so could protect her from the hurt. "The illusion being they're the ones being dumped because the true dumpee is too good for them."

Winnie rinsed out her glass in the sink, as if she were buying time in which to find something appropriate to say.

"Do you know Derek had sent me a card quoting the verse from Whitney Houston's song 'I Will Always Love You' about leaving so her ex-lover would then be free to do as he pleased? That's pure Kierkegaard. It's an easy out for the bastard who's trying to leave in the fastest and least messy way possible."

"Appears like you've been doing some figuring out all by yourself," Winnie said. "That's good. You've found the exact moment you lost your innocence, right?"

Hadley stared at the forest green cabinet in front of her, the color favored by camps situated deep in the woods. How perfectly such a color blended into a house in a town where trees and hills surrounded it, protecting them from outside trouble, yes, but also keeping some of the fun big city stuff out. She recalled a poem she had once published about her hometown:

The sun, like the hills, tempers the natives.
appearing only after cresting the Alleghenies,
and departs long before turning in for the night,
taking the sky with it.

Here there are no tales of sunsets like bloody yolks
or ones stippling the dusk with magenta—
such scenes unfailingly compromised
by mountains or mist.

The ring of hills surrounding the town
serves as a golden mean,
muscling back the kind of trouble,
born of unbounded heavens.

So the people here spend their lives longing
to feel a fire hot enough to burn diamonds—

All the while casting onto phantoms
their hooded glances, their bitten lips,
and swear they smell the sea in every remnant
of a hurricane that comes here to die.

She stirred the mixture on the stove and turned down the heat. "I don't think I ever lost my innocence."

"You believe it was taken from you instead? Is that it?"

"Yes."

"Get over it, Kathy." Winnie was back in guidance counselor mode.

Hadley widened her eyes at Winnie's tone. "What do you mean?"

Winnie removed two plates and two coffee cups from the cupboard. "It happens to everyone, this loss of innocence. That's the way of the world. Some learn it earlier, some later. Some by way of love affairs, some in other ways."

Hadley laid out silverware next to the plates. "I have never, ever in my life hurt anyone so bad as I've been hurt."

Winnie put her two hands on Hadley's shoulders. "What about Neil?"

"Neil? He's like my brother."

"But he's not your brother. You crushed him by not

loving him back. You might be sorry one day. He won't wait around forever."

Hadley became flushed, whether from the food cooking or what Winnie was saying, she couldn't tell which one.

"I can't help it if I'm not attracted to Neil in that way."

"All right, all right. The point is, you gotta move on, then. Heartbreak is part of life."

"It doesn't make it easier to know that. I know going forward, I need to remember to blacken someone's breast before he blackens mine, to quote Kierkegaard."

Winnie straightened the silverware on her table setting. "Let's hope that's not your final epiphany. C'mon, let's eat."

If Hadley hadn't been so hungry, she would have done something about Winnie always having the last word.

Chapter 17

The next day unwound slowly. She tried to read, to grade essays, to watch movies on TV, but her mind defaulted to a Saturday night in the Big Apple, Trey pointing out the Chrysler Building to Anise, or dining at the top of the Twin Towers, or going to a show together, then going to their hotel room and then…a knock at the door. Backdrop was all.

All at once, she was upright, like a Macy's parade doll infused with helium. Her hand grabbed the doorknob, as if she had floated there.

"Must be the booze," she said to her azalea on the mantel—when did she get that lovely plant? And how well it was doing at this time of year! She had never believed herself to have a green thumb, but this greenhouse gem certainly belied that.

She opened the door but a crack. And then, at the sight of Trey's coinworthy profile, she opened it all the way. He stood with one hand nonchalantly leaning against the street numbers of her apartment, which she was almost positive had fallen off last year.

"May I?"

"Of course." She had known, somewhere in her limbic brain, he'd come back, so it was easy to see him this time. She fell back against the door as she closed it behind him, feeling bolder than usual, almost languishing in the moment. Ah, it felt so good to give in to the feeling, to remove the silly strictures that had kept them *en garde*.

She leaned against the door seductively, remembering that scene in a famous mob movie when one of the boss's sons serviced a bridesmaid at his sister's wedding. He whisked her upstairs, lifted the bell of her skirt, yards of satin and tulle, and banged her against the closed door of an upstairs bedroom. The door deserved a best supporting actor nod.

He stepped closer to her and whispered, "Come with me."

"What?" She giggled from excitement.

"Take my hand and come go with me." He made reference to an old doo-wop song.

He held out his hand. Together, they air-surfed in the night like Peter Pan and Wendy. Incredibly, she didn't notice the chilliness. Before her were the streetlights against the inky sky filled with millions of tiny rhinestones—no, diamonds. Only diamonds could shine like that. When had it gotten dark so quickly? Where were the people? This was usually a busy street. Cars, kids, cacophony. But tonight it belonged to only the two of them...*Oh God, there you go again, thinking in cliches*. She promptly told the cynic in her head to shut up.

"What are you doing? Where are we going?" Her bare feet didn't seem to touch ground. Where were her shoes? Yet, she didn't remember stumbling on the stony sidewalks, humped up and uneven from decades of turning earth. She took a mouthful of night air, but she couldn't run any more. Her legs felt like sandbags. She leaned against a streetlight to catch her breath.

Trey's buttery jacket was gone. Hadn't he had it on

when they left? He faced her now, his shirt unbuttoned halfway. The streetlight exposed his golden chest hair. She became the village girl in the fairy tale that had spun gold out of straw. What was the name of that tale?

"Rumpelstiltskin. The fairy tale. Remember it?"

Trey clasped his long, strong arms behind her back and twirled her around once or twice before pressing her against the streetlight. His face was close to hers. There was no going back. He was stronger than she.

"You're a clever girl, did you know that? I like that about you."

"Really?" That was all she could manage to say. Her tongue seemed to thicken, to expand with each syllable like a sponge in bath water.

"Yes." He whispered the word, scanning her face. He licked his perfect lips.

For a moment, she took in his young luscious face and let her taut body relax against his strong arms. His beauty was almost too severe in its perfection—his green-blue eyes, his smooth skin with the "high color," his one dimple, deeper up close. Why does beauty come in spades for some people?

He kissed her, hesitantly at first, then completely. His lips were smooth and full. This time, he gently covered her mouth with his open mouth. What a wonderful kisser, the best ever, methodical, slow, gentle. If he could kiss like this, then… She put her hands on his magnificent head, feeling through his luxuriant mane like a phrenologist. Her motions seemed awkward compared to his, but her arms felt like ribbons.

At one point the streetlight morphed into the moon and then back again. They came up for air.

" 'O, swear not by the moon, the fickle moon.' Are

you familiar with those lines?"

He shook his head. He was still pressing her closely to his body.

" 'Lest that our love prove likewise variable.' Shakespeare. *Romeo and Juliet*."

"You English majors never quit, do you?"

She shook her head. Such bliss! "Hey, I've got to ask you something."

"Not now."

"But it's important. I want to know if you remember your last moment of innocence?"

"Shh." He put two fingers under her chin to tilt her head upward for another kiss, but she was soon distracted by the nonsensical tinkling of a celesta. It became louder, even frighteningly loud. The pitch changed as the sound neared—the Doppler shift, as she learned long ago in physics class—and then an ice cream truck appeared, the old panel truck of her childhood...at this hour? Who could want...? The distorted notes were loud and insistent...such an unpleasant noise for signaling something as wonderful as ice cream and kisses.

Hadley awoke to the sound of the phone ringing. For several minutes, she tried to get back to the dream, but it slipped away moment by moment, like the dissolving notes of a favorite song. She tried to remember it, but the unpleasant electronic tones of the phone dispelled any memory of it, other than Trey had been kissing her.

"Yes?" She could hear the grogginess in her own voice. "What time is it?"

"Wow. Sorry. It's 10:30-ish. Want me to leave you alone?"

It was Brenna. It was not like her to call at night, even late.

"No, no. That's OK. I must have drifted off. What's wrong?"

"I thought you were mad on Thursday and Friday. I couldn't find you."

What could she say? She didn't dare mention the dream…after all, she was furious at her subconscious for falling victim to Trey's wiles. Waking and sleeping, he had her.

A respite from thinking was what Hamlet had asked for in his soliloquy: "To sleep, perchance to dream." Yes, she understood that plea now. Sleep was never enough to beat back the dreaded emptiness, the weariness, the thinking. Without a dream, sleep was a reflex, a physiological function merely—like the gag reflex or a sneeze. It was like eating food for fuel, not for its taste. But a dream, a dream with its wild transmogrifications and lack of constraints, yes, a dream was as good as a drug or even the best moments in reality. To sleep, perchance to dream—why, that was good enough to push away reminders of the daily drudgery that seemed to define so much of life. And she was so tired lately, dreaming came easily.

"Not mad. Just preoccupied."

Brenna was one of those people who twisted the phone in her hand when she talked, which meant the listener heard squeaks and creaks from the plastic handset as the white noise behind Brenna's words.

"I have some dirt. Are you up for it? I think it'll cheer you up."

Where did people get this dirt? Again she wondered if there were some underground network they could tap into like pay-per-view T.V.? Did they live with their ear to the ground? When did they eat? Sleep? Dream? Was living vicariously, in truth, what people found to be the most exciting thing in their lives?

"Sure. Bring it on." She squared her shoulders.

"It's about Anise—and Trey." Squeak, squeak. Brenna had to be positioning the phone, but a portable phone would never fit comfortably against her ear. What she needed was a headset. Perhaps she'd get her one for Christmas. Or her birthday. Whichever came first. She could then talk, squeak-free, into the phone.

"And?"

"She and Trey flew off to New York City this weekend."

Hadley felt whatever effects of her quixotic dream remaining now dissipate in the cold reality Brenna brought back. Trey had no reason to be loyal to her. He was her paramour in a dream, an ephemeral lover in fairyland. *She* had been the silly village girl spinning gold out of straw—or chest hair, in this case.

"Hello? You there?" Brenna's voice sounded worried.

"Yeah. I was trying to wake up." Perhaps Brenna had more details to fill her in. "I mean what was it all about?"

"What was what about?"

"The trip. What do you know? And, by the way, who told you this?"

"Oh, sweetie. Do I detect a hint of hurt in your voice? I shouldn't have told you. I was hoping it would end all that talk you had about the pre-emptive strike or something."

Hadley must have been the most transparent person ever. A big sucker for the world to pity or laugh at. Brenna had come to all sorts of ridiculous conclusions based on her delivery of two measly questions. It was amazing how revealing the tone of her voice must be. At times, she believed her voice was analyzed more than the Zapruder film taken of Kennedy's assassination.

"Don't be silly." She tried to keep her voice steady. "Who told you?"

The informant, according to Brenna, had been Prue Eidelman, home economics teacher at the school. A veritable sieve when it came to gossip. Brenna said both Prue and George Herbert had been in the faculty room when Anise regaled them with details about her upcoming trip with Trey.

"Apparently, the trip was going to be rather decadent. Demo, drinks, diddling."

"Nice alliteration."

The reality that Trey was using *her*, as he was using all these women, made her nauseous—why had she let her guard down? But, hell! That was all part of the plan. She was using him, too.

Or was she? Hadley was falling for him, but he didn't see her as being distinctive. Instead, to him, she was but one of an army of broads, each fitting a different part of his personality or fulfilling a different need. She was now aligned with the hapless Sara as one of his utilitarian females, a caretaker. Momentarily, she had forgotten she was the Alexander slated to fell him in the battlefield of philandering and record it all for the innocents out there. Instead, she found herself reacting as she had to Derek's infidelities in the past—lost, alone, helpless. Trey had truly become Derek by proxy.

This could all end with the record executive giving Trey his due: a send-off that basically echoed what she had said. He wasn't ready for the big time. Her connection to Trey would be broken. She would move on with her writing and students.

"What else? I mean, what else did they plan to do there?"

The creaking of the plastic was discomfiting. Brenna must have been preparing to hang up, knowing no one would want to discourse with such annoyance.

"I dunno. Prue said she mainly talked about the hot sex, much to George's great pleasure. Let's face it. George's wife will play pinochle with him, but that's it. So this conversation saved him a 900 call."

When there was no reaction, Brenna finally came through with more detail. "I guess Anise told them she and Trey might even get it on in Central Park. Near Strawberry Fields. Where's the respect? Lennon, for Pete's sake."

When Hadley hung up, the last thing she wanted to do was go back to sleep on the odd chance she'd dream. After all, she needed the cold steel of reality to plan out every single detail of her trip to Hollywood with Trey.

Oh, yes. She planned to go with him, not just set up an introduction. She'd show him she was a different class of woman—one whose feelings were too fine to be trapped between the lines of one of his homemade songs. She'd show him with as much passion as she'd been unable to show all the others. But she still wanted at least one night with him.

She made a mental note to call Roxie and have her help set it all up.

Sunday morning, the phone rang again. She let the answering machine pick it up.

"Hadley, dear? This is Delores Malvern from the writing group. You never showed up this week when you were supposed to read your short story, but we're giving you a second chance to read it this week. Marsha, to say the least, was not happy you didn't show, but I stuck up for you. So be there. We'll save the whole night for you."

Such kindness on behalf of Delores, practically a stranger, made Hadley tear up. People ought to be acknowledged for their compassion—there was too little of it in the world. She wrote herself a note to call the accountant and thank her.

Chapter 18

Sunday morning, Hadley's heart skipped a beat when she noticed the answering machine had another message on it besides Delores Malvern's. Perhaps it would be good news, maybe a conciliatory call from Trey who would tell her he had, in fact, gone to New York and was dead-serious about working with her after having seen the light. Or maybe it would be a soothing check-in from Neil.

She eagerly pressed the message playback button.

"Baby, are you there? It's Bryce. How are you doing, my adorable one? God, but I miss you. Listen, I called to see how your play is coming along. I'm so excited about it. Let's talk. Soon. Call me 'cause I can't ever find you at home. Mm-wah."

Bryce in L.A. always had a project—or ten—in the works. He had written two books, had produced a movie, created his own CD, and was getting his own show on one of the satellite radio stations that featured divas only. Bryce, bottom line, was more connected than a spider web in an abandoned attic. What he wanted from her was a play to wrap a few of his zillion loose songs around. He'd start out producing in small groups, maybe a theater. It could be her big break...albeit one she'd have to enjoy long-distance. Or maybe he was feeling sorry for her and this, after all, was only a mercy commission.

Hadley moved from her computer chair to the wing

chair, one she had grabbed from her parents' home before they split up. She had no play to show Bryce. How many people had she disappointed lately? Certainly Neil had a right to be disappointed in her, but from what Brenna said, he was getting along without her just fine. Nevertheless, she could have helped him more…just as she could have helped all the people in her life.

She removed a round pillow from the back of the chair and gave it a wicked left-hand hook. Trey didn't know it, but she would also disappoint him. An insurgent ulcer burned in her stomach. She was using him. That wasn't right.

Hadley dialed Neil's number. She would talk to him now, find out what was up, what he wanted to talk to her about. Make up for lost time. Make things right.

But when she speed-dialed Neil's number, the only sound from the other end of the line was endless ringing. Not even an answering machine. Neil didn't like answering machines, but he usually put it on if he wasn't home. He couldn't still be at the paper. It was Sunday. The editorial staff didn't go in until later. Where would he be? She began counting the unanswered rings. That they had lost touch lately was entirely her fault. Yet he used to check in on her more persistently. Now, if she missed his call, he didn't even call back. Twenty-seven rings, 28 rings, 29… After 30, she hung up.

Her chest felt tight, as if it were swaddled in Ace bandages. She held her breath to control her breathing. It was 6:45, and Hadley needed to get dressed and write a bit. There was a lot she had to do today. But first she wanted to tell Neil she was going on a short vacation. She wanted him to care enough to worry about her while she was in California with Trey.

No return calls from Neil. Even without an answering machine, he could check his caller I.D. to see she had called. He must have caller I.D.—didn't everyone these days except her?

How little she knew of what Neil was up to lately. At one time, they had known the details of each other's lives. Even when she lived in L.A., they had spoken several times a week by phone. Now, a gap seemed to be widening between them, just when she wanted it least, but maybe Winnie was right. Maybe he realized it was hopeless and was pulling away. It was like that scene in the perennial favorite *It's a Wonderful Life*, where Jimmy Stewart and Donna Reed are dancing in the gym when all of a sudden the floor opens up between them and they fall in the pool.

If she and Trey left on the red-eye out of Buffalo Thursday night, they'd be in L.A. Friday morning. Roxie could set up the meeting with the shark at the record company, and the jig would be up. They'd be back by Sunday night, both a bit wiser. Maybe she'd even show up at a future writers' meeting, a suppliant, all penitent, with a fistful of *play* in her hand.

She glanced again at the clock. It would be 3:46 a.m. in L.A. Roxie would be up, insomniac that she was. If not, she'd leave a message. She pressed memory #2 in her phone's keypad and waited a few minutes.

"Hey, girl. Can you meet us Friday morning? Early? Maybe 1 a.m.? I think there's a plane arriving in L.A. at that time, if memory serves me right," she said, speaking into the air. "I'm gonna do this thing, and I want it to be over with. Don't be like me—call me back when you get this."

Hadley dressed quickly and ran to her car to fetch

some coffee downtown. She was concerned about Neil, so she drove by his apartment, only a few blocks from her own, on a sleepy little side street by the name of Elm, no less. His car was not in the driveway, as it usually was. Was he OK? Inside her torso there was nothing but emptiness. No internal organs, just emptiness, like a mummy's insides.

When she returned home, she paced her apartment, all the while weighing what Winnie had said about her father, that he had left a deep hole in Hadley's heart. She loved him, yes, but she had often had to navigate a twisty road to get at his love.

She remembered the time the lurid luminescent colors in the bar had intrigued her as a child. They could be found in the jukebox and in her orange soda pop before her and the various neon signs advertising beer common to this region: Utica Club, Ballentine, Carling Black Label.

Her father had taken her, a child, to a dive bar in the middle of the day so he might get buzzed, a need that often loomed larger than anything else in his life, including taking care of his non-school-age daughter while his wife worked.

The excitement of being in a bad place was implanted early. And she always associated it with her father. He was an alcoholic. Are there even degrees? He had times when he didn't drink, but it was always on his mind, like some men think of mistresses. He also gambled. Both liabilities consumed him. And that made it bad for a little girl. Most times, she sensed he preferred drinking and gambling to her.

She remembered sitting in the bar tipping the rim of the glass toward her mouth, hoping not to spill the liquid on her clothes. Her father was ahead of her in drinks of a different kind, his eyes getting rheumy the longer the two stayed. He spoke to some men in the bar, wetting his lips between sips of beer. She, on the other hand, had no one to talk to. The sound of sad music on the jukebox was loud. She recognized one of the old songs because her mother played it at home, something like, "Are You Leaving Now that Love has Gone?" No answer to the singer's question was forthcoming—here or at home. Why did people ask it then, especially in song? The bar was yellowish-dim and smelled of cigarette smoke and alcohol, odors she would forever associate with her father.

After a while, she wanted to go home. She wanted to tell her long-suffering mother that her father had taken her to a bad place. But her father was having a good time, singing along to the jukebox's selections, drinking beer after beer in filmy glasses. He never seemed to have a good time with her alone, reading stories to her at nap time or taking her to the park. Something was always lacking in regular activities.

This too—this need to find things to fill in the abyss—would be something she would internalize. Such wadding need not take the form of alcohol, she was to learn, but she would always seek out what was lacking, what needed extra effort on her part, a challenge, the lesson being, "Life isn't good enough as is."

And that expanded into "I'm not good enough as is."

Christmastimes were especially rough. Her father often got drunk, wouldn't come home, leaving her mother and her wondering where he was. The garishness of the Christmas decorations couldn't outdo him when he finally came home. She remembers one Christmas when he'd lost his shirt, literally, clad only in a thin white T-shirt, stained with Muscatel. She remembers the name because she had never heard the word before. Her mother adorned it with the adjective "cheap" before it, putting a point to it. He also brought his wife a new expensive robe and lingerie from the best store in town, one smelling faintly of moth balls because of the fur storage place above it. Such tokens, charged, never paid for, were meant to stand in as symbols of affection instead of real love that required steadfastness and perseverance, qualities that had not stood him well in his life.

That Christmas, he had taken his daughter on his knee and sang "Silent Night," his thick tongue eliding the sacred lyrics. She didn't want to be pressed against the cheap Muscatel stain on his T-shirt, which he wouldn't change in spite of her mother's pleas. It was revelry time. He said out loud, "Why do my wife and kid always want to spoil my fun?" Would they rather see him glum and reflective, thinking of all the Christmases he got nothing from *his* mother, dumped on a farm in the middle of nowhere?

Years later, she had come home from school one cold wintery afternoon to find him face down in the snow in the front yard. How long had he been there? Was he dead? She turned him over. Someone—perhaps those who had taken his shirt and his wallet and his car keys— had drawn the face of the devil in green permanent color on his face. She screamed. It wasn't often she got to see a visible manifestation of his transgressive nature. That he drank in spite of a hard-working, clean-living wife and an honor student for a daughter always confused her. Nothing she did pleased him as much as a bottle of wine or endless rounds of beer.

157

She had run to Neil's house and pulled him away from whatever he was doing to come help her. Neil was aware of her father's drinking and sympathetic to her mother and especially to her. It had taken a long time for both of them to get him into the house and a lot of soap and scrubbing to remove Satan's likeness from his visage. Perhaps it was under his skin naturally, she had thought at the time.

Hadley put her head in her hands, weighed down with the memories. He wasn't always bad, yet the bad was imprinted in her memory. She had done nothing wrong but try too hard to make him love her the way she was.

She was still trying too hard. She was still trying to win his unconditional love, just as she was, in turn, trying too hard for unavailable guys to love her, repeating the whole toxic process.

But the past couldn't be changed. Only the present. And the future.

Before she went to bed, she left another message for Roxie to call her tomorrow.

She was going to Hollywood with Trey. And then it would be over. It was time to move on.

Chapter 19

As Monday morning rolled around, Hadley dressed quickly, a black skirt, white blouse, black blazer—the standard grammar marm's uniform—and ran to her car.

She'd have to talk to Roxie about setting up the plan for her and Trey to meet her married boyfriend at the record company.

And she'd have to ask Roxie if they could stay a few days with her.

Then she'd have to tell Trey that she was going along with him when he was introduced to the A&R guy at the record company. She wanted to see it all unfold, come what may. She wanted a breakthrough. She also wanted a fling before he flung her over.

She'd let the chips fall where they may with Trey's future as a recording artist. If there was one thing you couldn't coerce a record guy into doing, it was signing someone they didn't like. It came with too much responsibility. If the act failed, the record guy could lose his job.

And no one was going to sign Trey. She knew that much. No matter how gorgeous he was. She rationalized her part by telling herself it would be a good wakeup call for him. Life in Hollywood was not life in Tillsdale.

Throughout the day, she searched for him, hoping he'd show up to see Anise after their weekend together. She wanted to set up the upcoming trip. She was receptive to any sparks that might ignite an idea.

Her hopes of seeing Trey never came through, however, until she walked out the door at 3:45 that afternoon. He was leaning against his car, his arms folded, a golden vision of youth and heat and possibility. When he spotted her, he ran over.

"Hey, Miss Todd," he said. He sauntered over to her, certainly none the worse for wear after what must have been one busy weekend. "You're the person I'm waiting to see."

She stopped and turned.

"Hi. How's kicks?" he asked, as effervescent as ever.

"No complaints," she said. She couldn't help thinking of what he and the elastic Anise had done the past weekend besides produce a demo and then reminding herself she mustn't care. Not anymore.

"I have the demo," he said. "I finished the demo this weekend. All I need is the name of your friend at the record company, according to our deal. We shook on it, remember?"

She resumed her walk to the car. "I haven't forgotten. I've got a call in to make the arrangements."

He smiled his crooked disarming smile, bringing his irrepressible dimple out for show. "Wonderful," he said. "That's great."

She fished for her keys in her purse, which required her putting her books and briefcase on the hood of her car. She had done something similar once, except she'd put her purse on the trunk of her car and then driven off. Some nice truck driver picked it up and honked his horn until she stopped to retrieve the goods, so she only plunked it on the hood ever since. One life lesson down.

A hundred million to go.

"There's been a change in plans," she said, averting his gaze.

She could feel his body heat. He was that close.

"Yes?"

She turned around to face him. "I'm going with you. I'll introduce you to the A&R guy in person."

He continued to stare at her. She imagined the plans he'd already made... If Sara was paying for the trip, she would have naturally been going with him. Now what? Hadley had never offered to pay his way. Would he still go?

"What made you change your mind?"

She stepped away and grabbed her books and purse from the hood of her car. "I have other business out there. I'm supposed to see a friend about something I'm writing for him."

He jangled the keys in his hand. She wished she knew what he would have to change now to accommodate this new revelation.

"When is this going to happen?" he asked. "I'll need to know soon because of work and—" He didn't finish.

"Soon. I've got a call in to my friend. I'll let you know."

He frowned.

"What's the matter? Most people would be thrilled with the in-person introduction."

"I'll have to make some last-minute arrangements at work. But I guess it's OK."

She was more in control than he. And that was good. Only because she wasn't succumbing to his will, his obvious preferences.

"Which girl were you going to take with you?" she

asked him. "On this trip, I mean? Until I interfered?"

He peered into her eyes. Did he see them as a warm hazel color, the brown part good at keeping her emotions in check? If she could only keep her mouth shut.

"Let me know as soon as you know the arrangements." He turned and walked to his car. Instead of starting the ignition, he sat behind the driver's side, plunking out a melody on the steering wheel. Soon, Sara came out of the school building, heading straight for the self-same car.

Hadley drove away so as not to seem interested.

When she got home, however, there were two messages—the first from Roxie saying to call her. She had the flight booked—not to worry about it.

"I'll be at the airport at 12:30 a.m.," she said. "And I can't wait to see you. Both of you. You can pay me back for the tickets when you get here."

The second message was from Delores Malvern. It seemed Hadley had been voted out of the writers' group. Marsha Culpepper was furious that she hadn't been there to read her short story since, in good-faith, the group had given her a second chance to redeem herself. Fortunately, Delores had brought the next chapter from her new novel, so the evening hadn't been a complete bust.

Just you wait.

Hadley dreaded the next task. In an ideal world, she would not recoil at the sound of a voice she usually thrilled to, but this was no ideal world. It was a made-up world, one of her making. She picked up the phone and slowly pressed the numbers into a keypad.

"Hello?"

"Hello, Trey?"

"Yes. Who's this?"

"Hadley."

"Hey. What's up?"

She hesitated. She could have 'fessed up right then and there, come clean, and put the wedge between them.

"I called to tell you the trip is set. We leave Thursday after school to get to the Buffalo airport."

"This Thursday?"

"Yes. Is there a problem?"

"What's wrong with Friday?"

"If we travel Friday, then we won't be able to see the record people. We have to be in L.A. by Friday morning so we can see them Friday afternoon. I'm taking a vacation day."

She heard from his end of the line what sounded like a lighter being opened and shut. He didn't smoke that she knew of, but Anise did.

"Maybe your friend would take me around to the record company on Monday instead."

"I don't have Monday off. We have to leave Sunday. Hey, the arrangements are all made. It'll be a short trip."

"I know you have to leave, but maybe I can stay another day or two out there. With your friend."

Clearly, he did not deem her as essential as she had hoped. These guys, she had forgotten until now, had unbelievable panache. The world was meant to accommodate them, not the other way around. Did humans crave beauty so much that it trumped every other quality?

"I'm sorry, but those are the arrangements. Record people are busy. And so am I. Take it or leave it."

He spoke softly into the phone, as if he did not want anyone to hear him. "I'll take it. What time should I be at your place?"

"I can pick you up. Though I don't know where you live."

"Not for lack of trying, am I right?" he said, adding a chuckle at the end.

She flushed. Was she that obvious?

"You come to my place. We have to leave for Buffalo, so be at my place before 5 p.m."

"I'll be there."

"Don't forget the demo."

"The what?" He seemed in a hurry to get off the phone. There was an edge to his voice.

"The demo. Your CD."

"Yeah, yeah. I'll see you then."

"OK. Good night."

No thank you, no ebullience, no message of gratitude or excitement. Perhaps he was nervous. Perhaps it was finally sinking in he was going to the record capital of the world to meet with a record company insider, albeit one who undoubtedly was treating this whole thing as a joke if Roxie had filled him in. Or perhaps it was something else.

Perhaps, for instance, he was falling for Anise and hated to leave her. She shouldn't care, she reminded herself.

Hadley then called her father to tell him she wouldn't be over to see him this weekend because she was going away.

"Hullo."

His tongue seemed thick. He had been drinking no doubt. Not eating right. He needed her, a fact that made her heart sink.

"Papa? You all right?"

"Why sure, I'm all right. Why wouldn't I be?" His breathing was heavy. Too many decades of cigarettes. What was it with those generations of smokers.

"Listen, I'm going out of town this weekend, and …"

"Where to?" He sounded like the properly concerned parent, as if she were going on a date at sixteen.

"Out of town. You know. All those papers and kids at school. I gotta get away."

She could hear him scratch his unshaven chin against the phone. "Dontcha think I oughta know where you're going?"

"A short weekend getaway." She wanted some distance. "I'll be back by Monday. I'll call you then. Remember—Neil's at the paper if you need him—or call Winifred."

"Winnie? She's old and sick. I don't need nobody. Not you, not your mother. Nobody."

He hung up the phone in her ear. She told herself not to cry.

She called him back, but the only response was an endless series of rings before the answering machine picked up, an answering machine she had set up for him.

"Papa," she said into the phone. "Please don't do this. Don't make me feel guilty. I'm not Mom. I didn't leave you. I mean, I left you, but I came back. And even though I'm so busy, and I don't get to see you… I love you. I have to get away."

She replaced the receiver. Something in her heart made her wish she had the guts, the strength, to call off the trip and stay at home with her father. Help him clean up his spaces. Cook him a big dinner. Give him a big hug and get one back. Do the same with Winnie.

She vowed she would make it up to them.

Chapter 20

On Tuesday night, Hadley was too wound up to do much. Maybe some food would help her to straighten up and think straight—or fly right, wasn't that what the song said? Nat King Cole had sung it first; then Linda Ronstadt covered it in the 1980s. Would Trivia Trey have known that?

She peered into her refrigerator, then her freezer. A TV dinner covered with frost made a lean-to against the freezer wall. She was in no mood to cook or wait for a TV dinner. Besides, the idea of such a meal was too pathetic. A triangular dessert wedge stuck in the middle of a desiccated chicken leg and mashed potatoes with the machine squiggles frozen right on them was too bleak. It was a wonder there wasn't a "Hi Loser!" sign printed on the peel-back film.

Realizing she was out of coffee, she grabbed her coat and headed for the car. The choices for a good cup of joe were limited in Tillsdale. For drive-throughs, a few fast food franchises, standard fare for small towns. Small-town people were supposed to be satisfied with these. No high-end coffee place here. It was an insult, really. A deep, cutting example of discrimination—in this case the unsophisticates who presumably fill small towns.

No, rubes weren't worthy of a coffee shop with its complicated hierarchy of drinks with French names. A "small" wasn't a "small" in coffee-shop-speak; it was a "tall." Not knowing the lingo meant exclusion from a select community, a dialect that deliberately kept out the yokels.

"Hey, Miss Todd. What can I getcha?"

Justin, the buck-toothed student from her first period class, was working the drive-through window. She was glad she had only ordered coffee since the young man's mullet was free and flowing. Weren't these kids supposed to wear the fast-food equivalent of a toque? A backwards baseball cap with a grinning death mask on it? Or some do-rag with dancing fries and milkshakes?

Perhaps Justin got away with loose hair since he had an *extreme* mullet—business in both the front *and* sides with only a *little* after-party in the back. It was as if his barber had put the bowl on his head and forgotten to take it off until that "uh-oh" moment. Still, no one in Tillsdale would consider Justin's hair to be out of place—or time. Here, hairstyles were held over from the 1970s. Too many young men, and, alas, women, were coiffed and attired as if they were ready to walk into a Foghat concert.

While in the drive-through, Hadley spotted Neil, of all people, coming out of the joint, accompanied by... who? The pointillistic dusk made it difficult to see who was with him. He must have been on his work break. His companions, therefore, must have been his co-workers—one a girl, an intern, possibly; the other a male reporter who had plodded along for years without more than a township meeting under his byline.

Neil carried a tray of milkshakes, walking next to his cohorts, who seemed to be chuckling and having a good-old time. Must be a working dinner at the *Crier*.

Even Neil was guffawing. It had been a while since she'd seen old Neil laughing that hard.

She found herself missing him again in her life of late, his steadfastness, the surety and availability of him. The way he always seemed interested in her, even though she questioned his intentions, always acting as if his unrequited love remained unspoken between them. Yet, he had been a good sounding board against which she might hear her voice, unless, of course, he disapproved, as he would have if he had been privy to her scheme with Trey. Was that why she had been avoiding him?

The last time she'd seen Neil at the school, she had been abrupt, the way one can be with a sibling. She had seen him after that a few times, trailed by a queue of ragtag misfits, but hadn't stopped to talk. In fact, he had become a frequent presence at the school. His anti-drug newspaper series and the surveys had stirred up the kids to the point where he was spending time after school with potential crack addicts as the ad hoc counselor of an anti-drug club of sorts. He took the kids to heart, something even their own loved ones had failed to do for the most part.

Hadley remembered a conversation she'd had with Brenna concerning Neil that had taken place during one of the days he had been at school.

"Rumor has it he talks a lot about love at these after-school meetings," Brenna had told her over a bologna sandwich in the faculty lunchroom.

"To the kids?"

She nodded, her mouth full of deli nitrites and spongy white bread.

"Do you mean *love* love? As in 'Let-me-count-the-ways love?' Or more of a Barney hug-me love?"

"Barney love?" Brenna spoke before catching herself in another display of pop culture deficiency.

"You know, family love, unconditional love, big, warm fuzzy purple love—all the things these kids don't have."

Brenna paused to chew and think. "Umm … more 'Only the Lonely' love." She smiled, as if pleased she'd come up with a pop reference, although it hailed from decades past.

"Oh God, you know what *that* means." Hadley regaled Brenna with the short version of Neil's unrequited passion for her, planted in high school, germinating ever since. "I've always considered him my brother. But I've always suspected he harbored more than brotherly feelings toward me."

Brenna put her sandwich down before dabbing her mouth delicately with a napkin. "Has he ever said as much?"

"No. At least not since we grew up. It's more of an unspoken thing."

"How many years have you know him?"

"All my life."

"Does he call you a lot?" She ran a blush-painted nail over her gums.

"No. In fact, I haven't heard from him since the school anti-drug thing. Maybe a message, but I didn't call him back."

She picked up her sandwich again. "Can't be you. If a guy's interested, he'll keep calling."

Hadley lifted her eyebrows, wanting to ask Brenna to elaborate, but she didn't. Instead, her remark ended the conversation. Thinking of love, though, brought Trey to mind, as she sat idling her engine in the drive-through, wondering how long it took a high school senior to pour a cup of coffee. Had Trey ever truly been in love? Can polyamorous guys really love? Certainly Derek hadn't ultimately been able to love her…

"Bastard." She spoke the word aloud, with emphasis.

"Hey, that's not Shakespeare I'm hearing," Justin needlessly pointed out. He grinned widely, as he handed over the cup of coffee, swaddled in a napkin. These kids pretended to think teachers were cool when they slipped up and became human and swore or drank or smoked or had an affair, but too often they'd use it as leverage when they got in trouble themselves. So, Hadley's response was measured.

She made a gesture as if to zip up her foul mouth while she took the coffee from him. All the talk of Shakespeare—did they see its worth, all those clever conceits and masterful metaphors? It made her sad… why tempt them at all with the finer things of life if it was merely to make them more aware of the rich world beyond their reach? Or would it make them miserable, as it had her? If anything, she had proven herself to be one of them.

She wanted to catch up with Neil and his posse, making their way on foot, and drink her coffee with others. She wanted to be with people, with him, with someone who knew her and knew her well. Maybe even loved her. Others, obviously, enjoyed his company. She understood that. Neil was dependable, a good listener, trustworthy. Maybe she could learn to love him as more than a friend…

She hit her car horn in a series of staccato beeps. Neil and the others turned around.

"Hey stranger!" She put her crooked elbow on the rolled-down window to appear folksy, as if she'd never spent time in L.A.

Neil responded by lifting up the tray, given that his hands were already in service. He offered her a big gap-toothed smile.

Hadley pulled up beside the trio. "You guys need a ride?"

Only Neil stopped. The others continued walking. *I'm that insignificant.*

"I guess not." He was eyeing his cohorts sauntering ahead. "We need the walk with the long night ahead of us. Thanks, though. How've you been?"

She was stung by the rudeness of Neil's co-workers. "Fine. OK, well, listen—I'm not going to interrupt your break."

"No problem. We got a hankering for milkshakes and had to act on it. Say, let's get together soon and have a talk." He glanced downward, reflecting on something not on the tray he was carrying. "I've been meaning to talk to you."

"Sure," she said. Her own desire for her hot coffee overtook her. Did Neil want to tell her again how he felt about her? Was that what was weighing on his mind? Then she recalled what Brenna had said, how if he had been interested, he would have moved heaven and earth. All she wanted was to go home and drink her coffee. Maybe even grade a few essays before she hit the sheets. "Give me a call."

"You bet," Neil said. He then hurried to catch up with the others.

She expected him to turn back, maybe lifting the tray again in a friendly goodbye gesture.

But he didn't.

Chapter 21

Hadley knew she'd have to stop in the school office first thing and tell Sara she would need Friday off, the day she planned to be in L.A. with Trey.

The school secretary was staring into her computer when she stepped up to the counter.

"How you doing, Sara?" Hadley's stomach tightened.

Sara didn't get up. She turned to Hadley. "How can I help you?"

"I need to request a personal day this Friday. So, you should get a substitute for my classes."

Sara remained seated. "You know, of course, Mr. Clymer would have to approve this before I call any substitute."

Hadley tapped her foot, an action Sara couldn't see but might hear. "I know. But it's important. I have some business to take care of."

Sara smiled what Hadley believed to be a knowing smile. She wished she could like this person, but even before knowing of her alleged connection to Trey, she hadn't warmed up to her. Maybe it was due to her being so calm and quiet. So unlike Hadley.

"OK, but if he gives you any trouble about it, please let him know it's imperative. I have to go out of town on business."

"I know," the school secretary said, cryptically.

174

Hadley hated not knowing what half the people in this school were thinking. She hurried to make it to her first class.

Most of the students were in their seats by the time she arrived at the citadel of learning, her classroom.

"Hey, were you going after Mr. Martin when I saw you?" It was Justin, who manned the burger joint's window, asking the question. He was supposed to be asking questions about Hamlet's lassitude vis-a-vis Ophelia, but he was obviously far more interested in the goings-on between her and Neil.

"I've known Mr. Martin since I was a kid," she told the class. It wasn't like her to be this open, but she wanted it to be known she was not the type to chase after anyone.

"So, are you sweet on him?" Justin beamed widely, showcasing his unbraced buck teeth.

"No, I'm not sweet on him."

"I heard you call him a bastard."

She was in too far. Never get into the game with the students. That was a given. Once in, never out. "All right, already. Let's get back to Shakespeare."

"I heard you call someone a bastard the other night at the drive-through window. Don't you remember when I said something about that not being Shakespeare?"

Some of the students snickered.

"Then you drove up to that guy who was in here with the drug survey. You practically ran him down trying to get to him."

"He doesn't like Miss Todd that way." It was Corynne speaking up. Brenna had told her the girl was an active member of Neil's after-school anti-drug club. Had even succeeded in getting her to lay off the weed, too, according to Brenna. Did she, also, know more than Hadley about the goings-on around here?

"OK, let's move on," Hadley said. She felt a tinge in her cheeks and hoped they weren't red.

Corynne spoke up again. "I'm letting Justin the Creep know that Mr. Martin says Miss Todd's like family to him. He told us so."

It had gone way too far, but Hadley didn't care anymore. "Now what would make Mr. Martin tell you that?"

Jennifer, also in Neil's sphere, took over this time. "We were just sitting around talking about school in our group and someone called you a name…"

"And it wasn't me," Justin said, eliciting waves of laughter. " 'Cause I'm not in that drug club."

"You should be!" someone yelled out.

"…and Mr. Martin told us never to refer to you again like that 'cause he grew up with you and stuff," Jennifer continued. "So none of us were ever allowed to call you a bitch in his presence. Whoops, sorry Miss Todd."

Justin laughed the loudest, no doubt thrilled that someone else had echoed his sentiments exactly.

She forced a smile. Don't let them know you're bothered by what they say—that's what Brenna had told her when she first started as a teacher. "It's good to know I have at least one friend." She stomped to the podium. "Now, let's get back to Hamlet. Does anyone remember the name of *his* friend?"

****

"Sheesh, what a morning. I thought it would never end," Brenna said. She busily unwrapped her lunch from a brown paper bag and squeezed into a student desk in the front row as her make-shift lunch table, close to Hadley's corner desk. The chair was old, the kind from the 1960s that was all one non-ergonomic unit, designed when a little suffering was considered an essential part of education.

"I've been dying to know what you've got to tell me."

"You didn't figure it out?" She wanted both Brenna and Neil to know she was going to L.A. in case the plane crashed or she was abducted by an alien from another planet. Or worst case scenario, ignored by Trey. She wanted someone to care. And since she couldn't locate Neil…

Brenna shrugged.

"I'm the one taking Trey to Hollywood this weekend."

"*You*?"

Hadley nodded. "I have a friend with connections, so we're flying out on the red-eye Thursday. I'll be back Sunday." She said it as matter-of-factly as she could.

Brenna wiped the corner of her mouth with her napkin even though she had yet to take a bite from her sandwich. "But *why*? After we spoke, I thought maybe you…"

"I'm going to see some friends. On business. About my play." Not all of this was true. She did want to see Bryce, but it wasn't her main reason, of course. *I'm getting rather adept at lying to myself*, she thought.

Brenna nodded. "Yes, the play, I forgot. Is there at long last a play? Last time we talked about it, you were suffering from writer's block."

"Of course there's a play! At least the beginnings of one in my head. Besides, I have to see this other thing through."

"What thing?"

Hadley took a sip from a can of soda. It was diet soda. Not as bad as the cyclamates once swimming in earlier versions of diet drinks, but still funny-tasting. "The Trey thing. I told you I promised him I'd introduce him to some record people." She gently put the can of soda, upright, in the waste can. "Frankly, I don't know how to get out of it. I gave my word."

Brenna said nothing. She toyed with the salad she'd brought in a tidy plastic container.

"I know how you feel, but what harm to introduce him to some people? He's already got the demo all done." Hadley hoped her friend would understand.

"Yes, we both know how that was accomplished."

Hadley nodded. "And he can rise and fall on the basis of that. When that's done, I'm through."

A sly little smile played on Brenna's lips. "Hollywood with the hunk. Just you and him?"

"What do you mean?"

"I mean, will you stay with him? In a hotel? Just the two of you?"

"No. We're staying at my friend Roxie's." A classroom window showcased a few leaves that were already turning yellow and orange. Winter was just around the corner. "It's not like that."

Brenna shrugged. "Good to hear. Like I said, he's trouble…"

"I already told you. I'm not going to be one of his girls. He's research for my play." *I'm lying. But so is Brenna. She's not telling all she knows.*

Brenna's smile quickly faded. "Darling, you already are one of his girls if you're doing this for him. Speaking of which, what about Anise? I mean, obviously she's telling people if the cafeteria crones are overhearing her."

"I don't know. I can't figure it out."

"So, I'm curious. Why did you let me in on your plans? You know how I feel down deep. No matter how you paint this trip, it's probably going to be bad for you." She took a bite from her sandwich. "Bad for all involved."

Hadley shivered. "Why do you say that? As I said, I have business with other friends out there."

Brenna covered the untouched salad with the plastic lid and wrapped up what was left of her sandwich. "Why are you doing this?"

"Why? I'm old enough to know what I'm doing."

"You only know how to get your heart broken, dear. And he's going to tear it wide open. The sad part is, he won't even know he's doing it."

"What do you mean?"

"You've told him you'd help him, right? So, he believes you. He thinks you want to help him because he's so damned pretty, and you're a mite taken with him."

"I'm using him for inspiration for my play." By this time, Hadley was halfway out of her chair. "He's so self-centered, he thinks it's because he's good at being a rock star. I guess there's only one way to educate him."

Her friend shook her head, her coral necklace providing a soundtrack. "Darling, he's young and beautiful and full of himself. He knows he's quite good at something else he does or he wouldn't have so many women willing to do things for him."

She ignored her friend's remark. "I see him as more

than a specimen."

"Does he know how you feel? He's egoistic, but he isn't stupid."

"He can't think I care for him. I mean, our relationship is business related."

Brenna shook her head again as she gathered up her meager lunch wrappings. "That's exactly what I'm saying. He's used to women falling all over him, spoiling him. In fact, that's how he survives, right?" She struggled to undo herself from the student chair and stand erect. "I don't understand why you're doing this? You—a girl who loves beautiful books and poems and paintings and cries at roadkill—you, my dear, are setting yourself up to be trampled again. By another jackass." She grasped her lunch bag tightly to her, as if it were her purse. "You are so vulnerable, you positively squeak. What's it going to take to get it? He's going to use you only because you're letting him. Can't you see?"

Hadley put her hands in the air. "I told you. I'm using him, too."

"How? You haven't mentioned anything lately about how he's helped you with your novel. All right, I'll shut up before you tell me to go straight to you-know-where. Be careful, OK? Make sure you get out of this thing without getting hurt again, that's all. Go to the beach. Make some new memories. Do some research. But don't get hurt." Brenna clip-clopped out of the room, her slim ankles fashionably showcased in a pair of high heels.

"Brenna?"

It was too late. She was gone. *It's a play, not a novel! Why do I even confide in her? She's not even hiding the fact she doesn't want me to be around Trey.*

180

What goes? She doesn't understand. No one does.

In less than a minute, Brenna was back. "At least take this with you," she said, setting down the English Department laptop next to Hadley. "Make sure you actually write, so it's not a total waste."

"Brenna?" Hadley wanted to draw her back in, to tell her she didn't know why she was going with Trey to Hollywood. Was it really for the play? Or was it for a quick fling? Or did she want something more, something she couldn't put her finger on? It didn't matter. Brenna was out of earshot.

****

On the way home from work, Hadley stopped in front of the *Tillsdale Town Crier* and left her car idling. In Los Angeles, leaving one's car with the keys in it was beyond foolhardy. It was like putting a sign in the back windshield that said, "Steal this." But in Tillsdale, people watch out for each other. No one would steal an idling car. Not so long as at least one person was driving by or one pedestrian was walking the streets.

She swept into the century-old building that smelled of burnt rubber from the press. "Hello, Madge. Is Neil here?"

" 'Lo, Kathy. How are you?"

Madge, the receptionist at the newspaper for four decades, had known Hadley when she had been Kathy. With some of the older folks, she let them call her by her birth name. They would never understand why anyone would want to change the name their parents had given them. Never. It was sacrilege. It was as good as a Bronx cheer to your parents.

Madge cupped her hands over her mouth and shouted, "Is Neil in the newsroom?" She directed her query to the girls in the back of the office who kept track of all the staff's comings and goings.

"He just left for lunch," was the reply. Only on a night shift could 4 p.m. be considered a lunch break.

Madge repeated the information even though Hadley had heard it as well as she had.

"OK, thanks." She turned to leave.

"Do you want to leave him a message?"

Did she? Did she want to burden him when he was obviously a busy man, trying hard to succeed as a reporter at a small-town paper? As humble a calling as it was, he was at least effecting positive changes in the lives of the young people, perhaps more than she, as their own teacher, was doing. She wanted to talk to him, to thank him for sticking up for her, for caring about her. She wanted to tell him she missed him because he and Brenna were the closest thing to family she had these days—and maybe ever. And now Brenna was scolding her. She reminded herself Brenna was just mothering her, as usual. That was different from scolding. But it hurt, nonetheless.

"No, no message. Thanks." Hadley left but not before noticing the drab tan walls that hadn't been painted in decades.

It seemed to her as if she missed all that was important by just a beat.

Chapter 22

When she got to school, she ran into Brenna's tidy classroom, the chairs and desk all in straight lines. Unlike herself, Brenna had to tend to a homeroom class, a border collie amidst sheep.

"Wow, look what the cat dragged in," she said under her breath, as Hadley approached her desk. "What happened to you, honey?"

Hadley ignored her. "I know, I could probably join them," she pointed to Brenna's Willa Cather and Lillian Hellman posters behind her desk, the touchstones for a bad hair day. "I haven't slept much, thinking about what's coming up."

Brenna had already crooked her index finger, signaling her to sit in the chair next to her desk, a place reserved for students who didn't understand the nuances of MLA formatting.

Hadley wanted to unload on Brenna, ask her for advice, but something, God knows what, prevented her from doing so. Was it because Brenna had never approved of her getting close to Trey because Hadley didn't need any more heartbreak? Or was the reason more nefarious? Maybe Brenna was falling in love with him. After all, if anything, Trey certainly showed he was open to relationships with all kinds of women.

"I forgot I had one more essay to grade before my next class," Hadley told her friend. "I'll talk to you later."

It was times like these she longed for her own mother, now residing with a real estate agent somewhere in the South, far away from her only daughter, her only child. Although her mother always seemed to put her father first when she was growing up, Hadley now understood why. Her mother was trying to keep the family together, to keep her father home instead of at the race track or at a bar or juke joint, so something had to give. And that something was time spent with her daughter. Growing up, Hadley wanted a carefree mother, one who would drop what she was doing and go shopping with her or go to a movie or lunch. She always seemed second best, her father coming first.

Hadley remembered the time her tall, thin mother had come into her second-grade class for a conference with her teacher and how proud she had been of her. She could have passed for a model in her ivory coat with big lapels and matching belt. She brought the winter-washed air in with her. How Hadley had wanted her for herself then and there, to run away with her, without her father.

Her mother did eventually run away, but not with her daughter.

And now, so far away. Didn't her mother realize how precious time was and how much had already been lost?

****

After classes ended for the day, Hadley sat at her desk instead of running like hell out of the school as she usually did. The room seemed bleaker than usual, what with the sky darkening. Brenna was always urging Hadley to decorate the room, put up student cut-outs of Shakespearean figures or portraits of literary greats. The posters of Lillian Hellman and Willa Cather, two of America's greatest literary wallflowers, that Brenna kept behind her desk made her look better by comparison, she told Hadley. But inside, they were powerhouses, Hadley reminded her. And that's what counted.

She sat with her head in her hands, wondering what in the world would happen in the next few days, going to L.A. and in the city itself. It was raining in Tillsdale. Soon, after a beautiful fall, the tree branches would be bare. Winter, the longest, and bleakest, season here, would settle in.

She had sat this way for God knows how long when her reverie was interrupted by a knock on her classroom door. "C'mon in."

In walked Jennifer, her thick black tresses now spilling over her shoulders. "Do you have a minute, Miss Todd?"

Hadley remembered how she had stood up the poor girl once when she asked to come in after school for help with her paper.

"Yes, of course, Jen. Come on over here and sit down." She pointed to the beat-up brown school chair next to her desk, one infrequently used in spite of its worn appearance.

The girl did as she was told, holding her books on her lap. "That paper, the last one. I got a 'D.' You wrote on it that I could rewrite it. But I don't know where to start."

Hadley's heart softened. The girl had come in for help, which few did. Hadley wanted to honor her effort. That's why she had been staying after school, in case Jennifer, or other students, came by. These kids deserved respect and help.

"I'm here for you, Jen," she told the girl in a soft voice. "As long as it takes, we're going to get that paper into working shape, OK?"

The girl raised an eyebrow. Hadley figured she might have been surprised this was the same Miss Todd who had stood her up a few days before.

"Sure," she said to Hadley, managing a weak smile.

And together, they worked through the "D" paper, bringing it out of the darkness into an above-average argument, a metaphor, perhaps, for what she knew teaching could be.

Jen stood at the classroom door before leaving. "Thank you so much, Miss Todd." She hesitated. "I'm sorry I said the kids called you a bitch." She stared at the floor. "You're not."

Hadley nodded. "Listen, do you think you'd like to meet again? This time before your next essay is due?"

"Yeah, I think so. I'll come by after class one of these days."

"Hey, Jen. Before you go, I've got to ask you something. Would you and maybe a few of the other kids in class ever like to start a writing club? I'd be there to keep things moving, but we could work on essays and maybe do some creative writing, too. Would you be interested?"

Jennifer's face betrayed nothing. Maybe she still didn't entirely trust Hadley. "Yeah, maybe."

"OK, so we might talk more about it when you come by again."

Jennifer walked out of the classroom, a girl too thin—and not fashionably thin either. It was from a poor diet or drugs or need for regular home-cooked meals that included coconut cream pie for dessert.

She was tempted to cancel the trip and let Trey go his way. He would be fine. Those guys always were. Her students needed her, not a substitute. This felt right what she did today, not running after a dead end who was going to hurt her and be just like the rest.

Don't you have enough experience from these guys to write an entire encyclopedia, not only one lousy play? What are you really after?

Where was Neil? She longed to talk to him over dinner, to spill her guts, to talk about these kids. She wanted to tell him more about her writing club idea. It would be a chance to see these kids blossom, to be able to express themselves at last without having to write about Shakespeare or Samuel Johnson. OK, maybe it was a fantasy writing club at this stage, but she could plunge in, inspire, and encourage these kids in a way the writing club she belonged to didn't. Jennifer had a story to tell. And others did, too. She couldn't wait to talk to Neil about her plan.

But he wasn't around much these days.

Chapter 23

Hadley glanced over at Trey sleeping in the seat next to her. The flight from Buffalo to Detroit had been short. But this leg—from Detroit to L.A.—would be unendurable unless Trey returned from the Land of Nod. Whichever concubine had been with him the night before had done the boy in. If, as she believed, it had been Anise, well, no wonder he was beat. Or if he had instead spent it with Sara, letting her mother him...

Stop it! Thoughts like that only make things worse.

His face was turned away from her, snuggled as he was against the window with his jacket bunched up for a pillow. He'd pulled the shade down. The day had been bleak and misty when they boarded the plane in Buffalo and the connecting flight at Detroit. He slept soundly, seemingly oblivious to the turbulence—real and imagined—going on about him.

"Something to drink?" A male flight attendant with a spiky hairstyle inquired.

"Coffee...and ice water, too, if I may."

"And your...?" He gestured, pencil in hand, toward a slumbering Trey.

"Nah...we'll let him sleep."

She still couldn't believe they—she and her "whatever"—were actually on the plane, headed for L.A. He had passed up the chance to be the plan's wrecking ball. She would have been an instant victor had he canceled.

And now she wished he had.

Instead, he had appeared at her door, a canvas duffel bag in one hand, his guitar case in the other. The woman he had spent the night with must have dropped him off. Both finally in her car, she drove in relative silence to Buffalo, where there would be no turning back. He had barely said a word, sleeping mostly, as she navigated the curvy two-lane roads 65 miles to the nearest mecca in a forest covering much of Western New York.

They arrived early, so Trey opted to drink overpriced coffee in the concourse and read the paper without so much as glancing up.

Hadley stepped away to call Bryce to tell him she would see him when she got to L.A.

"I'm thrilled, darling. It will be so dang good to see you! When will that be?"

"I'll call you when I get there, but probably Saturday. Will you be around?"

"Of course! For you," he said. "How's the play? I'm dying to see it."

Hadley played with the silver cord as thick and scaled as an armadillo tail connecting the receiver to the rest of the phone. She needed to get a cellphone. Even some of her students said their parents had them. She always did tend to lag behind the latest technology, still content with playing cassettes in her car and using an old-fashioned hair dryer to free her hands for reading.

"No, I don't have it done yet. But I can give you a progress report."

"Fine, fine. Whenever you've finished it. You're the artist," Bryce told her, his voice betraying a bit of disappointment. "It'll be good, nay, wonderful to see you. Like old times."

As she made her way back, Hadley hoped Trey wasn't still reading a newspaper. It was rude of him after all she was doing for him.

"By the way, where do you live and where *are* you from?" Hadley asked. She moved a section of the newspaper from her seat. "I know nothing about you!" Trey continued to check the sports scores, ignoring her question. "Hey! I asked you where you're from."

"Nowhere. Everywhere. My family moved around a lot," he said, not looking up from the paper. "Would you pass me the rest of the sports section?"

"Not until you at least tell me what city and state you're from."

He finally met her gaze. "Like I said. Nowhere. And everywhere. My father was in sales, so we moved around a lot. He was on the road a lot. My mother mostly raised me."

This had not been the first time she'd lost out to the charms of sports when it came to men. She remembered a poem she'd written about Derek titled "Torpor." She might forget a lot of things, but she never forgot her poems… "You took me to a movie," it started out, "and I sat still, as precious as an Easter bonnet, wondering if my lip gloss was too cherry or if you would ever notice the Gucci on my purse."

What was the rest of the poem? "And I assumed you were worrying about the razor cut on your chin or if you could afford more vodka gimlets after the show." She closed her eyes and visualized the last words of the poem as if she were typing them… "Imagine my surprise when you reached over and took my hand." That was the beauty of poems…you could end them as you liked.

How nice if Trey had magically sat up and smiled at her. But he didn't. Life was no poem. The obsession with sports was something Trey shared with Derek. Oh, there were other things, too—over-arching egotism, his expectation of being cared for and pampered. Those qualities make them seem so unattainable. And then the perfect face thrown in. Lord, she couldn't wait for this to end just to be done with it. The words Brenna had spoken to her a few days before had lodged in her brain. "Why are you setting yourself up to get your heart trampled on again?" Brenna, clearly, would not. Or would she?

And you don't even have your play in any cohesive shape to show Bryce.

Who said that? She turned around, but no one could possibly be telling her this. Did she think out loud? She touched her foot to the laptop, making sure the gateway to her independence was still there.

Once they boarded and the plane took off, Trey said he planned to catch up on lost sleep. Trey's six-foot frame didn't fit comfortably in these too-small seats. His shoulder blades strained through his shirt. The boy was out cold, even though he had told her that he was a night owl through and through. Here it was, the beginning of the flight, and he would be one with the Sandman. She, on the other hand, was a confirmed morning lark. Hardly birds of a feather. No wonder Anise and Sara let him run loose in the morning after their evenings with him.

She had never been able to reach Neil before leaving. Had she told him, he would have tried to stop her out of brotherly or loverly concern—or maybe not. He had seemed rather detached the last time she'd seen him at the burger place. Since her brush-off that day at school, he'd adopted a more distant attitude with her, so uncharacteristic of him. Oh well, if the plane crashed, at least Brenna would know. And her father.

Of course, waiting on the other end would be Roxie, who had assured her repeatedly that she would handle the details once they arrived, that Trey would get his comeuppance in no time at the record company, and that she, Hadley, would only have to sit back and take mental notes and her play would write itself.

True to her word, Roxie's connections had handled the flight and her apartment would serve as a hotel while they were in L.A., but the nagging doubts remained. The more she was around Trey, the less she knew him. The idea of building a play around him, as a representative of his kind, no longer seemed as fetching. The concept she was finding much more interesting was, amazingly enough, herself. At least she had moved beyond being merely a player...she was also now an observer. Maybe she was learning something about herself after all.

Anyway, the trip would proceed, and the plan would unravel—or be fulfilled, depending on the perspective. She would observe his reactions when Benny played his demo and leveled the truth: "You're not good enough, kid." She'd watch his reaction and put it down on paper later. It would be comparable to how he dropped girls in his life who were no longer exciting enough, rich enough, sexy enough, young enough. Fill in the blanks. After that, she hoped he would move on—just not stand still in Tillsdale. If he stuck around, she'd have to face him—the living embodiment of what? Her naiveté? Her stupidity? Her own self-centeredness? Her muse? Her lack of judgment? Her deep-seated need for revenge? Her unresolved problems with her father?

A sudden pocket of turbulence made Trey stir at last.

He opened up the window shade, peering down at the cloud floor.

"Won't it be great to get to the land of sunshine?" He gave her a game-show-host smile. He rubbed his eyes. "Hey, by the way. I really appreciate the keys."

"What keys?"

"To the city." He nudged her upper arm, as a brother would a sister.

"Yeah, sure," she said, smiling in spite of herself. *Why didn't he repeat the kiss he gave her that night at The Cork?*

"Listen," he said, patting her hand, "I want you to know that when I make it, I won't forget what you've done. I'll repay your investment in me."

She grimaced. "You mean with your earnings as a rock star?" The words had escaped her mouth before she'd had time to think.

He sat upright. "Well, yeah, what else would I be?"

Indeed. *Perhaps an actor in one of the unwatchable sit-coms so popular nowadays.* She waved off the question.

"It's funny you said that. I've often wondered if I'd be any good on a game show," he said. He craned his neck to stare up the dress of a flight attendant who was bending over an elderly man to open up his tray table.

A game show! Why he'd be a natural! Hadn't that been her initial impression? A host waiting for a quiz show? Then how committed was he to being a rock star?

Hadley didn't like the fact that he'd unknowingly drummed up his own Plan B to her Plan A. Could he have been smart enough to have developed a contingency plan? Something she, herself, had even failed to do, other than the trap door through which she might fall.

"Go ahead. Try me." He gave her his signature half-crooked smile that could have driven her crazy had she let it.

She raised an eyebrow. *The fact that he always defaulted to trivia should make you wonder. It's called "trivia" because it isn't deep! He prefers to stay on the surface. Maybe that's all you need to know about him.*

"Try to stump me. G'ahead." He was persistent.

As promised at their first meeting, he was putting her to the test as much as he seemed to be asking her to test him. If she refused to play, then he'd think her to be unequal to the challenge. Yet, to play would be to give in to him.

"I think I'll pass," she said, trying for a condescending tone.

"Ah, c'mon. Just one. Go on."

"Just one. What area? Music?"

"Nah, we did that already. Don't you remember? I killed you. Donny Osmond? David Cassidy? Choose another."

Hadley searched her mind. *What area might she be better at than he? Literature? Poetry? Yet he had known John Donne.* "It's your challenge. You choose the subject."

"How about mythology. Hit me."

Mythology was one of the few weak spots in her knowledge of the literary canon. It was especially shameful since all English teachers were supposed to know mythology. She searched her mind in an effort to throw him.

"OK, what was Oedipus Rex's hamartia?" She remembered that much from her reading.

"Hamartia?"

"Tragic flaw."

"Oh, that's easy. He slept with his mother."

Hadley met him eye to eye. "Wouldn't you say it was his pride instead? His short-sighted, overweening pride?"

"But those aren't necessarily flaws. Pride gets you places."

"It got him blind."

Just in time, a flight attendant came by taking dinner orders—Chicken Kiev or beef tips. Hadley chose the chicken; Trey, the beef.

"Hit me with another one."

"I don't feel like drumming up questions so you can show off," Hadley said. "How 'bout an actual conversation instead? The first of the trip."

"OK. What do you want to talk about?"

Hadley felt tired all of a sudden. She cleared her throat. "You said you'd been in love. Tell me about it."

He paused for several beats before answering. "Yeah, sure. Lots of times. Joni Mitchell wrote the song 'Help Me, I Think I'm Falling' just for me. How 'bout yourself?"

He must have forgotten he had asked her this question before, the night at the school.

"I don't know. I don't know if what I felt was real love. I wonder if Joni had been inspired by the song 'I Fall in Love Too Easily.' "

"Sounds depressing. Falling in love should be a cause for celebration, not moroseness." He sat up in his seat and pulled his dinner tray down from the back of the seat in front of him. "Sounds like you know a bit too much about sad love songs. Hey, how's this for a topic. What's the worst musical invention ever?"

It was a segue all right. And perhaps for the better. She wished he had taken her hand instead. After all, she wasn't ruling out a fling with him. "The worst musical invention ever? What do you mean, like the Theremin?"

"Yeah, something used in a record that shouldn't have been. The Theremin was used in 'Good Vibrations.' It was perfect there, so that wouldn't count. Gimme me another one."

"All right, the wah-wah pedal. It's ruined every record it's been used in."

"Like?"

"Like 'Show me the Way' by Frampton."

He shifted in his seat to better face her. "That wasn't a wah-wah pedal. It was a talk box."

"Yeah, but there was wah-wah in 'Walk, Don't Run.' "

Again, a moment of silence, as he appeared to ruminate. "I love the Ventures. I love all that Dick Dale surfin' shit."

"What about you?" she asked. "What's the worst musical invention?"

"That's hard. I kinda like it all. Even the mistakes."

That was an odd thing to say! Maybe she'd read him wrong.

"What's your favorite Sinatra song?" she asked, genuinely interested.

"God, that's tough. I love so many." He tapped his fingers and closed his eyes momentarily. "Maybe this one." With that, he launched into one of Sinatra's tunes, as if the airline had hired him to initiate a singalong.

The stewardess with the half a skirt stood up when Trey began singing. They shared a smile. Others began to chuckle with all eyes on the singer. No one, however, shushed him. With one exception.

Hadley turned to him. "You're a little loud, you know."

He ignored her and began snapping his fingers along with his vocal, something Sinatra would have done.

A little boy in the row ahead of them turned around and clapped his hands in glee. The stewardess continued to giggle. Soon, more and more people began clapping along with Trey. Hadley even heard a few remarks along with the laughter like, "Sing it, brother."

A rousing round of applause and some wolf whistles signaled the audience's approval. One of those clapping and laughing, in spite of herself, was Hadley.

****

After dinner, conversation was erased by the monoglycerides in the microwaved food. Trey snuggled back into his makeshift pillow. "Wake me when we get to L.A." were his last words.

Hadley calculated at least two more hours must pass before they landed in Los Angeles around 1 a.m., Pacific Time. If Trey slept the rest of the distance, he would be anxious to go out and explore the town, when all she wanted was to crash at Roxie's and sleep until she had to go to the record company for the official curtailment of his fantasy. She didn't dare let him go unchained at night without her—and how could she ask Roxie to lend him her car, which she shouldn't do anyway. His persistence would undoubtedly turn ugly. She sighed. She was getting too old for this.

"Terribly long flight, isn't it?"

Hadley turned to the woman sitting in the seat to her left. She was elderly, white hair, red lips, mother-of pearl eyeglass frames.

"Yes, it seems so."

"It's the first time I've flown since my husband died."

Hadley dreaded the idea of being roped in for the remainder of the flight, listening to a stranger's reminiscences. And isn't that what most people did? Talk about themselves rather than carry on a conversation? But she hated rudeness to old people more than she loved her privacy.

"I'm sorry to hear that."

"Oh yes. A lovely man. He drowned last winter."

"I'm so sorry."

"Yes. He was walking the dog on a lake that appeared to be frozen. But it wasn't. Not all of it."

"Tragic."

"Yes, but the dog wouldn't budge from the spot. He stayed there barking until someone heard him and came by."

Had Hadley herself ever known such loyalty from either man or beast? Her dog Butterscotch had run away and she couldn't tell how many cats had gone, never to return. She thought of Neil. He could have been a freckled springer spaniel in another life. Oh, loyal Neil. What did he want to tell her? Usually he was the dogged one, calling, pestering her, keeping the link alive. But now…well, now, he was busy with the paper and the kids in the anti-drug club. Or she must have truly disappointed him.

Hadley dozed off after that, dreaming wildly of pink toy poodles with grosgrain ribbons in their fluffed up fur barking madly at a hockey game. She was glad to be awakened.

"Any garbage?" The flight attendant with the two-toned hair held open a white plastic bag, awaiting Hadley's lipstick-stained coffee cup, which she gladly donated. Shortly thereafter, the brunette walked up the aisle.

"Sir," she said to Trey, speaking over Hadley. "Sir, you'll have to sit up and buckle up for landing. Make sure your seat is upright and your tray secured."

At the sound of a young female's dulcet tones, Trey roused himself, blinking. "Oh, yeah, sure," he said, obeying her command, possibly from reflex.

The thud of the landing gear dropping meant their destination was not far off. Roxie would be waiting at LAX, ready to assume the guise of mentor to Trey, only to turn into Lady Macbeth before the trip was over. It would be good to see her. Like any true friend, she would be the grout to fill in the heart's holes.

"Prepare for landing," the pilot told the attendants who hustled to their stations and buckled up against unforeseen disaster.

Hadley couldn't help scolding Trey. "Except for your matinee performance, you've slept practically the whole flight. You know that, don't you?"

"Yeah, sorry. Didn't get much shut-eye last night."

"Oh?"

"At least I'll be wide awake when we land. I hope you intend on taking me for a quick tour of the City of Light."

"The City of Lights is Paris, not L.A."

"I said, 'City of Light,' not 'Lights.' You don't know your Doors, obviously. No wonder you didn't last long here." Sealing his remark with a devilishly crooked grin, he once again stared out the window, this time confronted by a magical display of colored lights, quite unlike the gray mist they had left behind in the east.

She couldn't blame him for fixing his gaze on the city at night. There *was* something magically alluring about flying into Los Angeles with its electric expanse of lights, stretching endlessly in all directions. From an airplane, Los Angeles was like a cheap hooker, its massive bosom bedizened with gaudy costume jewelry promising a grand time for all the desperate johns who frequented her. Unlike New York with its prickly verticality, L.A. was horizontal, lying on its back, sprawling and spreading, its winking lights tempting even the strongest of souls. It made people feel special without their earning it. Just like a whore.

"Wow, amazing." Trey remained glued to the display beyond his grasp. "I want to know this city, and the city to know me."

Out of compassion, perhaps, or humanity, Hadley softened. "Listen, you're aware that, connections or not, 90 percent of all the people who shop their wares here never make it. I mean, you are aware of that?"

"I'll be in the 10 percent. Just get me through the door, and I'll do the rest."

Hadley touched her forehead, which was damp. Taking off and landing were not her cup of tea. It had been a long flight. Maybe her conscience was bothering her, too.

"I wish we'd touch down already," she said to no one in particular.

Trey faced her. "You OK?"

"Yeah, I think so. I prefer being on the ground."

"Like Antaeus."

"Who?"

"Antaeus. The giant in mythology."

"Never heard of him." The bile rose in her throat.

"He was able to defeat anyone as long as he was touching the earth."

"How interesting." Hadley fought back the nausea.

"But then when Heracles discovered his secret, he lifted him off the ground, and then guess what?" He waited patiently until Hadley sighed. "He strangled him."

Hadley tried to distract her mind from her body's betrayal. "Everyone has a weakness. Is that the moral of the story?"

"Right you are. It's only a matter of finding out what that weakness is." Trey peered intently into her eyes before returning his gaze to the colored lights drawing nearer by the second.

Chapter 24

"Girl!" It was the unmistakable, paint-peeling scream of one Roxie Sanchez. She executed a quick wave with her undoubtedly highly moisturized hand, then she flew toward her friend—one she hadn't seen for over a year. "Oh my God, you're really here!" She grabbed Hadley by the shoulders and spun her around before giving her a bear hug. "I'm so glad to see you. And you must be...Todd." She extended her prized hand.

"Todd? Todd's *my* last name, remember? He's Trey," Hadley said, flashing a half-smile.

"Shit, that's one too many 't's,' wouldn't you say?" Roxie laughed nervously. "Hey, Trey. Wait a minute—that rhymes! How you doing?" She planted a friendly kiss on his cheek—the one with the dimple.

Hadley thought Roxie was going way overboard in the meet-nice department. It was Trey, after all, the dog, the dirty dog archetype they had long discussed. It was as if seeing him in the flesh had made her too flustered.

"I've heard so much about you." Trey was beaming. Hadley suspected it was because he knew Roxie was a necessary link in the chain and was appropriately oily. "Roxie. Is that your real name?"

She put her arm on her hip in mock indignation. "Of course it is! Named after my hometown."

"I thought you might have been named for that place on Sunset Strip."

"Wow. I shoulda been." She laughed and shifted her weight from one boot to the other. "I practically own it."

"She was born in Rosamond, California. It's short for that," Hadley said. She scanned the airport, as if Derek were about to appear any moment from a nearby gate. It was ridiculous to associate L.A. proper with Derek. People can easily hide in such a city, never to be seen again. She wasn't even sure she wanted to see him again. *Besides, he's in Branson!*

Trey was checking out Roxie. Hadley followed his gaze. Roxie was tall—and quite thin, no doubt helped along by the cigarettes. The thinness belied her age, though, which had to be around Hadley's, 35. She could have passed for someone in her late 20's in spite of her miles. Her endless legs, madly showcased in a short Burberry pleated skirt and black leather boots, complemented a red tank top and black leather jacket.

Her hair was appropriately "record company cool," a thick black shag standing up all over her head—like the coat of a black Labrador brushed backwards. She had beautiful brown eyes framed by dark lashes and dark eyebrows. She blended in perfectly in L.A., but she must have seemed an anomaly to Trey, accustomed as he was to the small-town outfitting of Anise and Sara and, if she were honest, Hadley herself, of late.

"I can't believe it. We're really here," he said. "Don't move. I'll be right back."

"Where are you going?" Hadley plucked at his jacket, as he hurried by. People were pouring out of planes. He could get lost, or he could be caught up in the crowd. She was too tired to sit in an airport and wait for an errant knight to return.

"I'll be right back."

He blended in with the crowd, his head turning upward for signs and sideways for arrows.

"Jesus, Joseph, and Mary, you didn't tell me he was so gorgeous!" Roxie said, breathlessly, which brought on a slight coughing fit. "It's gonna be tough to crush *him*."

"From your perspective—or his?"

"Oh, what are we doing? C'mere and give me another hug, you! I'm so glad you're here."

Hadley motioned Roxie to a line of seats. "It's great to see you, too. In spite of the fact you practically swooned in front of The Boy Wonder."

"Listen," Roxie said, simultaneously making a motion like she was lighting up a cigarette. "Anything that gets you here for a goddam visit can't be that evil. I promise to get meaner."

Roxie, like seemingly all those within an inch of Trey, had gone over to his side. And Hadley was tired and hungry. She was lagged out and yearned for the stillness of Tillsdale, a hot roast beef sandwich at The Cork and Kettle, a cup of Joe from Mickey D's. A medium, black.

"Now what? We wait here? We can't even go to baggage. Oh God, I knew this would happen."

"Relax, sweetie. You just got here. C'mon. Let me get a look at you…a bit peaked, but I'll make that better. Sit down. I'll get you some coffee—something to eat?"

"Coffee. Black."

"OK. Wait here."

Roxie's skirt flew up like a cheerleader's down the concourse toward the first concession stand. Hadley needed a moment. When she lived here, she had picked up Derek numerous times at this airport. Short visits to his family. She had remembered the time she had kissed him upon one such return and smeared lipstick on his shirt—how angry he'd been.

She leaned back and took in the people filing by. During the day, the airport here was unlike any other airport in America. It was as colorful and vibrant as a bazaar in Timbuktu—an emporium of the senses. Girls in short dresses and fishnet stockings hung around decked out like hookers; others walked primly past in tight pastel tank tops and cargo pants. Guys in gangsta garb with low-rider bloated jeans shuffled among the racks of magazines and concession stands. Well-heeled executives with expensive shoes and attaché cases hurried past, large cellphones to ears. An occasional celebrity or two ambled by. And always movement… always people in the process of becoming, never content to just *be*, as Aunt Winnie had once said.

"Here you go." Roxie was back, a cup in her hands. "Black, like your heart, you bitch you."

"God. You might be right," Hadley said, laughing in spite of herself. "Have I told you it's good to see you?"

"Yup. Hey, I saw him."

"Who?"

"Todd, Ted, whatever his name is."

"Trey? Where?"

"He's on his way. He was calling someone. I gestured for the son of a bitch to hurry it up."

Phone call. To whom? Anise? Sara? Sara would have supplied him with phone cards. "Call me as soon as you arrive—and every hour after," she would have said, pressing cards worth 1,000 minutes in his hands.

"Listen, I booked your return flight for Sunday. We don't have much time, do we?"

"No. I've got to get back to school Monday. I'm a

teacher, after all. This is a lark, remember? A lark that toppled from a tree and lies dead with its feet stuck up in the air."

Roxie flashed her brown eyes at her that seemed to say, "It's your doing." She straightened up, her leather jacket squeaking in the process. "So, later today we take him to Benny the bastard, play the demo, la-de-da. Then Benny gives him the hook, we all do a little hand-holding, then have fun tonight and Saturday. That's the plan, right?"

"Benny's doing the dirty work for sure?" Hadley asked.

"Yeah. Said he'd give him a fair listen and tell him the truth. He gives the boot to a million of these losers a day. I gave him the backstory about the small town and stuff like that, and he shrugged and said, 'You owe me.' " She cast a slit-eyed glance at her friend before guffawing.

"What if Benny likes Trey?" Hadley asked. She let the steam from the coffee clear her sinuses. A sudden scene whereby Benny thinks Trey has talent made her heart race. Trey could be disarming.

Roxie fluffed up her already fluffed-up hair. "Benny doesn't like anybody. Except the people he discovers himself."

Benny Miles was an A&R man fit for all the stereotypes. When Hadley worked there, he took her and Roxie to expensive restaurants along Melrose and in Beverly Hills—along with half a dozen other girls—and was famous for having the best parties in Hollywood. He'd tried to come on to Hadley at the beginning, as he did with all the new girls, but she let him know she wasn't interested in anyone or anything but Derek—

including the cocaine he offered her. He told her he liked her glasses, the one time she'd forgotten to put in her contact lenses. "I know how wild librarians are between the sheets," he said, no matter how many times she told him she was no librarian. "They've all read 'Lady Chatterley's Lover.'"

"I don't have to go with you guys, do I?" Hadley asked, feeling guilty about the whole setup finally coming to its fruition.

"Where?"

"To Benny's office? Can't you do all that?"

"What? Hell, yes, you're coming. Benny wants to see you. It was all your idea, anyway! Whaddya going to do otherwise? Sit in my apartment and watch Oprah? C'mon. It'll be fun. Heads up, here he comes."

Trey loped down the concourse, looking for all the world like a rock star already. Like a million other wannabees.

"Ready?" Hadley asked her friend and confidante.

"Absolutely." Roxie jumped up and slipped her arm through Trey's. "Are *you*?"

Hadley capped her cup of coffee, convinced her sojourn in Tillsdale had been a dream and, in fact, she'd never left L.A.

"Where we gonna eat?" Trey asked, once the trio were finally in Roxie's car. "I'm feeling peckish."

"I dunno. Where do you want to go, Had?"

Where, indeed? Did she feel like impressing Trey? Maybe a hip spot in Beverly Hills? Or Hollywood? Or go local. Canter's, maybe. She was in no mood for a trendy oasis with beautiful teenagers and their perfect bodies.

"How 'bout…"

"Someplace cool…to see and be seen." Trey's head was spinning, trying to peer into every car on the 405 Freeway.

It was late, close to 2 a.m. Their options were limited. She'd be in bed back home. She was on Tillsdale time, wishing she were under her covers, sound asleep. Maybe she was too old for L.A. Maybe she belonged back home.

"Whatsa matter? Too many friggin' choices?" Roxie asked. "You guys are used to one lousy diner back in the sticks, right?"

"God. Don't even bring it up," Trey said. "I'm never going back."

As they walked toward the parking garage, she glanced heavenward. The sky was different here. At night, it absorbed the lights from the city. But she remembered the sunsets were magnificent—all bright pink—magenta. Palm trees, not pine trees as in Tillsdale. Pine trees and oak, ash, maple, cherry trees. The trees back there had a vast tangled network of roots under the forest land. They belonged there, deep in the dirt, intertangled, root clasping root. On the other hand, the palm trees in L.A. were transplants—not even native to the area. Spaced far apart and showing up in spurts, they were decoration only.

"God, this is so amazing," Trey said. "So much traffic here. I can feel the city."

Roxie caught Hadley's eye in the rear-view mirror.

"Speaking of feeling, let's see if we can spot any hookers on Hollywood Boulevard," Roxie said, adding a laugh at the end.

Hadley slumped back in the back seat. Had she had the strength, she would have fastened her seat belt.

"Let's eat first."

"Old Had's tired, Trey. What did you do to the poor girl?"

"Nothing." He sounded defensive.

"I'll tell you what, let's drop Had off at my place. You and I will go out after that. Sound like a plan?" Roxie nodded to Hadley in the rear-view mirror.

Should she? Roxie was a tried and true friend, but Trey was young and terribly gullible as far as L.A. was concerned. But, on the other hand, Hadley was beat—and beaten down. The last thing she wanted to do was go sight-seeing. L.A. was different from New York in that way. New York energized her, but L.A. enervated her. Besides, she'd need all her strength for her appointment with Benny in a few hours. Two more days and nights of this before she could relinquish her controls behind the curtain and return to Kansas.

"You guys go. Just drop me off."

"Fine with me," Trey said a little too quickly for Hadley's taste.

"You sure?" Roxie braked for an exit. "Let's take a short cut through Brentwood. I'll show you where O.J. and Nicole lived."

Hadley closed her eyes and groaned.

****

After Roxie and Trey left to explore the city and Hadley found herself alone in her friend's spacious Santa Monica apartment, she did something she told herself she would not do. She called Derek's best friend, Dave. She had introduced the two of them, in fact. He worked at the record company in the production department. She had lined him up to record Derek's demo. Sheesh—a yenta even back then, making the arrangements, taking care of all the things Derek should have done himself.

Her hands trembled as she pushed the numbers on the phone. It was, after all, a link to the past, to Derek.

"Hi…is this Dave? Hi. It's Hadley. Remember me?"

"Ah, no, not really. Can you give me a clue?" he asked.

She identified herself through Derek, finding it difficult to mention his name. Why did it still hurt? Why was she still searching for a link?

"I'm in L.A. for a few days and happen to be free tomorrow. Would you like to meet me for coffee or a drink? We could catch up, you know, with things."

It sounded like a come-on, exactly the opposite of what she intended.

"It's the wee hours of the morning…did you know?"

Why hadn't you planned for that?

"Gosh, I'm so sorry. I'm all mixed up on time, having just flown in. Please forgive me."

"Don't worry. I'm an insomniac, but as for tomorrow, I've got plans with my girlfriend."

"No problem," she said, slowly, to sound casual. Hooked-up people have an automatic excuse. "I was taking a chance you'd be free."

He asked her how she was doing.

"I'm fine. Great, actually," she said. She hoped he'd convey it to Derek. "I love teaching. And I must say I'm happy to be back East. It's good to be out of the madness that is L.A."

"To each his own, I guess. I love it here," he said, justifying his existence. "By the way, have you heard from Derek?"

The vasovagal nerve twitched again. "No, no, I haven't. Have you?"

Another chuckle. "Yes, he's in Branson."

"Wow, who knew?" she asked rhetorically.

"C'mon. Isn't that why you called?"

She was silent. She hated being so transparent. "Yeah, sure. I guess so."

"He and Rachel, you remember Rachel, don't you? Anyway, he and Rachel went together there. She's pregnant with triplets or something. I guess they'll get married after the kids are born."

She cleared her throat. She hadn't known about the pregnancy. "Amazing. Hard to believe Derek would be a father. I guess we can hope one of them is a boy, the way he wanted a boy."

"Do you want me to tell him you called?"

Her face flushed. They hadn't parted as friends. "No, please don't mention my name at all. It was a long time ago…things change, you know how that goes." She was babbling.

"You got it."

"Listen, it's been great talking to you. I'll let you go."

He seemed more animated now that the call was finished. "Yeah. Definitely. Next time call with a warning, so we can meet for a drink. You take care."

"Absolutely. Same to you. Good night."

She shouldn't have called. Guys tell guys things. He would tell Derek, and Derek would make some comment about Hadley finding it impossible to give up on him. Now with triplets coming, there was never any hope.

"There never was any hope," she told herself. "Never."

She didn't remember unpacking, taking a shower, and falling into the guest bed. The pillows and blankets stacked on the sofa were for Trey, whether he liked it or not. You reach a certain age and sleepovers aren't fun.

Chapter 25

A mother of a cramp in her leg woke her up. It wasn't just any cramp. It was as if her muscles had created a cloverleaf in her leg. She tried flexing her calf, but to no avail. She would have to get up and hop around like a human pogo stick. Yes, that would help. Or maybe drink some milk. She had read somewhere that was good for leg cramps. She hoped it wasn't a blood clot...all those hours on the plane. She'd seen the profiles on the Discovery Channel—woman takes trip she'd planned all her life, gets home, and boom! A blood clot in her leg does her in. She needed to get her karma in order before that happened.

The hall lights were still blazing, made evident by the light coming through the opening under the door. No clock visible. Just like Roxie. She kept her own time. She finally found a watch on the bed stand—6:42 a.m. She slipped her feet into flip-flops and grabbed a robe and ran into the hall.

Roxie's door was open, so she went in.

"Rox?"

No answer. Hadley turned on the light. The bed still had several different changes of clothes strewn across it. She then went back into the living room. The corner light was on, exactly as Hadley had left it. She shivered. The bedding and pillows were still stacked on the couch, awaiting Trey's beautiful form.

"Where could they be?" she said in a whisper. The cramp in her legs continued. She opened the door to Roxie's refrigerator and was greeted by a six-pack of lime-flavored mineral water, some hot sauce, some eggs, a few bottles of imported beer, but no milk.

She started walking across Roxie's front room, a rather spacious affair. The dining room morphed into the living room at one point. There was a large bay window, which, if one craned one's neck, provided a glimpse of the main drag where the Santa Monica hotels were located, close to the beach. There were no books, no shelves. A "W" magazine lay on the mid-century coffee table shaped like an amoeba. This was not the condo of a nester. Roxie came here only to sleep, shower, change clothes, and leave again.

Just as Hadley was about to pore through the pages of "W," someone began fumbling at the lock. A former wary L.A. resident herself, Hadley's nerve endings starting in her heart and going outward to her fingers and toes were on the "qui vive." Hers was the reflex system of someone who'd been mugged twice.

A few giggles ensued, then a "Shh-h," then a low chuckle before the duo made their entrance.

"Girl, what are you doing up? I was shushing this boy here so he wouldn't wake you."

Roxie was visibly pickled. For a neatnik, her black hair was uncharacteristically disheveled, the button on the back of her skirt now positioned right beneath her belly button. Her jacket was halfway off her shoulder. Trey helped her extricate herself from the other sleeve.

Hadley feared the worst. "I woke up and when I saw how late, or early, it was, I got worried."

Roxie stepped behind Trey and winked in an

exaggerated manner. She mouthed something, but Hadley couldn't make it out. Trey must have seen Hadley's expression since he turned quickly to see what Roxie was doing. Having been busted, she let loose with an explosion of bawdy laughter. Soon, the two of them, laughed uncontrollably before falling on top of each other in the nearest chair. Hadley noticed the sweat stains on Trey's shirt.

"I'm going back to bed." Hadley hoped they sensed her disgust.

Roxie crawled from beneath Trey and staggered over to her friend, who remained seated. "Wait—hey, now wait a minute there. Don't you get any ideas." She put her hand on top of Hadley's. "I was only showing the boy the sights. Remember, you said you didn't want to."

She was right. Hadley had seen the sights of L.A. over and over, had even worked at a few of the landmarks, and had felt no compunction leaving them. Roxie had done her a favor, toting a wide-eyed tourist around the town, getting drunk with him, doing all the things Hadley no longer wished to do. Her youth seemed as if it had been lived by someone else.

"C'mere." Roxie dragged her friend to the closet and shut the door behind both of them. "This is all a part of the plan, can't you see?" She hiccupped. Her breath smelled of alcohol.

Hadley only shook her head. "You're popping your p's."

"Of course, I've got to pee. But listen—this is more important. That boy out there is gonna look like shit when we drag him into see Benny tomorrow."

"Today, you mean. Tomorrow is today, remember?"

"Oh shit." Roxie held onto the bar holding many of

her coats to steady herself, all the while peering intently into her friend's eyes with the singular intensity only drunken people possess. "He'll be hung over and have big, black circles under his baby blues."

"Green. His eyes are green. Or green-ish. They change."

"Whatever. They're beautiful." She turned to open the door. "And he may even smell like a liquor cabinet, if we're lucky, making it easier for Benny." She swung the door with too much intensity, causing it to slam against the outside wall. "It's over for that one."

As if smelling like a liquor cabinet was ever a bad thing in a record company. Hadley caught a glimpse of herself in the mirror on the wall where somebody's mother stared back at her. She feared that ineffable youth was slowing fading.

Upon emerging, Roxie had beelined for Trey. "How 'bout a bottle of the hair of the dog that bit you?"

Trey never answered. He was already lying on the sofa, clutching a still-folded blanket on top of him. Hadley walked over to the door, bolted it like any conscientious L.A. woman, then helped Roxie down the hall to her bed.

****

It was a beautiful morning in Los Angeles, unlike the cold, scary mornings back East. How would Roxie feel after a few hours' sleep? Hadley had known Roxie for eight of the ten years she'd spent in Los Angeles, and believed they were as close as two friends—as different as they were—could be. So, she left her a note saying she'd fished out her car keys from her bag and was going in search of bagels and coffee and would be back. "Probably before they even get up," she muttered.

Anywhere people have lived and then left, they always leave an imprint or else residual hauntings that keep looping over and over. Once behind the wheel, Hadley remembered the different routes. The surface streets to get to the "10" freeway, the side streets through to Venice Boulevard, a few quick cuts to La Cienega. She drove through West Hollywood, then on to Hollywood, then onto the 101 Hollywood Freeway to the Valley. She wanted to drive past a few landmarks of her own.

The old apartment Derck had lived in was still there, but with different curtains in the windows and different cars in the driveway. She drove by the restaurants they had frequented together, and had fought in together. There was much more here now, but the lay of the land was still familiar. It was an uncomfortable feeling, like discovering a yellowed wedding dress packed away from a failed marriage.

She traversed the side streets of Encino and Studio City, eventually pulling back onto Ventura Highway then over Coldwater Canyon to avoid the 405 traffic in getting back to Santa Monica. She remembered how foreign L.A. had seemed to her when she first moved out here. She frequented places she had discovered: the same pastry shop to get a daily donut and coffee. On one such trip, she had seen a man lying on a sidewalk, a human being who could have been dead or alive.

All of a sudden, she no longer wished to go back to Roxie's right away, but she must. She could go back by way of Silver Lake to see Bryce, but she remembered he wouldn't be up this early. Besides, she didn't want to see him without crafting an explanation for having no play. Had she ever been serious about writing it? Or was she falling into the unwanted role of a woman seeking the love of an unavailable man, explanations be damned?

Much to Hadley's surprise, Roxie was up and making coffee when she returned home. She was dressed in a short white waffle kimono robe, with nothing but a sash keeping her from being charged with indecent exposure.

"God, you brought coffee? How sweet! And bagels. Yummy, yummy."

"So, what damage did you two do last night?"

Roxie narrowed her eyes. "Do you think I wanted to go out all night and entertain Luke Duke?" She shrugged. "Cute yokel, but yokel, regardless." She turned her back, scouting in the refrigerator for something. "Shit, man. I did it for you, so don't get all pissed. You have a real knack for blaming others for shit you started."

Hadley waved her off. "Don't screw with me. You'd have been out anyway."

"Yeah, but not with him. Not that he's not easy on the eyes." She yawned loudly. "And entertaining. And sweet. Not like the other one, Derek. Wasn't that his name?"

Hadley sat down on one of the stools facing the kitchen bar. "What's that supposed to mean?"

Instead of waiting for the coffee she made to stop brewing, Roxie opened one of the coffee cups Hadley had brought and poured in three containers of cream she discovered in the tray the coffee came in. "It means he's just a wide-eyed kid with big ideas. Derek was, I don't know, motivated maybe."

"And you don't think the fact this kid is using me isn't mean?"

Roxie curled two shapely legs around another of the

kitchen stools and took a big bite out of one of the still-warm bagels. "Mmn. Needs some cream cheese and lox. Did you bring any?"

Hadley nodded. "Cream cheese. In the bag. With plastic knives."

"Mmn. Found 'em." She grabbed a sharp knife from a drawer instead and expertly sliced the bagel in two, offering her friend one half. Hadley shook her head.

"You're the one who offered to help this kid. Why? I dunno. But I'm glad to play along because I miss you and wanted you to come out, and I know how you are. Without some screwy reason like needing to break this kid's spirit, you'd never leave the backwoods and come see me." She licked the tips of her fingers. "I'm not worthy of your efforts by myself. Am I right?"

Hadley shook her head and took a drink of coffee. "I hope that's not true."

"I only wish we could ditch the kid and go shopping or see some friends."

"I don't see how. The last thing we need is to have him go out on his own and have something happen."

Roxie laughed. A low, guttural dirty laugh.

"What's so funny?"

She shrugged. "You sell him short. He's really quite smart. And funny. We actually had a pretty good time last night."

Hadley cocked an eyebrow. Maybe she didn't know her friend after all.

"Oh for God's sake, not like that," Roxie said, while not meeting her eyes.

"Your skirt, though. It was completely turned around."

Roxie wagged a finger, but Trey began to stir. He

219

shifted his position so he now faced the girls, his eyes still closed. Neither Roxie nor Hadley said anything for what seemed the longest time. Hadley noticed that instead of the black circles, his skin was flawless, tinged pink with the remains of the booze from earlier that morning. His long lashes fringed his cheeks, his bow-like lips pale and pursed in sleep, as if he were kissing someone. His long, thick hair cascaded over his eyes. He still wore his watch, on the right-hand wrist, the hand of which was clutching a blanket, with Roxie's jacket on top. One foot was on the floor. Visible were the blue stripes of his boxers. Derek used to say that men only wore tighty-whiteys when they wanted to get things done. "It pushes up all the equipment, making it uncomfortable. You have no choice but to get busy." Obviously, Trey wasn't too worried about his upcoming audition.

"I wish you could see yourself," Roxie said after at least five minutes of silence.

"Whaddaya mean?"

"You're staring at him like he was the Mona Lisa or something." She put her finger under Hadley's chin, turning her to face her. "You've got to get over Derek, sweetie. You've got to let it go."

What Roxie said made Hadley think of something Derek had once told her, that life meted out only a limited number of purely happy moments. He said he was glad he got to spend some of them with her. Were happy moments really like coins in one's pocket to spend? Had he simply gone through all the happiness coins he could with her and was now spending the rest of them with someone else? It didn't matter. She had her own pocket change to spend.

Hadley slammed the lid on the coffee cup with more force than necessary. "Why are you saying that? He's over."

"Listen, if I can get you into my shrink today, will you go? He's so amazing."

A shrink? Some nerve! "No. Of course not. I'm fine."

"You're not fine. You keep repeating the same behavior over and over. There are guys out there who like you, who would love you, if you'd only give them a chance."

"You're a great one to talk. You've been screwing a married man for how long?"

"Yeah, but I'm seeing a shrink. I'm trying to figure it out. It's just, what you're doing here, for this guy…do you know he thinks you're doing it because you're a good person? Did you know that?"

Hadley voluntarily turned to face her friend this time. "What?"

"Just what I said. He thinks you think he has talent, well, some talent, and want to see him succeed." She licked her fingers again and dotted the tissue paper to pick up any crumbs. "He thinks he blew it by kissing you 'cause most of the older women, so he says, do things for the attention, whatever form that may take. Not you, though. You're different."

"He told you that?"

"Yeah. And you never did tell me. What happened to no secrets?" She pointed two fingers at Hadley, then herself.

"It wasn't like that. He was excited about my offer to help."

Roxie jumped off the stool and stood close to her

friend's face. "That's what I mean! Nobody does that! It's weird. And the kid here thinks you, this Hollywood person with connections, really believe he's the next big thing in spite of some constructive criticism."

Hadley groaned, putting her head in her hands.

"And you know what else?" Roxie leaned down on the counter so she could see Hadley. "You're all caught up in him. A guy with so-so talent, who's sizzling hot, yes, but no next big thing. Yeah, he's smart and gorgeous, but he's a little young, don't you think? I mean, why don't you pick on someone more like yourself?"

"You're not the first person who's said that lately. And I'm not so sure he doesn't have talent."

"Whaddaya mean?" She buried her face in her coffee cup.

"He can work a room. He had the whole plane singing."

Roxie nodded. "What about you, though? What's in it for you?"

"See, what nobody seems to understand is…I like men who are young and beautiful and somehow unapproachable." The words came automatically. She tried to remember where she had heard them.

"Because? Lemme guess." She wiped her hands on a dish towel. "If you get a young guy to approach you, that makes you feel so damn special, right?"

With her index finger, Hadley followed the outlines of the boomerangs in the Formica pattern. "I don't know why I need to see a shrink if I'm attracted to someone who's young and gorgeous and virile. And he's my inspiration. I told you as much. Why is that so pathological? I'm not the only one who likes beauty and charm and…and everyone knows all men are dogs."

Roxie shook her head.

"Hey, what's going on over there? Can you keep it down?" Trey opened one eye, exposing a glint of emerald.

In a barely audible whisper, Hadley asked her friend, "Would you rather wake up to that or Benny?"

Roxie stared into Hadley's eyes without blinking.

****

At 2 p.m., Roxie had pulled herself together remarkably well for someone who had only had an hour or two of sleep. Hadley, in tight black slacks and a boat-neck black sweater, sat on the couch. Both were waiting for Trey, who was still in the bathroom getting ready for the grand denouement at the record company.

"What time did Benny say?"

"2:30, 3:00. Said he wanted to make sure he was well-tanked from lunch before he took this on." She stood, her leather hobo bag slung over her shoulder, her car keys in hand.

"You might as well sit down."

"Sit down? Sleeping Beauty here is on West Virginia time. I'm getting sick of this boy. Who the hell does he think he is? What if we miss Benny?"

Hadley scowled. "Oh, so that's the real problem, isn't it? You got plans with Benny tonight?"

"No, no. I'm with you guys, remember?" She crinkled her mouth, making her lower jaw seem more sunken in than usual.

Hadley opened her eyes wider. "Listen, you've been so amazing putting us up and all. You go out with Benny after the big blow-off with Trey, then if I can borrow your car, I'll do the honors of wiping away his tears and hand-holding and all the rest."

"I told you. He's not right for you. I need to chaperone you two."

Hadley could tell by the sound of her voice that she could easily be talked into such an arrangement. "You know what? It's not what you're thinking. I'm writing a play, you see, and…"

She couldn't forget what Trey had told Roxie: That she, Hadley, was doing this out of the goodness of her heart.

"So you said. When do I get to see it?"

"No, I mean, yes, someday, when I write it, but it's not… I'm using Trey as a specimen for the protagonist. I thought I told you all this…"

Roxie scowled. "I remember. Sounded sinister then. Still does. Especially since he thinks you're his fairy godmother."

A few minutes later, Trey walked into the room. He was dressed inappropriately, more for the late 1980s than a decade hence, but it was his vision of a rock star: tight leather pants, a black AC/DC T-shirt, a black leather jacket, black cowboy boots.

Hadley sat at the edge of the couch, poised to make a comment, but Roxie put her hand, her delicate hand that she usually protected from any untoward movement, firmly on Hadley's forearm.

"Nice boots," Roxie said. "Everybody ready?"

Chapter 26

Record companies make a person remember all the good things that ever happened to them.

Maybe it's the power that lies within their walls: the power to make or break an artist's career.

The power that resonates from the stars who once walked these halls, some of the greatest entertainers ever.

The power that music has over people.

Or maybe it's the inexpressible wonder of it all.

Photos of the great artists who had been associated with the company plastered the walls. Gone were the shots of groups or individuals who were signed and then flopped. A record company's interior was all about success.

And the A&R guy at such a big label had an office that reflected his power. Lots of windows, lots of photographs and gold records on the wall, furniture that invited stars to sit down and linger. A liquor cabinet. Recessed lighting. Stereo equipment to make any geek pass out.

Benny, A&R guru, was the same as the last time Hadley had seen him. Long hair, wire glasses, porcelain veneers on his teeth, and a slight paunch presaging a dad belly in years to come. His voice, a booming FM radio voice, had not yet been ravaged by cigarettes, cocaine, and screaming over noise in bars.

A&R guys, however, don't have to be handsome

and charming. They are flush with power and cool and money.

"Sweet God, look who's here? It's the librarian!"

He emerged from his tall leather chair and took long strides over to Hadley, engulfing her in a bear hug that always included a quick feel to the ass. He kissed her on the mouth, as she remembered too many record people had done in the past. The lips—or often the mouth and throat—were the cheeks to record company executives.

"How are you, baby? Have you saved yourself for me?" He was so close, she could see the spittle on his veneers. "How do you like being back in the woods? Didn't they make a movie about your hometown called *Deliverance* or something?"

Hadley was at a loss for words. She had regressed, coming back to such talk, such superficiality.

"Hey," he said, at last acknowledging Trey and extending his hand. "Bon Jovi, right? Have a seat, buddy."

Trey was visibly uncomfortable. Perhaps it was the get-up, more likely the combination of Benny and the idea of at last being in a record executive's office. This was not Anise's bedroom or The Cork and Kettle. This was the big time.

"His name is Trey. Trey—what's your last name?" Roxie appeared jumpier than usual.

"Harding." His voice cracked, even after he cleared it. She noticed he had spoken in a lower voice than usual.

"Trey. That's a good name for a rock star. Well, I can see you've brought your harem."

Roxie, with a bit too much familiarity, grabbed Benny's flaccid bicep and said, "Be nice."

"Whatcha got for me, besides these two red-hot

pussies?" he asked Trey as matter-of-factly as if he were commenting on the weather.

"I brought my CD," Trey said. He fetched it from the pocket of his leather jacket.

Benny turned it over once or twice. "OK, good. I mean you, not the packaging. Where'd you have this done?"

Trey cast a furtive glance toward Hadley before saying, "New York."

"City or state?"

"City."

Roxie shot Hadley a glance, which was greeted by what could only be compared to an upside-down happy face.

Benny took the CD out of its jewel case and flipped it onto a player behind his desk. "Sweetheart," he said to Hadley. "Can you close the door?"

She knew the drill. Trey's song would be blasted all over the floor of the record company, regardless of who else was listening to what. This was the music business and that meant music was business.

Roxie exchanged a look with Hadley, as if to say, "Maybe we should have listened to this alone together first? Maybe it'll be good."

Trey's guitar work, sweetened though it had been with the help of the engineer in New York, was mixed low, even Hadley could tell that. The introduction sounded ever so unsteady. Within minutes, Trey's voice came through the speakers. It might hold up well in her boombox back home, but its weaknesses, especially pitch, were evident here. Benny wouldn't have to lie in order to dismiss him. Hadley realized she had been holding her breath, so she released it, inaudible over the speakers. The whole thing would soon be over. Hadley sighed with relief.

Benny listened to it through the middle eight before taking it out and returning it to its case. "You got anything else?"

Roxie's eyes darted from Hadley to Trey.

"That was the hit," Hadley said.

Benny never took his eyes off Trey. "Whatsa matter, son, you letting these girls do your talking?" He rapped his knuckles—his fingers adorned with ostentatious rings like Ringo—on his desk. "Well?"

"No," Trey said. He shifted in the large comfy chair. He seemed ridiculous in his outfit, like a bride who wears her wedding gown to a diner. Timing was everything. "No, but what did you think?"

Benny, his gaze still intent, continued to drum his fingers on the desk. "You sleeping with both these girls or just one?"

Roxie jumped up. "C'mon, Benny. Enough, already."

"You sleeping with the librarian? She find you in the woods back in West Virginny? Call in her connections, did she, so you'd keep fucking her?"

Hadley was going to respond in kind, but pinched her lips instead. She was used to record company executives talking entirely non-PC lingo, but the fact she hadn't slept with Trey seemed to make the situation more unnerving, not to mention desperate. "We're from New York state. Hardly the backwoods."

Benny stopped his tapping and sat up straight in his chair. "OK. Here's what I think. You work at a regular job, kid?"

Trey nodded. "I'm a sports broadcaster."

"Oh, a sports broadcaster," Benny said, in a patronizing tone. "Lots of high school football back there?"

"Oh for God's sake, Benny, cut it out," Roxie said. "He's probably drunk," she said to Trey. "Or feeling good."

"I hope I'm drunk," Benny said, "because what I'm about to tell you isn't good. Son, keep your day job."

Silence ensued. *Anyone who wasn't from New York or Chicago or L.A. was a hick.* She had felt it when she had lived and worked out here. But these guys had to come from somewhere, too! A lot of them hailed from the Midwest, hardly a cosmopolite's haven.

Knowing the record business, neither Roxie nor Hadley had felt the need to tell Benny to reject Trey. They both knew he would. But the jousting about where they were from felt gratuitous. Why did Benny always have to be such a sneering bastard? What did Roxie see in such a jerk besides the money and status?

"Hey, that's OK," Trey mumbled. "Thanks for giving it a listen." He rose from his chair, reaching out for Benny's hand.

Hadley examined his face. He seemed to be fighting back emotion, his mouth turned down, his eyes half shut. *Remember this reaction.* That's what girls did when guys dump them. The exterior only half indicates what's churning inside. Sometimes the delicate slips through unexpectedly. Was this *his* moment of losing the innocence? Would he ever be the same again, having been rejected by a major record company? How would he proceed? *He tried too hard.* His photo, had it been taken, would have been shelved with the others who had failed to make the grade. Nothing like a Poison knock-off to incite pity.

"Sit down," Benny told him. "I didn't say all was lost, did I?"

Roxie and Hadley exchanged glances again. Roxie shrugged.

"You can't sing and you can't play real well," he said. "But I like that song, although the lyrics need work. Did you write it?"

Trey nodded.

"Got anymore?"

"Yeah, sure. I don't have them produced, but sure, I've got 'em."

Benny swiveled in his chair and put his feet up on a shelf filled with CDs. "I like your look." He faced him. "If you get rid of the '80s metal get-up and join the rest of us in the '90s…"

Roxie groaned.

"…yeah, I'm thinking." He rifled through a calendar on his desk. "You staying in L.A. for a while?"

Trey's eyes darted first to Hadley, then Roxie. "Yeah, sure, I can stay as long as I like, I mean, as you need me."

"I don't need you, kid. You need me. Let's see," he tapped his calendar with his index finger.

Hadley nudged Roxie and shook her head. "Hey, Benny, they gotta be going back Sunday. They're staying with me, and, uh, they gotta be out of my place 'cause my mom and sister are coming down from Rosamond, so he can't stay, and Hadley here has to teach Monday."

"You're a teacher? Not a librarian?"

"Yeah. While I'm doing other things."

He wagged a finger at Trey. "Yeah, I'll bet I know what you're doing. So, go back and teach, and Trey here can stay in my guest house for a few days." He turned in his seat and spoke directly to Roxie. "I need some seat fillers for a music awards show that's coming up next week, and this kid's got the physical goods."

Trey grinned broadly, showcasing his heart-breaking dimple.

Hadley sat stone-faced and immovable. Not only would she be returning to Tillsdale alone, but she had indeed come through, her plan notwithstanding, as Trey's stepping stone to success—even as a seat filler. The actual reverse of her plan. But certainly indicative of the "good soul" she appeared to be to Trey.

"When can you bring your stuff by?"

Roxie was ashen-faced. "You sure about all this? I mean, your wife and all?"

Benny laughed. "It's for a few days. Besides, my wife's out of town. You of all people know that. Anyway," he said, smiling widely to showcase his sparkling veneers, "you've got your mother and sister to entertain."

"Wow," Trey said. He slapped his knee. "This is fantastic. Thank you, Benny. Can I call you Benny? Thank you so much."

"Bring your stuff by tomorrow morning around noon. Roxie knows where I live," he said, winking.

"Man," Trey said. "This is the best day of my life."

"Hey, I didn't say I was giving you a contract. I need some hot young people to fill my row at this show, that's all. Maybe I'll listen to your other songs. Now, get out of here, all of you."

Hadley expected Roxie to protest, but she was the first to the door. "C'mon, let's blow," she said to Trey and Hadley. "Drop me off at home. I need to sleep for twelve hours."

Outside the door, Trey hugged Hadley. "Damn!" He raised his hand, searching for another palm to slap. "It's all because of you. And, you!" He whirled around to Roxie and lifted her off her feet before kissing her. Apparently it was OK to kiss Roxie. This set about as well with Hadley as had that morning's coffee.

"Listen," Roxie said to her friend, once grounded, "run to the restroom with me?"

"Sure. Where'll we meet you?" She asked the question of Trey.

"I'll be in the lobby…finding a space for my gold record." He grinned.

Once in the restroom, Roxie leaned against the sink, arms akimbo. "Now what the hell are we going to do? Any ideas?" Her tone was unmistakably cool.

"I'm sorry. It's all my fault."

"Right. You know my family isn't coming down, don't you?"

Hadley nodded, a penitent child.

"And you know Benny's wife's gone, right?"

She nodded again, obedient.

"However, now that Benny's got himself a new roommate…not to mention spy. Who's to say this naïve kid won't spill to wifey when she comes home if I were to go over there and stay with Benny like I planned?" Roxie buried her head in her hands and sobbed. "This is a perfect time for Benny to dump me. He's tired of me anyway."

"Why, is he acting that way?" Hadley asked. She knew full well the answer. She wanted to say something about knowing better to get involved with guys like Benny, but she didn't. After all, she had a few moral incongruities herself lately.

Roxie nodded before fishing in her bag for a tissue. "You know, I had my doubts about this whole thing from the beginning. It's bad karma messin' with people. That's a lesson for you, too." She blew her nose, making a honking sound. "And now all the bad karma is coming back on us—or at least me."

Hadley wanted to say that sleeping with a married man was hardly good for karma, but instead gave her friend a shoulder to cry on. In doing so, she caught a glimpse of her reflection in the mirror over the sink. She didn't recognize the person reflected back at her. How could she have involved her friend in such an imbroglio when she had her own messes to deal with? Trey was too young and faithless. He was a kid who truthfully didn't know what he wanted. And she did. And it wasn't a younger guy who didn't love her. She was ashamed to think he'd be the answer to her problems—or even a gateway. She whispered "I'm so sorry" into her friend's ear and hugged her tightly.

Roxie pulled herself together, then asked to be dropped off at her apartment, so Hadley and Trey could spend the rest of the day sightseeing. The sky was filled with smog. She longed for the clear, sweet air of the woods back home but would have to settle for a long drive on Pacific Coast Highway where the ocean kept the filth at arm's length.

Chapter 27

"Where you taking me?" Trey asked, as Hadley pointed the car west on Sunset.

The afternoon sun cast a daguerreotype hue over the scenery. She glanced at Trey who, with somewhat of a victory under his belt, now truly seemed like he belonged here. He had flattened down his spiked hair and peeled off the leather jacket. He could now pass for a beautiful Hollywood specimen in a land lousy with them.

Hadley gripped the leather-skinned steering wheel of Roxie's Cabriolet convertible.

"Deadman's Curve."

"What?"

"Deadman's Curve, Mr. Trivia. Don't you know that?"

Trey preened in the side-view mirror. "Of course I know it. It's an old Jan and Dean song."

"Did you know that's where Jan had his accident?

"Are you talking about the fictional Deadman's Curve or the one where he had the real accident?"

Hadley smiled. "Same thing."

"You're wrong." Trey was halfway out his window. "Cast your eyes on these shacks. The Beverly Hills Hotel. Hey, do you mind slowing down...maybe just for the landmarks?" He sounded churlish.

Only to a tourist would the Beverly Hills Hotel be slow-down-worthy. Its freshness gone for her, it was more like an upscale insane asylum from street level.

Hadley sniffed. "People don't slow down on Sunset. This isn't Elm Street." Why had she said Elm Street? That was the name of the street Neil lived on. "Besides, we're past Dead Man's Curve. And if you take a gander over there, you'll see the park where another celebrity got into trouble."

Trey turned to her. "Did you hear me before when I said you were wrong?"

"I'm not wrong. I remember reading about it."

"About Jan's crash? The day it happened? Damn, you are old!" He laughed and tickled her ribs before drawing back his hand.

Don't tickle me! I'm not to be patronized!

"No, I didn't read it on the day it happened."

"And I was talking about the real versus fictional Deadman's Curve being one and the same. They're not, you know."

"They're the same."

"You're wrong. What streets did we pass that made you say we're at Deadman's Curve?"

"Doheny." She recited the lyrics of the old 1965 hit.

"Right. But that's not where Jan crashed."

This was her adopted town, not his. "Who said?"

"Research it." He stared straight ahead. "I told you not to mess with me. I know my trivia."

Hadley drove on in silence. In a few minutes, Trey asked her where Benny lived. "In the hills. Back there." She pointed behind her. "Unless you know more about that than I do."

"Close to the clubs?"

Hadley nodded.

"Can you believe all this? I mean, I'll be staying

with a record executive!" He turned to face her, his elbow positioned perfectly on the car door. "I told you I'd make it out here. Or at least get my heels dug in."

She kept her eyes focused on the road. She tried to think of something else. It had worked out better than both of them expected, so she needn't feel guilty any more. She reflected on how this whole thing had made Roxie cry; that troubled her. It was a beautiful fall day, after all, although still high summer in Tillsdale terms. "How are you getting home? We leave day after tomorrow. The tickets are non-refundable, you know. And we owe Roxie."

He turned to face her, his eyes hidden by his wraparound sunglasses. He could have been Robert Wagner in *It Takes a Thief*. What was the character? Alexander Mundy. Wonder if Mr. Trivia would know that nugget.

"If you think I'm going home tomorrow, you're dead wrong. Why would I blow my chance to make it in Hollywood? That's my entire life's dream. You go ahead and go, but I'm staying."

Hadley's knuckles were white against the black leather steering wheel cover. "Benny's using you. He needs you to fill a seat at an awards show. Once you've done that, you're gone. That's how it usually works out here." Once again, she kept quiet about the obvious fact that Benny used people whenever he felt the need. And maybe she was as bad as Benny. But that would all stop now, with this trip.

"That's how it works wherever you go. You scratch my back, I'll scratch yours." Trey waved to a beautiful girl in a BMW convertible.

Hadley noticed the beautiful young thing waved

back.

"There is no way I'm leaving this place. After all it's taken me to get here."

You? She raised her left eyebrow, the more flexible of the two. "Then you're on your own. Roxie can't pay for two tickets back home for you."

She was tired of his not paying for his good luck. Did all beautiful people get comped?

"She didn't pay for this one."

Hadley's heart was racing, a metronome to her thoughts. "Where'd you get that idea?"

"She told me. Last night. It was expensed to the record company or something. Benny told her to do it. Hey, slow down, will ya?" He squeezed her arm too tightly.

How had she finagled that? Was it ever doable? Or had she expensed Trey's ticket? It was true Roxie hadn't asked her to pay her back, and Hadley had forgotten in all the chaos.

"I assumed you'd want to experience Dead Man's Curve," she said. The blood thundered in her head. *Why was she mad at him?*

"What are you trying to do? Kill me before I even get started? I didn't sign up for the Jan Berry tour, thank you very much."

She opened her mouth, but bit her lip instead. "Are you really and truly happy?"

"I can honestly say, before you tried to kill me back there, this is the happiest I've been in my life. Thanks to you and Roxie." He turned back to take in the scenery. "God, I'm happy."

She made a mental note: Few get a cushion after having lost their innocence.

****

By the time they got to Malibu, Trey was fidgeting in his seat. Even the sight of the magnificent Pacific Ocean wasn't enough to change his mood.

"Let's go there." He pointed to a famous fish joint. "I could eat a whale."

"Tourist trap. We're going someplace else." She was thinking of a more romantic place next to the ocean, with better lighting and atmosphere.

"But I'm a tourist, and I'm trapped. I feel like I've been in this car all day."

That was cold. She made a turn, heading up the Pacific Coast Highway. "What'sa matter? You anxious to make a call or something?"

Trey said nothing for several minutes. When she turned on her signal to turn into the lot next to a nondescript building, he sat up straight. "What's the name of this place?"

"Does it matter?"

He grabbed her arm. "Listen, don't turn. Keep going."

"Do you know how hard it is to get across this highway? Now we missed our turn."

"Let's stop at a place, pick up some burgers and Cokes, and eat on a stretch of beach."

It was still afternoon, so the ocean glittered with a thousand rhinestones. Back in Tillsdale, the rhinestones were in the sky, but in L.A., the reverse was true—you could only find them on the ocean. The only time Hadley had ever seen the stars in the L.A. sky was in Griffith Park Observatory. And one other time, during an earthquake when the city lights defaulted to Mother Nature.

A picnic on the beach? Not a nice, early dinner where she could try to salvage what was left of the trip by positioning the candle on the table and controlling the conversation without competing with the crashing of waves and breeze blowing her already unmanageable hair to Medusa levels? A quiet place to talk to Trey, to really get to know him. Pick his brain for her own creative purposes before he slipped away. But he was insistent.

"Here. Pull in."

"It's a gas station."

"I gotta hit the head. Besides, they have food, don't they?"

With the car still rolling, Trey sprung out. "Listen, pick up some hot dogs and some sodas, and I'll be right out. Thanks, hon."

Reluctantly, she got out of the car, her purse slung tightly over her shoulder and held in the front—in New York City mode. Naturally, he assumed she would pay. Didn't Sara give him any mad money for the trip?

Once inside, she wandered to the food section. None of it appeared fresh, especially the thick-skinned glistening dogs that must have been spinning on the metal rotors for a week or so. She picked up some wrapped sandwiches, some water and soda, some chips, a pack of gum, and headed toward the cash register.

Trey still hadn't returned. How long did it take to admire himself in the mirror? She turned her face upwards to the warm sunshine. Already late afternoon. It was nighttime back in Tillsdale. She would be reading about this time, getting ready for bed. Maybe this trip was good for her. It forced her to stay awake. To stay alive, as it were.

"Hey, you. J'get everything?" He seemed exuberant as he grabbed the plastic bag from her to view the contents inside. "Where's dessert?"

Nothing was ever enough with him. "Dessert's *your* call, buster."

"Buster, heh? Is it 1936 or something?" He smiled widely, crookedly, disarmingly. She gazed up at him. He had used his sunglasses as a hair band, pushing his mane away from his face. It gave him an uncustomary schoolboy appearance. Gone was the fidgeting, the edge. He must have made his victory phone calls to his girls. That must have been what took up his time. He must have said, "The top record guy loves me and my stuff! In fact, he's invited me to stay with him!" How might that sound to anyone, let alone a Tillsdale girl? "Let's go. Any public beaches around here?"

She remembered the general location of a few spots. She had driven, at risk of life and limb, to Malibu many times herself, climbing over rocks, wishing to escape from the heartbreak of Derek. She had done that until she had read about the murders of young women in the area, even in broad daylight in beach houses. Beauty, it seemed, always belied the danger beneath it.

The car was headed north. She needed to turn around, first to get her bearings, then drive along, hugging the berm of the road as much as she could get away with, hoping to spot a familiar cove. At last, she found a good place to pull over that was more private than public. Trey was soon out of the car, a wild man, already negotiating the rocks like a goat on a mountain.

A twinge in her lower back as she got out of the car reminded her of her mortality. Traveling wasn't as easy as it once had been.

"Hey. Come back here and help me!" She had earned a command or two.

He already blended in beautifully with the breathtaking landscape. He retraced his path, grabbed the bag of food and drinks, and extended a large hand like a gentleman, helping her down the side to the beach.

The ocean mesmerized her. She remembered the first time she'd seen it. It had taken her breath away. She remembered, too, a birthday at the Malibu Inn, alone, on the balcony, watching the sun go down, fresh from being dumped by Derek. She had written a poem about the experience, too. Called it "Mimesis." She even remembered it, word for word:

> People become instant artists at the seashore,
> carving Picasso's mandolin in the sand
> with a mere footprint.
> Imprints of seagulls fast become
> tiny kites in a grainy skyshore
> a spray of sea is a Turner painting,
> all the better for its immediacy.
> But art so easily done is easily lost —
> Better left to the museum of memory than to
> a canvas at the mercy of waves
> and the impasto of fog.

"Whatsa matter?"

"I was remembering. You can't erase memories, can you?"

He didn't answer. Gold streaked the firmament, as if the sun were holding a buttercup under the sky's chin.

"I swear I've never seen anything more spectacular in my life." He closed his eyes and took a deep breath of sea air. "And it's going to be my backyard."

Another rush of blood flooded her ears. "You're a

dreamer. You're here for a week at least, no more." She regretted saying it. She had used her teacher's voice. She didn't want to leave mad at him.

"Oh, you think so?" His light eyes caught the sun's reflection. "Why so negative? If I didn't know better, I'd think you wanted me to fail."

The boy appeared to know more than trivia. She bent down, picked up a smooth stone and attempted to skim it across the waves.

"C'mere."

"Where?"

She motioned him down to the edge of the sand and cupped some seawater in her hands. "Bend down."

Frowning, he crouched down. She sprinkled him with some drops of water.

"Hey, don't hit my hair!"

She laughed, catching the allusion to a popular movie. Was there nothing trivial he didn't know? "I was making it official."

He used the bottom edge of his T-shirt to wipe his forehead. "What? That you've gotten me all wet and turned me into a geek?"

"No, silly. Now you've been baptized in the Pacific Ocean." The best she could come up with was a well-meaning smile. What had her words meant? He belonged here.

Their eyes met. She tried to remember when they had locked eyes like that. She remembered … the dream when he had whisked her off her feet and floated with her, down the street, telling her how clever she was. The dream had replicated it perfectly. Or perhaps, he had tapped into her dream somehow. Whatever the case, she imagined for a moment he was that dream.

He put his hand on her shoulder. "You should have put all such useless knowledge to good effect."

"Oh, thank you very much! What makes you think it's so useless?" She tried for a playful tone in her voice, but feared it came out as defensive.

He continued his steadfast gaze into her eyes. He seemed dead serious. "Because it's an investment that ultimately doesn't pay."

She stared back at him intently. "*You* seem to appreciate it."

He turned away from her. She must have stepped over the line in the sand, as it were. All resemblances to the dream had ended. "I do. I like sharp minds." He was staring at the ocean now. "What I meant was, you should have gone on a game show and won a wad of cash—for yourself."

"That's not me."

"That's what I intend to do." He raised his hand to block the sun.

Hadley felt the vasovagal nerve come alive again. She was tired and yearned to go home. She was more of a Tillsdale girl than an L.A. woman. She sensed the futility of this, realizing the men she'd fallen for weren't good for her. They didn't care about her interests, her future, her goals. What she liked for dessert. Where she wanted to travel to. What books she loved. If her play would materialize. Except for Neil, of course. Maybe the questions he asked her were the ones she should be interested in hearing.

She wrapped her arms around herself in the absence of anyone else doing so. "What do you mean?" she asked him. She remembered he had been talking about going on shows where he might make a buck for knowing so much useless information. "You're only here for a week. You have to schedule those auditions in advance... it takes weeks, even months, sometimes, to even take the test."

She had tried a few herself, upon first coming to California, but never was able to muster the fake enthusiasm the producers always wanted in their contestants. She surmised, however, that Trey could probably fake anything.

"I know." His lips seemed uncharacteristically colorless. The bag filled with the food was slung over his shoulder. "I'm going to be staying out here. Sara's moving out here." He said it as if he were making a pronouncement about war. "I'm not going back to Tillsdale... ever."

She flinched at his multi-pronged revelation. "Listen, you can't live on dreams and illusions, especially out here. And two of you." She couldn't bear to say her name.

He chuckled. "Millions do." He pressed his lips together, draining them even more of color. "But I won't have to."

She was, to say the least, addled. "What are you saying?"

He put down the bag of food, in spite of the overwhelming presence of seagulls, and grabbed both her hands. He stared into her eyes again. "I want to ask you something. In fact, I've been meaning to ask you..."

She squeezed his hands, feeling the tensile strength of the fingers and the fleshy mounds under his thumbs, the barometers of a person's sensuality, some say. "What?" she said, drawing out the moment. "What do you want to ask me?" Her heart beat in double time.

He stared past her, first at the cloud-splotched firmament, then at the waves, which were periodically laminating the sand.

Hadley felt a confluence of emotions brewing in the caldron of her stomach. Was he going to tell her that, in spite of it all, they had a true connection, that their brief relationship was offbeat, but fun. That she was always going to be a special memory to him, so how could they always stay in touch and in what way?

"What's your question?"

"What's the real reason you did all this for me?"

What was the reason? Could she even boil it down to one reason even? "I told you. You had talent, I had connections." She didn't move. "Besides, I wanted to see my friends. And …"

"You'll have to speak up. I can't hear you with the ocean."

"I had business out here."

A quick grin flitted across his face then disappeared, like a distant bird. "What business is that?"

"My own business," she said.

"OK, whatever. I hope you got something out of it, too."

She studied his perfect dimple. When he pursed his lips in a certain way, it became more prominent, as it was now. She shivered from the breeze. "It wasn't entirely selfless. I'm writing a play, you see, and I'm considering the subject of innocence. I'm studying *you*, in fact."

"Innocence?" A sly smile spread across his face. "I'm the wrong subject if you're using me as your guinea pig."

She laughed, joyously. She loved his straightforwardness that seemed to occasionally surface.

"I actually think you're more innocent than you know," she said, adopting a matronly tone to her voice. She remembered his unfiltered exuberance on Sunset Boulevard earlier. "And that's what intrigues me."

"Innocent in what way?"

"You don't seem to realize how hard life can be, even for someone as beautiful and charming as you." She smiled as she said it, but he continued to give her an intent but expressionless stare. "You think all the pieces will fall in place for you, without realizing the odds are stacked against you. Against everyone. Astronomically so."

"Oh yes I do," he said. His voice sounded deeper and more authoritative than it had all day. "Realize, I mean. That's why I long ago swallowed whatever self-respect I had and plan on selling my soul if necessary to make my life easier." He shoved his hands in his back jeans' pockets. "I have plans."

"Plans?"

"Sure. I have a plan for my life. But I have feelings, too."

"Yes?"

"Yes. I love Sara. The minute she spoke to me, I wanted to know her."

"But Sara? She's hardly your type."

"Why? Because she's a bit overweight? Quiet? Not flashy?"

The wind whipped her hair into strings. "I guess. If I'm being perfectly honest."

"Thanks to Brenna, I got to really know her."

"Brenna's involved?"

"Yeah. She'd ask me to come to dinner, and Sara would be there. Several times. It's almost as if she'd set us up."

Hadley's suspicion was right. Brenna was behind their union, which meant she was against Hadley's plans with Trey for reasons of her own. Her hands reflexively turned into fists. "I see. I didn't know you were that serious. I mean, having her come out here."

"I need an anchor in my life. Someone who's going to take care of me. I can't run around L.A. and pursue my career without someone who'll be there for me, to steady me, to love me. She understands me. She sees me as a person, not a type. Do *you* understand?"

The waves seemed to reflect the turmoil going on inside her gut. "I guess I had you wrong."

"I guess you did."

The bile rose in her throat. It matched her anger at that moment. "But you think nothing of using other people in the meantime."

"Like you, for instance? Is that what you're saying? You led me to believe you wanted to help because you could. I took you at your word."

"Fair enough."

"And you just said you were using me for your play. I'm flattered. I hope you got the scene you wanted."

She loved how the sun sprinkled the ocean with light. "I think so."

"Listen," he said, taking her by the shoulders, "use me all you want. I'd love to be in your play. I told you someday I'd pay you back. I'll write a song about you someday. And you'll hear it and know."

She smiled weakly. Experience had taught her how these guys turned out. They appeared to be hellbent for stardom, but often became convention itself, marriage, two kids, a mortgage.

If anything, she was the rebel, the outsider, the one who wanted more than anything to write, to create a play that would make the audience shake their heads and say, "Ah, that's it."

"We should get back," she said.

"To where you once belonged, right?" He nudged her and laughed, two trivia experts in the know.

She decided that Neil was the real rock star, initiating a drug program to help wayward youth, using his limited connections to change people's lives, mixed in with his solid goodness and drive. Yet he was the nondescript guy who lived on Elm Street.

She wanted to go home.

Trey grabbed her hand and retraced their indented steps in the sand, the trail of Picasso's mandolins they'd carved on their way in.

Chapter 28

The next morning, Trey made bright conversation with Hadley while he readied himself to move into Benny's digs. He made no reference to the day before or their conversation on the beach. Roxie offered to serve as chauffeur once again, hoping to get a chance to corner Benny and give him the send-off because she interpreted his moving in Trey as a way to keep her from spending the night.

Hadley said there was no point in her going to the "drop off." Benny always made her nervous with his X-ray stare and blunt talk. Instead, she wanted to see her friend Bryce who lived in Silver Lake, so the plans were that Roxie would deliver Trey into his uncertain future and bring the car back for Hadley. She wasn't going to stick around for Hollywood talk. She'd heard all she ever wanted to hear.

Hadley was relieved to be done with the whole Trey incident, knowing her part was over, that his loss of innocence may have already happened—and maybe long before she knew him. She surmised that Trey wasn't aware of what the women in his life felt or how they reacted when he left them to twist in the wind. It was all about him, really. He enjoyed his flings and imagined his women did, too.

Hadley realized guys like him didn't feel the same way about losing their innocence as girls did. Or as this girl did. She needed to be open to love that wasn't such a challenge, that required so much work. Love shouldn't be such work. She was writing the play in her head as she waited for them to leave.

"I guess this is where we say goodbye."

"Bye, toots," he said. He then gave her an expansive hug. "I'll call you or drop you a postcard."

She gave him an extra-tight squeeze, feeling his shoulder blades and muscles, confirming his humanness, knowing he, too, would change because that's what people do. She wouldn't be around, however, to see it. She turned so as not to watch him go out the door. It bothered her when she saw someone leaving whom she'd never see again, even one who hadn't exercised her heart as he had.

Instead of evaporating into the mist, though, he came back. "C'mere," he said, after momentarily hesitating. "You know the damn world's waiting for a woman like you."

He kissed her. On the mouth. The only way a drop-dead gorgeous golden boy can kiss a girl. But what anatomy books don't tell people about hearts being the size of fists is that they can clench like fists, too.

She wasn't sorry to see him go. He was part of the past she was giving up. He wasn't the bad guy. He was young. And self-obsessed.

And maybe he even understood her better than a lot of people.

She'd write the play without him. It had always been in her power to do so.

The damn world *was* waiting for her.

****

Her friend Bryce lived in a beautiful home on a

sloping incline in the Silver Lake area of Los Angeles. The home had been featured once in an architectural magazine, and deservedly so. It was a place where he worried about cakes being taken out of the oven at a certain time so they could "breathe."

For the first three minutes after Bryce came into view, she hugged him, twirling him around in a clumsy embrace. She buried her head in his shoulder and smelled his expensive cologne.

She always felt so under-dressed compared to him. He was a dandy of sorts. Like his cakes, his fabrics had to breathe. But dressing well flattered him. His hair was short with a few brown gelled wisps in front. He had a nice face, a familiar face, like a weatherman in a Midwestern TV station. He was, after all, from Ohio, not so far from her upstate New York.

Bryce, in addition to his many other resume listings, including literary agent, had been an assistant to one of the so-called stars at the record company where Hadley had worked. The girl, a vanity act signed to the label because one of the executives was sleeping with her, had put out one album that subsequently tanked. Bryce had then gotten lucky by selling a few songs he'd written himself. In fact, he had asked Hadley to write a play that could showcase a few of his songs. This opportunity was a billet-doux to her, but she wanted to do it as much for herself as for him.

"It's so wonderful to see you," he said. He then steered her inside, one arm around her waist.

"And?" she prompted.

He tilted his head. "You confuse me, as usual."

"I was waiting for you to say something like, 'You look tired or drab,' or 'Get the hay out of your mouth.'

All the locals here think I live on a farm."

He pointed her to a massive circular sofa. "You need a friend, don't you? Come on in and let me hydrate you."

The house was as magnificent as she remembered it. Flower arrangements in statement vases were positioned all around the house.

"Did I interrupt your program?" She jerked her head toward the large TV, the picture on, but the sound off.

"Nah. It's a new game show. *Trivia Train.* I'm in love with the host. What can I get you to drink?" He didn't wait for the answer, instead bringing back a plastic bottle of ginger ale and two glasses. That was the Ohio coming out in him. For all his careful cultivation, his favorite drink remained ginger ale, not always an easy drink to find next to the effervescent mineral water in Southern California refrigerators. "Something nice and stiff to add to this?"

"I don't drink much anymore," she said. "Just a finger or two of the swill you're imbibing."

He smiled as he grabbed a highball glass and filled it with some ice cubes, a lemon wedge and ginger ale.

"I might as well remind you I don't have the play with me."

"Did I ask?" He handed her the glass.

"No, but it's there, between us. It's like a… as if we had once slept together and I had been the reason for your going gay, or something like that. You know, something terribly unspoken and life altering."

He laughed. "Sounds like the story line to 'Careless Whisper.'"

She finished off the drink and grabbed a coaster. "I've got writer's block or something."

"It's those damn woods. I don't know how you live

there. No inspiration, no wit."

She fluffed up a teal satin pillow before positioning it in the small of her back. "Oh, there's wit. You have to peel away the layers to find it, though. Do you know what I couldn't find the other day at the grocery store? A bottle of *Herbes de Provence*. They don't sell it. Apparently us woods people aspire only to salt, pepper and the odd pinch of parsley."

"Oh, the humanity! A free and open marketplace is worth the crime and traffic we put up with out here. But listen, dear. Don't let the play come between us. We've always got each other, even if your masterpiece remains in perpetual development." He sat beside her and pushed her hair behind her ears, something her grandmother used to do. "Besides, it's not like I'm waiting for it."

She stared at her glass on the coaster. Bryce had put ice cubes in her drink, as he liked it. She preferred her soda neat, straight up. "Does that mean it's just something to keep me busy? A vanity project? You don't really need it—or me—after all?"

He grabbed a pillow and threw it at her. "I'm so glad I'm used to dealing with a diva whenever I see my reflection in the mirror. Otherwise, I'd have to eject you from the premises." He put his feet up on an ottoman. "Now, talk to me. What's going on with your life? Are you still teaching? You should be writing. You're too big for the classroom. But go on, tell me about your life."

"I'd rather hear about yours."

"Oh God, same old same old. Men, the filthy pigs. Where shall I begin? You said you're only in town until when?"

"I leave tomorrow. Alone."

Bryce cocked a perfectly arched eyebrow. "What's

that supposed to mean? You didn't come here solo?"

"No," she said. She finished off the drink. "I came here with the protagonist of my yet-to-be written play."

Bryce got up and brought back not a platter of crudités, but a bag of cheese puffs, another vestige of his Ohio days. "You are so damn cryptic, but that's what I love about you. Now talk to me."

She settled in to tell him about Trey, the set-up, the premise of exploring him to test for his innocence and at what point a girl might lose it.

Bryce sat there impassively, other than offering a "Fascinating" every now and then.

"And, what did you discover?" he asked when Hadley was done.

"Meaning?"

"Is he a hardened criminal vis-à-vis innocence? And when is the tipping point for a girl to lose it to him? Tell me how it ends!"

She loved his house. In spite of its affectation, its precision, its carefully arranged fresh bouquets, she found it homey. She had, after all, spent many a night here, in the guest room, after sobbing her eyes out to Bryce and his gang after the end of her coupling with Derek. It felt more like home than her own place had.

"As usual, I've overthought it. He doesn't spend much time on other people's sensibilities. He's too caught up in his own pleasure. But yesterday, as he and I were driving on Sunset, I realized something."

"Which was?"

"There are different kinds of innocence. And he has yet to lose his kind. Or at least I believed so at the time."

"What on earth are you talking about? What's his kind of innocence?"

She slumped back into the cushions, feeling the small button in the center of one pillow push into her back. "Belief in a happiness that doesn't involve someone else."

Bryce waved his hand. "As usual, you're complicating things."

Hadley shrugged.

"Innocence is a stage of life we all grow out of." Bryce stared into her eyes.

"That makes me feel even worse. It makes me feel like I can't write something I don't understand."

"But of course you understand it. It's in the genes. Besides, writing is all about making stuff up. That's what I love about fiction. Even if you have bruised fruit, you can still make a mean Sangria."

Hadley burst out laughing and couldn't stop. It had been so long since she'd laughed so freely. She cozied up to her friend. "I love you."

"And I you," he said. He popped a cheese puff into her mouth. "Now, tell me about this guy. Is he handsome?"

"Very, unfortunately."

"More than Derek?"

"Really similar. Uncannily so."

"In his appearance or temperament?"

"Both. I mean, forget what Fitzgerald said about people in stories being individuals, not types. All the men I've loved have been types—blackguards all."

He accented the air with a sweep of his hand. "That line goes in the play." He grabbed her by the shoulders. "Even if it never gets written."

She snuggled back into his shoulder and peered out the scene-framing window: The horizon was a parfait of smog and sky above a jagged line of houses and hills. "I don't know if I'll ever get the play written. I don't think it's in me."

"It's in you, silly. You have to tell yourself to do it. You were never meant to be a teacher. You've never had any tolerance for the benighted—but plenty for the naïve."

"Say," she said, channeling Neil. "What did you mean when you said a minute ago that none of us is innocent?"

"It's in the genes. We're all doomed to lose our innocence. We couldn't grow up and move on if we all stayed naïve. And it's only after we lose it that we realize it's gone."

"Elaborate. I might steal it."

"Just as we're born with all these little stem cells that will grow into kidneys and liver and femur bones, we've got some marked 'horny,' 'greedy,' 'lascivious,' 'selfish,' along with others marked 'loving,' 'forgiving,' 'kind,' and so forth. Innocence is neither ours to keep nor ours to destroy. We all outgrow it. I mean, your kidneys don't stay little kidney stem cells. They grow. Same with innocence. You grow up and away from it. Listen, write your play about stuff we all go through, and you'll be fine. And if you don't want to write it, that will be fine, too." He gave her the eyebrow arch again.

She thought of Tillsdale. "I must have missed the stem cell line marked 'selflessness,' or 'dedication,' " she said. "Or at least could have been nicer to the people who got a double dose of it."

"Oh my God, you're even more of a drama queen than…some people I know." He crunched his ice. "Don't over romanticize everything, dear. We all have to grow up and lose our innocence. That's our fate. Including you, Miss Priss. So, if someone's around to act as a catalyst…"

"Wait a minute. What do you mean?" She was intrigued with the idea. It sounded like something she could explore.

"Derek, for instance. He may have whisked you down that path to jadedness a bit faster than you may have wished, but you would have gotten there regardless. Perhaps not with the speed of the Concorde, but we're all done in eventually. We have to move on."

How similar this sounds to what Roxie had told her, that we all lose our innocence whether it's forced on us or we outgrow it.

She thought of something that seemed to fit in. "I read once that a woman in a coma for decades continued to age."

"See? Things go on, regardless of our awareness."

"Yes, I see now. And Trey?"

"Who?"

"This guy. The one I brought with me. My protagonist."

"Oh, him. Yes, well, you're using each other for your own selfish ends, whatever they may be. Oh, my God. Did you see that contestant?" Bryce hit volume up on the TV remote.

Hadley felt a pang of remorse. "I'm not using him anymore. In fact, he more or less told me yesterday he was using me."

"Oh, so we're back to him, are we? Darling, be reasonable. You wouldn't have come all this way with him if you hadn't had an ulterior motive. Knowing your tendency for drama, I'll bet you secretly wish he'd become Val Kilmer and profess his undying love to you and you alone. That would make you feel ever so special, am I right, Cher?"

"You're full of shit." She had a funny premotion that something wasn't right back home. All the artifice of L.A. contrasted with the realness of her hometown and her responsibilities. She sat up straight, got up from the couch and walked over to one of Bryce's many phones. "Do you mind if I check my messages on your dime? Not that I'm expecting any, but…"

"Don't even ask." He carried the glasses into the kitchen, clinking them in the process.

Hadley's fingers flew over the keypad. She waited to hear her voice on the machine and pressed her secret code to retrieve her messages.

"You have five messages," the machine said.

She pressed the key to access them.

"Hi, it's Brenna. I was hoping you'd check your messages. I, uh, I wanted you to know I missed you and worry about you and hope you're having fun."

The second message was from Neil. Her heartbeat became almost audible when his familiar voice said her name.

"Hi. Did you try to call me? Madge said you stopped by the office, so I figured you'd try to call. I'll try again. Hope all is well with you."

Who could be the third message? She pressed the code.

It was her mother, asking her to call her. She wanted to set up plane reservations for Hadley to join her and her second husband for Thanksgiving.

There was a hang up. Then more messages.

"Hadley? Hi, Dee Dee Malvern. Both Sal and I stuck

up for you in the writing group, and we want you to come back and give it a go. Just show up. Even if you don't have your whole short story. We still want you there with what you've written. So, please come, dear. We'll be expecting you."

Still, Hadley felt a surge of warmth for this woman. Maybe she and the whole lot of them deserved another chance.

She listened to the fifth, and last, message and grabbed a nearby chair for support upon hearing it. It was Neil again. She quickly tried two different telephone numbers, but got no answer from either.

She turned to Bryce, who had re-entered the room. "I need to go home now."

"Are you kidding? Aren't you leaving tomorrow?"

"I want to do a standby flight. I need to get home."

"But think of the movies and restaurants we need to do. Ones that use *Herbes de Provence* in their dishes."

"On my next trip, promise. I'll have the play done, then. But I need to get my stuff at Roxie's then go home."

Bryce put one hand on his wrist and shifted his weight to one leg. "Are you angry with me?"

"For what?"

"For what I said back there. About you needing to feel special. Sweetheart, we all need to feel special, but we at least try to find a place, real or imagined, where there's a chance of it happening. Stay a while. Hang out with your friends who love you."

Hadley kissed him. "I adore you. And appreciate you. I have to do something important back home."

"OK, but you just got here. And I'm going with you. Roxie can drive me back here," he said.

In the meantime, Hadley pulled out a pen and an old

piece of scrap paper from her purse and jotted down some information, which she put in a secret compartment in her wallet.

****

Even though Roxie had given Hadley an extra key to her apartment, there was no need to use it. Roxie had the door open when she and Bryce had approached the stair landing.

"Bryce, baby!" Roxie wrapped her slender arms around him, careful to protect her hands lest she break a nail.

"My God, you're a vision," Bryce said. He whirled her around. "Who's that you're wearing?"

"Shabby chic. Estate sales and flea markets," she said. "Why is it we live mere minutes away, and it takes our friend from back East to bring us together?"

"It's an outrage. We can do better than that."

Hadley came in and headed to the guest room to pack her things.

"Whoa, where do you think you're going so fast?" Roxie called after her. "For God's sake, sit down a minute. Don't you even want to hear about your protégé? One I've chauffeured all over this damn town?"

Hadley reluctantly retraced her steps and sat on an over-stuffed arm of the sofa. "It's the least I can do. I've screwed up everyone's life, it seems, including my own."

"You didn't. Bryce, for God's sake, sit down and make yourself comfortable. And shut that door. I don't trust my neighbors." She turned back to Hadley. "As I was saying, I should thank you and what's his name for helping me see the light."

"What are you talking about?" Hadley was anxious to get to the airport. Besides, she felt terribly guilty involving her dear friends in all this entanglement.

"Darling," Bryce said, "before you spin this evil tale, you must let me take you someplace besides Ikea when next you shop."

Roxie put a cigarette in her mouth, then took it out again. "Here, take these," she said. Thereupon she handed him the pack and the lighter. "Do something with them."

Bryce recoiled, putting his hands and arms up to his face. "Eew! I would never put anything so vile in my mouth."

Roxie shot Hadley a look followed by a burst of laughter from both. "Do you want to take that line or shall I?"

Hadley laughed heartily, the second time in one day. It had to have been a record for the past six months—two unforced guffaws in a matter of hours. She took the items from Roxie's hand. "What's the deal?"

"I quit. I quit cigarettes—and Benny—both in one day."

"Are you kidding me? You've been smoking since you were sixteen, haven't you?"

"Thirteen. But who's counting."

"And Benny? What happened?"

Roxie leaned up against her kitchen counter, one leg curled around the other. "On the way over, Trey told me smoking made me look hard. He said he knew someone who smoked back home—."

"Anise," Hadley interrupted.

"Whoever, and she would be beautiful if she only didn't smoke. He said, 'But I sleep with her anyway because it's a two-way street. Occasionally, she can even be fun.' That's what he said."

Hearing Roxie talk about what Trey said made Hadley feel discouraged. What Trey was saying had nothing to do with knowing a person. She stared at her hands, tracing the veins in her right hand with her left hand, tributaries of blood, the bas relief on the map of life. "What's that got to do with Benny?"

"He's like Benny, don't you see? Sure, a younger and prettier Benny, but Benny just the same."

Bryce got up and slinked to the kitchenette to retrieve a small bottle of lime-flavored mineral water. He had told Hadley once it was mainly the fizz he had the jones for in these drinks.

Hadley threw up her hands. "I don't see. Build a bridge over my troubled synapses because I'm not getting it."

Roxie threw the nearest pillow at her friend, missing Bryce by a millimeter. "I'm that girl to Benny. Tough, fun, but ultimately disposable. Screw him!"

"You girls. Did you get college credit for Men 101? Where have you been? Obviously, you both should have sat through the lectures and written the research paper for extra credit."

Hadley looked at the phone. "Not all men are like them."

"That's right," Roxie said. "That's right. But how the hell am I gonna meet any of them if I'm mooning over this bastard?"

"And Trey? How does he come into all this?" Bryce took off his shoes and tucked his legs under him.

"On the way over, I realized what he was saying about this girl back home was how Benny talks about me. I mean, it was like Benny was the ventriloquist to Trey's dummy."

"Filth. The lot of 'em," Bryce said. He grasped his legs. "Wonderful, crazy, delicious filth."

"Listen, girl," Roxie said, pointing a freshly French-manicured digit at her friend. "You're lucky to be rid of him, Trey, I mean. He's lovely in some ways, but he and Benny aren't meant for us. They'll either kill each other or become best buds. But either way, we're both going to move on. We'll all be lucky to be rid of them and still have each other, aren't we?"

"My God, yes," Bryce said. "Group hug?"

Hadley hung back at first, but soon found herself in the middle of a huddle. "Now, will someone please take me to the airport? My dad's in the hospital."

"But you're leaving tomorrow! Won't he be OK until then?" Roxie asked.

"I want to try for standby. Tonight. I need to get home. I want to be with him."

Bryce put his palm against her forehead, as if checking for a fever. "Darling, you are worse than Dorothy Gale mewling to the Wizard. All you need is the damn ruby slippers. Of course we'll get you to the airport."

Roxie approached her and grabbed her hands. "Sounds like a *new* plan."

Hadley was silent.

"Does this mean this old plan is officially over?" Roxie asked.

Hadley nodded. Trey was on his own. With his own plans. And so was she—with her plans. She made a secret vow to check up on Roxie more often.

"Hallelujah! OK, purge ceremony. Like when dumped divorcees burn their wedding dress in a bonfire on the beach," Roxie exclaimed. "Next time, we all go to dinner to celebrate, then a movie."

"The cheesiest ever so we can make fun of it afterwards," Bryce said. "I know! Maybe *Brenda Starr* will be playing someplace then."

"In that case, we'd have to make comments *during*!" Hadley said. "Next time. But now, take me to the airport."

"Who's got my keys?" Roxie asked, pointing at Bryce.

Hadley put both hands on her friend's shoulders and managed to whisper "I'm proud of you" in Roxie's ear. "And I love you both more than you can ever imagine." Hadley untangled herself from the six-armed entity they had created. "Let's go."

Chapter 29

By the time she arrived back in Tillsdale after a long, uneventful flight, Hadley drove home from Buffalo on seemingly endless two-lane highways and country roads. It wasn't quite the midnight hour, but awfully close. Instead of going home, she went straight to the hospital. She had called while still in California to confirm her father had been admitted.

The front door was locked because of the late hour. A sign told her to use the back entrance and sign in at the Emergency Room.

"More delay," she said under her breath.

The moon was bright, lighting her steps to the back of the hospital. Was it a waning gibbous or a waning crescent? Calendars used to have lunar phases printed above the dates. When did it become no longer important to know these things?

When she arrived at the emergency room, she told the receptionist she needed to know the status of a patient who had been admitted earlier, her father.

"I'll check." The woman punched in a number and asked the person on the other line about such a patient. "He's in Room 327," the woman told her.

"Thank you," Hadley said. She scouted around for an elevator or a staircase, whichever was faster.

"Wait!" the E.R. woman said, leaning her head out the reception window. "You can't go up there now. It's too late. The nurses won't let you in."

Hadley froze in her steps. "You don't understand. It's my father. I found out he was sick, and I was away. I'm all he has." She could feel the tears welling up. He had gotten ill, and Hadley hadn't been there for him. Neil had assured her on one of his calls that he would get him to the hospital, one way or the other.

"Wait a minute, OK?" the woman said. "I'll call the nurses' station and see if I can't get an update."

Hadley dragged herself back to the E.R. window, thinking she was too late. It was all her fault. Neil would have helped him. Yes, wonderful Neil. Of course. She would check in with him again. He hadn't answered the phone when she had tried to call him earlier.

"Miss?" the woman said. "He's resting, the nurse said. He's comfortable and sleeping. You can come see him during visiting hours, but he's doing well. You might as well go home, now. They won't let you in."

Hadley nodded. "Thank you. I'm so grateful for your help."

The woman smiled. "Go home, dear. You're undoubtedly tired. Your father is in good hands."

Hadley pretended to be rummaging in her purse, waiting for the receptionist to get distracted. The moment came when her phone rang. Hadley slowly crept away, into the belly of the hospital, determined to find a way up to the third floor. When the staircase came into view, she quickly walked up the three flights.

Fortunately, when she entered the third floor, she wasn't greeted by a nurse's station lit up like NASA's Mission Control. That was down the hall. She sidled along the walls, searching for Room 327. When she found it, she slipped in quietly.

Her father was lying in bed in a darkened room. He had an oxygen tube running into his nose. Damn, those cigarettes! Hadley wanted to cry. She grabbed her dad's hand and bent over to his ear. "Papa, Papa, it's Kathy. I'm here. I'm home."

He must have been sedated. There was no response save for the slow rising and falling of his chest. Hadley wouldn't cry. Not yet.

"Listen, Papa. I'm going to be back in a few hours, OK? So rest. I'll see you later."

She still held his hand, warmer than hers. She'd have to leave soon or be unceremoniously tossed out by a nurse.

She leaned over one more time and whispered in his ear. "I love you."

Her father's face remained expressionless. But as Hadley withdrew her hand, she was sure his hand squeezed hers. Only a little. But that was enough.

****

Back in her car, Hadley went straight to Elm Street.

Neil's car was in the driveway. His front room light was on. She could see him through the front window, talking on the phone. She parked and climbed the two steps to his porch. If he were on the phone... Nevertheless, she knocked. At least a minute had passed, and Hadley knocked again. She was sure she heard Neil laughing.

Hadley had already turned to walk back to her car when the door opened. Neil appeared, dressed in a V-neck white T-shirt and draw-string plaid flannel pants. He was barefoot. The red hairs peeked out of his T-shirt. Out of the nerd's uniform, he was different, sexual even.

"Hello there, stranger," he said. "C'mon in. It's cold

out there."

Hadley obeyed, feeling at last both chilled and fatigued. She was surprised he had opted to speak of the weather instead of her absence.

"Did I wake you?" She hoped he'd mention whom he had been chatting to when she had tried to call him earlier.

"Wake me? Hardly. You must have heard," he said before taking her arm and leading her into his house.

"About my father? Only what you left me on voice mails, that he was in the hospital, but I was in L.A. and couldn't get you or him on the phone. So I took the red-eye out of there. I went straight to the hospital, but they wouldn't let me see him. But they told me he was OK, you know, sleeping."

He motioned for her to sit down on the couch.

"I snuck up to see him anyway. He was sleeping."

Neil nodded.

The place seemed neater. A few lamps. A patterned throw over his easy chair. "That new?" She pointed to a framed picture over his couch, a rustic scene of an abandoned wagon wheel in a field overgrown with timothy and clover.

Neil ignored her question. "Did you have a good time? I'm sorry your trip had to be cut short. I was out of town, too, when your dad called me."

"How did he? I mean, who helped him?"

"I'll tell you in a bit. Are you sure you're OK? You're awfully pale."

"I'm OK. I know it's late. I'm so thankful Papa's all right. And when I couldn't reach you or him... I feel like we've lost touch. We keep missing each other."

Neil hiked up his pants as he sat down. "Yeah, I've

268

been meaning to speak to you about a couple of things. Did you get my message a while back?"

"Yes. What did you want to talk to me about?"

"First of all, please don't worry about your Pops. I know you said you saw him, but when I got his phone call, I called the ambulance to go over there and take him up to the hospital until I got back into town. I went up to see him when I got home. He was coughing, bronchitis, I think they said." He smiled and tapped Hadley's knee. "But he's going to be fine if he lays off those smokes. Can I get you something to drink or eat?"

Hadley leaned back, taking it all in. "Wow. I guess that really was some news to relate."

Neil moved to sit closer to her. "There's something else."

She liked the warmth of the little cottage, the coziness. It felt like home. It was like she was seeing his world in a new light. "I know about the after-school anti-drug club. I wanted to apologize for not helping you more."

"Apologize? Heck, you've got nothing to apologize for. In fact, I wanted to thank you for letting me talk to your class. Because of that, I was able to make a connection with some of those kids."

"I'm so glad." *I could sleep here. I could sleep on this couch all night.*

"Yeah, it's going great guns, but even better, because of that day at school, I…" He sat at the edge of the couch, bent forward, rubbing his hands together nervously.

"Yes?"

"Are you sure you don't want something to drink or eat?" He clasped and unclasped his hands.

He was so close, she felt the heat from his body. She was at last ready to listen, to hear what she hoped he'd say. "Go on."

"I met someone. That's what I've been trying to tell you when I called before. A student teacher there at the school, Darla Buchanan. Do you know her?"

Hadley searched her memory. "Prue Eidelman's student teacher? Home Ec?"

"The very one." He grinned.

Hadley's heart played the percussion line of a fast march. "What do you mean, you met her. You dating her?"

Neil turned his trusting eyes to her. "More than that. I'm going to marry her."

Hadley felt woozy, like trying to act brave after riding the Zipper at the carnival but caving in to sea legs, nonetheless. She tried to concentrate on the jaunty ruffled valance on Neil's front window that she had never noticed before, but exhaustion, bad coffee, fatigue, worry—and something inexplicable—got the better of her. The last thing she remembered was the white noise filling her ears.

When she came to, Neil was crouched beside her. A wet washcloth was on her forehead, and a glass of orange juice sat on the coffee table.

"I'm going to take you to the emergency room," he said. His brow was furrowed, one of his big, freckled hands holding hers.

Hadley slowly shook her head. "No, I'm fine. Honestly." She adjusted the washcloth. "I'm tired from the weekend."

"Thank God you're all right. You're staying here. I'll get my bed straightened up, and you can sleep in there. I'll sleep out here."

She looked up at him, something she had done for as long as she could remember. "No. I'll be all right. I want to go home. I'm beat, and I've got to go to school tomorrow."

"I'll take you. Just lie there while I get my shirt and shoes."

"No. C'mon. I'm a few blocks away," she said. She sat up slowly. "I'll be fine."

Neil handed her the glass of orange juice, which she dutifully drank. He always took care of her.

"Will you come over for dinner tomorrow night? Darla's cooking, and I'd like you to get to know her."

Memories flooded her brain. "Isn't she the one working with you down at the paper?"

"Yep. She's working there part time. I got her the job. Doing real well, too, but she's quitting soon."

"To plan the wedding?"

Neil's face flushed, erasing his freckles in the process with a red wave. "That and the fact she's pregnant."

Hadley was thankful she had had an infusion of instant sugar. Otherwise, she wasn't sure she wouldn't have fainted at that as well. What was next? Neil was full of surprises. A *pregnant girlfriend? Neil had found passion?* A rush of happiness transformed into a hug. She wasn't in love with Neil, she'd told herself, but something had happened in California. Maybe she did love him. Maybe this was what real love felt like. He was home, or had been up to now. Like Winnie, he was a part of her jerry-built family. But it was family, nonetheless.

"Oh, I'm so happy for you." She sat up and threw both arms around his neck. She was crying and laughing at the same time. "Hold me."

He returned her hug, pulling her closely to him.

"By the way," he said through her hair. "Your father will be all right."

Hadley opened her eyes widely. She tightened her grip on Neil, as if she could make up for all the physical closeness she'd denied him, and herself, throughout the years.

Chapter 30

When she returned to her apartment later that night, she re-played her messages. Besides Winnie, inquiring about her father, and Neil, there had been calls from Brenna, and Delores, plus a couple new ones from Roxie and Bryce seeing if she'd arrived home safely. In spite of the late hour, Hadley dialed Dee Dee Malvern's number, knowing she quit answering after 9 p.m. because she had said as much once in the writing class. Hadley surmised a late call wouldn't disturb her.

"Delores? Hadley here. Thanks for your message. And thanks for sticking up for me at the writing group. You've done that a couple of times, and it's always been brave of you when you didn't know me well or whether I could even string a few words together." She hesitated. "What I guess I'm trying to say is thanks for the vote of confidence. Guess what? I'll be at the meeting this week. And I'll have at least the *first* scene of my play to read. And thanks, again, for not giving up on me."

She turned back toward her desk. She would see her father as soon as she could, later that day.

Knowing he was hospitalized, she had thought a lot about him on the plane ride home. The lesson she learned from him—that she wasn't as important to him growing up compared to his addictions—made their relationship somewhat uneasy throughout the years, true enough. That and his quick temper. He was often mad and unpredictable. Hadley determined that someone who wanted to spend his life dependent on things that could never return happiness was bound to be edgy.

More important, she could now see the various ways he had influenced what she had yearned for in love—someone in the present to correct the deficiencies in her relationship with him, to make it right at last. She shuddered to think of how she once approached relationships with that agenda in mind, bubbling under the surface though it be. She was through settling, determined to quit longing for what wasn't to be. Like her father, the men she had fallen for in the past hadn't loved her enough or had found her wanting, especially in giving them with what they thought *they* needed. They were with their wives now, she thought, and a whole new set of friends who fit their needs and agendas.

How to translate this into her writing? How should she begin? As if in answer to her question, she remembered a time in L.A. with Derek when she had bought him a guitar. The guitar shop was small for L.A. and unadorned. The sun shone through all the streaks on the windows and highlighted the fine layer of dust coating the sills. L.A.—*the* city of dreams, but dreams real enough to become subject to the daily nuisance of things like dust.

Hadley had written out the check for the last payment, whereupon the guitar—a black electric acoustic—was handed over, first to her, the legal owner, then as a gift into the hands of Derek.

She had expected some fanfare, given the grinding payments. Hadley was far from rich. In fact, she was in debt. She was unhappy and unfulfilled in her job, in her life. But she was sure she loved Derek and could feel him slipping away. This guitar was meant to be a dam in the stream, a means by which he would re-evaluate the relationship. Hadley hoped he would have an epiphany once that piece of stringed wood sat on his lap, the feminine curve, the bout, fitting perfectly on his thigh.

But there was nothing for her in the exchange. She was only the midwife to the moment. He had skipped the reflection step and was already trying out the instrument, his fingers plucking away at its strings. It was now his. It would go into his house, be placed with his belongings, provide accompaniment for new scenes in his life involving new women. He would soon forget who brought it into his world. All of this came to her at the time as he neglected the thanking-her part, like a syllogism skips a premise, assuming the audience will make the leap.

How she had longed to fill the role of facilitator, helping to realize his dream of becoming a singer/songwriter or a member of some up and coming band. With her, he could bypass most of this grimy world in getting there. She would do the necessary intercessional work. And he would love her for this. She may have been fading as his muse, but she would be an indispensable part of his artistic fulfillment.

Surely, he would see that.

But he hadn't, even after she'd bought him a used electric guitar years before, the standard one for rock musicians. That, as well, had a two-fold purpose: to help him kickstart his career and to stanch a relationship bleeding-out, even then.

That guitar had been a black and white beauty, a surefire all-access pass in the hands of an ambitious go-getter. It was Manichean in its colors, no ambiguity.

Means and Ends. Success and Failure. Love and Indifference.

But he had only played it at his house or at a few pick-up gigs around town. It was similar to his having professional photos taken before he had done anything to warrant publicity. His plans for the future had no bounding lines as did the two-tone pattern in the guitar.

"I need a band," he told her. "You can't play a guitar like this alone."

Enter a new guitar. Hadley believed this electric acoustic guitar would be more suited to his artistic nature. It had more nuance, the electricity only amplifying the strings, not blasting sound like the other one. He could take it out to stages as a solo act and sing his songs.

That was her justification for going into debt for him—again.

But as she drove him back to the Valley on the Hollywood Freeway, she realized she had once again miscalculated. Why had it been so difficult to give him up?

She remembered something Brenna had said to her, something she was never able to forget: "If someone loves you, they will move heaven and earth to be with you."

And the man Hadley loved back then was becoming even more unavailable, notwithstanding the fact she'd given him strings to woo her anew, as troubadours with lutes had done centuries before with their ladies, or the Aeolian harp in translating the wind.

Hadley remembered the personal ads she read in the *L.A. Weekly* mere weeks after giving him the latest guitar, an ad that he might have written about his being cuter than Evan Dando of the Lemonheads. That it was steeped in both his bravado and his vulnerability touched her. At the time, she was still championing him. She wanted to answer the ad.

A woman named Rachel must have done so because he took off with her shortly thereafter.

Hadley had had plenty of time to think about her ex who had convinced himself he was destined for something big. He wasn't cut out to make it in the Hollywood sense, in spite of the guitars or connections or whatever else brought him closer to the inside track. Perhaps the whole "dream" he believed in was a rite of passage for certain young men, those with a combination of passion, swagger, looks. If so, is it something they outgrow once they've learned how difficult it is, requiring a level of persistence and self-confidence they lacked? She had never asked herself that before.

Clearly, the rapidity with which Derek hooked up with someone made her wonder whether "the dream" had been a toothless exercise all along, an excuse to wriggle free of commitments with her or to wrest free of the relationship overall. It may have been subconscious, but it was there, nonetheless, convenient as all hell. "I can't meet you. I've got to prepare some songs for an audition that may come up." "I need to be available in case someone calls me back about a song I wrote."

Or maybe the "dream" was just that, a dream, satisfying a jones to make it seem like he would one day become the rock star or balladeer he fancied himself to be. Maybe it was as much a self-delusion as the ephemera he had her believe.

Perhaps it was only a string of pretty words. One of the poets she loved, Yeats, wrote a poem that described how he, being poor, had only his "dreams" to spread under his love's feet, warning her to "tread softly" on them for that reason. In gauzy language, he turned over to her his soul, his vulnerable—because spoken out loud—hopes, but what were those dreams? They remain abstract, clouds full of lovely language but enchanting and effective, nonetheless. If a girl had but a dollop of romance in her, such talk would have won her over, wouldn't it?

Or maybe Derek's "dream" had actually been to be taken care of by someone else, to enjoy an upper-middle-class lifestyle without having to work for it.

He was already settling down, the dream then having dissipated like a fireworks bouquet in a night sky. Such a realization made her regretful. She had wasted her time and his. He didn't have the necessary staying power or talent or whatever it took after all.

Of course, all of made Hadley remorseful for having believed in Derek so ardently when, in fact, it might well have been indicative of something lacking within herself. Could her subconscious have made her do so many things she was now ashamed of? She probably knew deep down he didn't have the wherewithal to make it, just as such a lopsided relationship could never be deemed real love. Instead, his problems had kept her from thinking too much about her own. It was a tradeoff.

All along, she should have been putting her energy into her own future—or into people who appreciated her.

She would do that now. She was no longer trying to fix the past.

Rachel and Derek, Trey and Sara. Those women would have their own problems to deal with.

She was glad not to be those women, to have to

contend with a dreamer who sells out. Perhaps such dreamers sensed these women would not push them into being something bigger than themselves. They would provide a life for them, as companions, with all the comforts. And that's why these guys married them.

The dreamers don't forget the dream, though. What she knew in her bones was that the regret of an unfulfilled life would intensify even, or especially, as life—artistic or biologic—runs out, a thought purified by the tension and pressure of time. The options, however, are gone, as are the people who once believed in them. All except for their wives and families and mutual friends who never mention the long-ago aspirations.

That would not be Hadley's fate. She had already left that party. It was not too late for her. She would find the resolve to teach, to write, to publish—these were her goals from long ago. She would act upon them now.

Dreams—or *the* dream—is indestructible, Stilled like Keats' sylvan piper or immortal nightingale in the midst of their aliveness, the unfulfilled quest never really dies.

Hadley remembered reading that the greatest regret of dying people is not having been true to themselves, to the pursuit of their dream. She would not be among those.

She was ready. But sadness, too, overcame her. She had given something up, even as she gained insight.

Maybe it was innocence.

She would always remember walking down a tree-lined Valley lane late at night with Derek. It was springtime. They were singing.

He would take the melody. Hadley would harmonize. And somehow they made it work, their voices intertwining, without the want of guitars for inspiration, or debts to be squared, or other people on the scene.

And it had sounded quite good, untrammeled by the thick layer of dust eventually coating those earthly things that remain undisturbed, almost as if it had come from another world, quite possibly one made up solely of dreams.

But now her dreams were her own, not someone else's.

Part of those dreams involved her students. She would organize the writing club soon and ask them to sign up. She would ask Jennifer personally if she would join. She could make a difference in their lives, a positive difference.

And her writing. *I'm going to finish my play by starting it.* She no longer felt intimidated by the millennium—or the fact she would be 40 in a few years. Arbitrary deadlines, she told herself. She put them there; she could take them away.

What she had learned was that no one, as Bryce had intimated, could feel one's innocence in the moment or prior to its loss. Such an understanding required a backward glance. There was no way to avoid the fall.

There was, of course, a way to avoid falling like Alice down the rabbit hole: By *watching out for rabbit holes.*

She was fantastic just as she was—eccentric, smart, funny, talented, quirky, compassionate. And if no one found that out or ever understood that, she was content to be without a partner. She didn't feel alone; instead, she liked what challenges the future held.

She pushed aside the school's laptop Brenna had

lent her and faced her own computer. Soon, the illumination from the screen lit up the room.

Her hands suspended over the keyboard, she took a long, slow breath. She'd worry about changing names later. She needed to type, to write, to put into words what she and others had talked about, now interpreted through her own sensibility. She would weigh all the voices in her head, but now she was listening to only one: her own.

A word about the author…

Jude Hopkins has published essays in The Los Angeles Times, Medium, and elsewhere, as well as poetry in numerous journals and magazines. Her work can be found on her website judehopkinswriting.net. https://www.judehopkinswriting.net/

Printed in the USA
CPSIA information can be obtained
at www.ICGtesting.com
LVHW012333090923
757267LV00009B/514

9 781509 248438